# WON'T BACK DOWN

## A Jack Keller Novel

# J.D. Rhoades

The following is a work of fiction. Names, characters, places, events and incidents are either the product of the author's imagination or used in an entirely fictitious manner. Any resemblance to actual persons, living or dead, is entirely coincidental.

ISBN 978-1-947993-71-6
eISBN: 978-1-947993-99-0
Library of Congress Control Number: tk

First hardcover edition October 2019 by Polis Books, LLC
221 River St., 9th Fl., #9070
Hoboken, NJ 07030
www.PolisBooks.com

POLIS BOOKS

# ONE

"Hey, *raghead*."

The girl in the headscarf stiffens, but she keeps walking, eyes fixed on the door of the school. The only sign that she's heard the taunt comes when she moves behind the boy walking beside her so that he's walking ahead of her and her body is between him and the owner of the voice. "Hey," the younger boy protests, but she shushes him. "Keep going. Ignore them."

"I'm *talkin'* to you," the voice says again, raised and harsh.

The girl still doesn't respond, even when a stone the size of a ping pong ball strikes her between the shoulder blades. She only stops when a pair of grinning young men come out of the front door where she'd thought she'd find refuge. They take up a position in front of her, arms folded across their chests. She stops, regarding them, then sighs and turns her back on them to face her tormentor.

The source of the voice, a stocky young man who's already developing a pronounced gut, is sauntering toward her, savoring her discomfort, making it last. He's dressed in jeans, a plaid shirt, and an Atlanta Braves baseball cap. His curly red hair sticks out from under the cap in odd directions, and a cocky grin is plastered across his face.

"Brandon," the girl says, "please leave us alone." Her voice is calm, but she can't disguise the fear in her big dark eyes. The boy she holds in front of her starts to go for the bigger boy headed their way, but the girl pulls him back against her.

"It's you who needs to leave, bitch," the red-haired boy says. "You need to get the fuck out of my country."

The look on the girl's face says that nothing would make her happier than to be far away, but all she says is, "We need to get to class."

The young man in the ball cap reaches for the scarf covering the girl's head. "Take that thing off."

She flinches away from him and backs into the boys standing behind. One of them gives her a shove and she stumbles forward into her brother, whose handsome face darkens with rage. He balls up his fists and starts toward Brandon.

"Hey," another voice says, "leave them alone."

Brandon turns. The man approaching is tall, a little over six feet. There are streaks of gray in the long blond hair he wears pulled back, but his body is still lean and fit. Brandon isn't intimidated. "Who the fuck are you?"

The man stops and regards Brandon with calm blue eyes. "My name's Jack. What's yours?"

"My name is fuck you, asshole," Brandon snaps. "Mind your business."

The man doesn't react to the insult. "Kind of a long name. What do you go by on the street?"

"Hey, dumbass," one of the other boys says. "He told you to fuck off." He advances slightly, the girl momentarily forgotten. She and her brother take the opportunity to slip between the two who'd been blocking her and run to the door.

The one who hadn't spoken makes as if to go after them, but Brandon calls to him. "Forget it. We'll deal with those sand-niggers later."

The blonde man looks amused as the two blockers come up to stand beside Brandon. "Sand-nigger. Haven't heard that one in a while."

Brandon cracks his knuckles ostentatiously. "Three on one, dipshit." He gives the blond man a nasty grin. "Looks like it's not your day."

"Looks like." The man doesn't move, his arms held loosely by his sides. Brandon and his two cohorts hesitate for a moment. Brandon is the one who eventually starts forward, but he stops when the blond man speaks, his previously calm voice hard. "Here's the thing. Maybe, just maybe, the three of you can lay a beatdown on me. Three on one's not good odds. But I'm one hundred percent sure that I'm going to put the first one who throws a punch in the hospital. Possibly the second one, too. And I'm not talking ER and out. I mean busted all to fuck, long-term rehab, permanent damage. I've done it before, to harder motherfuckers than you drooling redneck assholes ever dreamed of being." He gives them a smile that makes the two on either side of Brandon actually take a step back, a smile that says he's not only going to do what he promises, he's going to have a good time doing it. "So. Who wants a ride in the ambulance today?"

As the man speaks, other students begin to gather, attracted by the growing confrontation. A murmur runs through the crowd. "Fuck him up, Brandon," someone calls out. Brandon and the other two stand as if they've grown roots, afraid to go forward, too stiff-necked to back down in front of their peers. The blond man doesn't move either, just stands and regards them with that calm yet terrifying smile.

"Okay, okay, break it up." A woman's voice cuts through the hubbub. The crowd parts, the spell broken. The woman steps between the blond man and the three boys. She wears a holstered pistol, a taser, and handcuffs on the belt of her black jeans, but the badge on her chest is embroidered into the fabric of her grey polo shirt. "What's going on here?"

The three look at each other, then at the man still standing there, still smiling. None of them speak. The woman shakes her head. "Brandon, Jayden, Jerrard, get your butts to class. Now." The boys move off, unable to disguise their relief at being able to leave without losing face. The woman turns to the crowd, which is already beginning to disperse. The woman nods, then turns to the tall man.

"What the hell, Keller?" she says. "You fighting children now?"

# TWO

A few miles away, two men sit in a white Ford F-150 and watch a man go into a warehouse. The man is about five foot six, with light brown skin and a fussy little mustache. He's dressed in off-the-rack dress slacks and a short-sleeved white shirt. There are other cars parked in front, but no one else comes in or out.

The two men know each other as Waller and Tench. Neither believes it's the other's real name, even though they've worked together before. Waller puts down his binoculars and continues to watch the door of the warehouse.

"Well," Tench demands, "is it him?"

Waller takes an envelope from the glove box and slides a picture out of it. He looks at it, purses his lips thoughtfully, and stares, enjoying the sound of Tench impatiently tapping his fingers on the steering wheel. He knows that it's their target, but he enjoys winding Tench up. "I believe it is," he eventually says, and puts the envelope away.

"So what now?" Tench says.

Waller pulls out a cell phone. "We report back and wait for further orders. Drive."

Tench starts the truck and puts it in gear.

Waller dials. The person on the other end picks up after one ring. "Yes," Waller says, "this is Mr. Petty from the realtor's office? I believe we've located the property you were interested in. Yes. It's in a bit of a rural location, but very accessible."

6

Their employer's answer is slightly fuzzy, as if he might be using encryption on his end. His voice is clipped, with what sounds like a trace of a British accent. "How many bedrooms?"

Waller thinks back to the boy and girl they'd followed to school earlier. "Three. As you suggested." He pauses. "The asking price is one hundred and fifty thousand. Do you want us to put in an offer?"

"No. I want to see the property myself."

That surprises Waller. Most of his employers wish to stay as far away from the actual "transaction" as possible. Then again, this is the first time he's ever worked for this particular client. "Yes, sir. One of us can pick you up at the airport if you like."

"I will call with the flight number and time."

"Very good, sir." Waller breaks the connection and looks at Tench. "He wants to come down and have a look."

"Huh." Tench makes a right turn. They're headed for the town's main street. "Wonder why that is." Waller doesn't answer, so Tench supplies his own suggestion. "Maybe he's got some kind of personal grudge against this target. You know these people and their feuds. I knew an IGF sergeant back in the Sandbox who straight up murdered another dude because one of their grandfathers shot the other." He shakes his head. "Savages."

"Swing back by the warehouse," Waller says.

"You sure?" Tench doesn't wait for an answer, just takes the next right. "I don't want this guy to make us."

"Maybe our employer's interested in whatever's in the warehouse."

"You think?" Tench looks interested. They cruise back by. Now, the big front roll-up door is raised and a large truck is parked out front. Workers with hand trucks are loading crates into the back of the truck. Tench starts to slow down until Waller shoots him an incredulous look. "Sorry." Tench speeds back up.

Waller shakes his head. He's not liking this particular mission one bit.

# THREE

Jack Keller nods at the retreating trio. "Those three were messing with some girl and what looked like her little brother. I walked up on them and put a stop to it." He smiles, more easily this time. "And there wasn't going to be any fight. They didn't have the stones for it. Even three on one."

"And what if you were wrong?" she demands, hands on hips. "Would you really have beaten up three eleventh graders?"

Keller evades the question. "They look awfully big to be in the eleventh grade."

"Yeah, well. They're older. All three of them got held back a grade. Some of the other kids pick on them for that. So they got together…"

"And they pick on someone else. Same old story." Keller sighed. "Sorry, Marie. I just don't like bullies. Whatever their story."

"Don't I know it." She quickly represses her smile with a stern look. "But I'm the school resource officer, not you. Dealing with that shit is my job, Keller. Let me do it."

He nods, looking contrite. "Okay. Sorry."

"Apology accepted. Now tell me about who they were bullying."

"Young girl and her brother. She was wearing a headscarf. Looked Arab."

Marie grimaces. "Alia Khoury. She's a sophomore. Her brother Bassim's a freshman."

"Refugees?"

She nods. "Iraqi. Came here about three months ago. But not straight from Iraq. I think they'd been living in Pittsburgh."

8

"A lot of changes, really fast."

"Yeah. She's a sweet kid. She's made some friends, but her family's really strict, so…"

"She doesn't get out much," Keller says. "Which makes it worse." Keller knows what it's like to have trouble fitting in. "What about the boy?"

Marie smiles. "He's a character. The class clown. He's having an easier time adjusting. Gets along with everyone." The smile vanishes. "Speaking of which, I have an appointment with the vice principal."

"About Ben?"

"Yeah."

Keller doesn't speak. He knows Ben's problems, and he knows why Ben has them. Keller believes he's mostly to blame. He realizes Marie is still speaking to him. "So what brings you here?"

"I've got a job interview."

She blinks in surprise. "What. Here?"

Keller nods. "Custodian. Saw it in the paper." He sees her look and frowns. "Would me working here be a problem?"

"No. No," she says, but her expression says otherwise. "I'm just surprised you'd want that job."

He shrugs. "Work is work. Got to do something."

"Yeah, but…" She stops. Keller knows what she's going to say. *You have money.*

"Can't just live on what my father left me," he says. He smiles. "I never wanted the life of a trust fund baby."

"I know. But mopping up teenager's puke and cleaning toilets just doesn't seem like something Jack Keller would be interested in."

"Yeah. Well. Like I said. Can't just sit around the house all day."

"Uh-huh. Well. Good luck." She steps aside.

He doesn't meet her eyes as he passes. "Yeah. You, too."

# FOUR

"You're late, Miss Khoury," Miss Othmar, the homeroom teacher, says as Alia slides into her seat.

"Yes, ma'am, sorry, ma'am," Alia says, face burning as she takes out her notebook. The teacher doesn't pursue it. She turns back to the smart board at the front of the room and proceeds with the lesson on quadratic equations. Alia is sure the teacher knows about the bullying, but she's a timid young woman in her first teaching job and does nothing about it. None of them do. *Some of them probably even approve of it*, Alia thinks bitterly.

She hates it here in this stupid little town with its stupid little people. She'd just begun adjusting in Pittsburgh. She'd made a few friends and was even working up the nerve to try to convince Father to let her try out for a school play. Then the American man who she'd learned to hate had come to the door again. He and Father had spent an hour in the kitchen downstairs, with Alia banished to her room to do homework. She'd already done her homework, but there was no use arguing with Father. She'd sat by her bedroom door, ear to the wood, straining to hear the conversation and failing, but knowing all the while what it meant.

"We're going to have to move again," Bassim said from where he sat cross-legged on her bed. He didn't even seem angry this time, just resigned. Alia hated that. She hopes she never loses the capacity for anger.

He was right, of course. After the American left, Father had called them down to the kitchen. He was composed as always, almost emotionless, but Alia had learned to read his moods and she could sense the anger in him. A new employment opportunity, he'd told them. A better life for them. Bassim didn't speak, just looked down at the table. Alia had finally lost her temper, raged at her father, told him she hated him for what he'd done to the family. She knew she'd gone too far when she shouted that he was the one responsible for her mother's death. She'd expected a slap for that, would have almost welcomed it, because the shattered look in her father's eyes broke her worse than any blow. She'd fallen silent.

"Everything I do," he said quietly, "I do to keep you and your brother safe." He stood up. "Now go start packing."

The harsh ringing of the class bell interrupts her memory. She stuffs her notebook in her bag and stands up. As she walks down the aisle between the rows of desks, a blue-jeaned leg suddenly appears in front of her. Alia had half expected it; she deftly steps over it and smiles sweetly at the blonde girl who glowers at her from the seat, her round, sulky face a mask of contempt. "Good morning, Amber," she says. She doesn't stay for the response, which she knows will be some variation on "fuck you." She and her boyfriend Brandon are perfect for one another.

In the hallway, Alia tenses as she sees the policewoman standing, waiting for her. She doesn't dislike Officer Jones; for all her outer toughness, she has kind eyes, and she does seem to truly care about the students. But that caring will only attract more attention to her, and the last thing Alia wants right now is more attention. But she can't very well ignore it when the woman motions her over. Alia pushes her way through the throng of students in the hall. Officer Jones is standing by her locker. "Hey," she says.

"Good morning, Officer."

Jones smiles at her. "You can call me Marie."

She keeps her tone formal. "Okay. Good morning, Marie."

"You want to talk about what happened this morning?"

Alia fumbles her locker open. "Nothing happened this morning."

Jones sighs. "I know you're being picked on, Alia. And I want to stop it."

Alia takes out her history book and closes the locker. For the first time, she looks the policewoman directly in the eye. "You can't. No one can."

Jones's jaw tightens. "Well, I have to try. If Jack…" She stops herself and starts over. "If that man hadn't stepped in, you and your brother might have gotten hurt."

Despite her desire to be anywhere else, Alia's curiosity is piqued. "You know him?"

Jones looks so taken aback, then embarrassed, that Alia almost laughs. "He…he's a friend."

There's a certain pleasure in seeing the usually no-nonsense Officer Jones off-balance, and Alia can't help but indulge it just a little. She arches an eyebrow at the resource officer. "A good friend?"

To her surprise, Jones actually smiles. Alia can't remember ever having seen her smile before. It's actually a very pleasant smile. "Nice try changing the subject, kid." Jones's face turns serious again. "But really. Help me stop this. If not for me, for your little brother."

The thought of someone trying to hurt Bassim—sweet, funny, charming Bassim—makes Alia feel sick to her stomach.

Jones sees the look on her face and nods. "Think it over, Alia. Let me help you."

"I have to get to class," Alia says.

Jones lets her pass. "You know where to find me. Anytime you want to talk."

In all the times she's been bullied in this place, she's never shed a tear. It took an act of kindness to bring that sting to her eyes. Alia considers taking Jones up on her offer. Maybe she could protect her and Bassim. She ruthlessly pushes the thought aside. *Police can't help you,* she thinks. Her father had been a policeman, back in Iraq, a high ranking one, even. And look where that had gotten them.

# FIVE

"It's a funny world, you know?" Tench takes a sip of his iced tea and stares out the window of the barbecue joint at the river a few hundred yards away.

*Here we go again*, Waller thinks. He's never been a reflective man. He takes a hush-puppy, drags it through the miniature tub of butter on the place mat in front of him, and pops it in his mouth without answering.

Tench, as always, fails to notice the lack of response. "I mean, look at who we're working for. Wasn't so long ago we would have been trying to hunt this guy down."

"Nah," Waller said. "This guy's a player over there. The bad ones, the Ba'athists, all got run out."

Tench snorts. "You sure about that? I heard some of them switched sides just in time. They got fat and happy turning in their old buddies. And you know what, Waller?"

"I don't, but I guess you're gonna tell me."

"That's the kind I worry about. If he'll sell out the people he'd been with for years, people like him, how the hell can we trust him?"

Waller sighs. "So, you want to give back the money? Tell our employer thanks, but no, thanks, we think you're a bad guy?"

The food arrives before Tench can answer, large plates of juicy pulled pork with vegetables on the side. When the waitress bustles away, Tench answers. "No. I don't want to give the money back. But consider a minute. Why does our employer want to eyeball the, ah,

13

property himself?" No one is paying their conversation any attention, but Waller appreciates that Tench is still careful enough to use the euphemism. "We could have closed the deal without him. Why's he coming down?"

Waller takes a bite. "You have an idea."

Tench nods, but takes a bite from his own plate before answering. "I think this may not just be payback. I think there's something on the property. Maybe there's money there that we haven't been told about. He wants to sweat the—I mean, explore the property. You know, dig a few holes."

"And?"

"And why shouldn't we get that ourselves?"

Waller shakes his head. "You just got finished slamming our employer for turning on his people, now you're talking about us doing the same thing?"

"Why the hell not? I mean, he could turn on us."

"Look, bro." Waller's been looking forward to coming back to this restaurant since he found out where this mission was going to take them, but Tench is beginning to spoil his appetite. "I may have done some shit I'm not proud of, but I got some principles. And one of those is, when I'm bought, I stay bought."

"I'm just saying. Keep it in mind."

"Yeah," Waller says. "I'll do that." The two of them eat in silence. Finally, Waller pushes his plate away, half eaten. "Okay," he says, "just for the sake of argument. There's money on the property." Finally, sick of the increasingly clumsy code words, he drops the euphemism. "Say this guy has some cash stashed away. And our employer wants it. What do we do?"

Tench has been steadily putting his meal away. He pauses only long enough to wash his last mouthful down with a swig of the sweet tea. He smiles, and Waller can see a bit of pink meat stuck between his teeth. "What about this…" he begins.

# SIX

"Come in, Ms. Jones," the vice principal says as he opens the door to his office.

Marie enters, even though being called into the school office doesn't exactly bring back good memories. She takes a seat as the vice principal does the same. The nameplate on his desk looks as if he keeps it polished daily. MR. BURNHAM, the gold letters read.

"So tell me," Burnham smiles at her, "do you like working here?"

No good conversation ever began this way, Marie thinks, but then realizes he's not her boss—the head of the county school's police force is—so he's just making small talk. He goes on. "I imagine it's different from being a patrol officer."

"Yes, sir," she answers. "It is. But I like it fine. I like working with the kids."

"And they seem to respect you. That's important." The smile on his long, jowly face fades, and he clears his throat. *Now for the bad news.*

"Ms. Jones, we need to have a talk about Ben."

She sighs. "What's he done now?"

"Oh, no," he says hurriedly. "It's nothing specific. This time. But... well...you know the kinds of problems he's been having. Cursing at teachers, fighting...we haven't actually caught him at it, but we're reasonably sure he's smoking marijuana. I just wanted to see if you could give us some insight into what makes Ben so angry." He gives her a look that's supposed to be open and sympathetic, but it makes him look so much like a basset hound that Marie almost laughs. The urge fades quickly. She looks away from him, unsure of where to begin.

He gives her a prompt. "What about Ben's father? Is he in the picture?"

She shakes her head. "No." *Fuck it, I might as well get it all out.* "Ben's father was shot to death in front of him when he was five."

"Oh," Burnham says, and shakes his head. "That's—"

Marie interrupts him. "Then the man who shot his father, a man named DeGroot, took him hostage by putting him in an explosive suicide vest. When I and…some friends got him out of that, we had to take refuge with some crazy survivalist in the mountains. DeGroot tracked us. We ran to another place. DeGroot followed us there, too. He set the house we were in on fire. When we came out, he threatened to shoot Ben in the spine and cripple him. Should you be writing this down?"

Burnham looks as if he's been poleaxed. "I…um…"

Marie can't help but feel a malicious glee at his discomfort. "The reason he didn't do it is that the man I'd been seeing, a man who Ben was really beginning to bond with, rescued us and shot DeGroot. It happened in front of Ben. Did I mention he was only five at the time?" She stands up, her eyes filling with tears. "So that's probably why he's screwed up. I try to cut him a little slack. Maybe you should, too." She turns to the door, groping blindly for the doorknob she can't see through her tears.

"Ms. Jones," Burnham says. The gentleness in his voice stops her. She turns back, wiping her eyes with the back of her hand. She feels suddenly wretched and ashamed for having teed off on Burnham like that. The man's only doing his job. He silently hands her a tissue from the box on his desk. "Won't you sit back down?"

"Thank you." Marie wipes her eyes, then blows her nose as she sits back down. "Sorry. It just…"

"No apologies necessary," Burnham says. He gives her a chance to collect herself before speaking again. "Is Ben in any kind of therapy?"

"Ben's been in every kind of therapy, Mr. Burnham. He's been on every kind of meds there are, until he was like a zombie." She feels her eyes filling with tears again.

"Ah. And what about you?"

She's startled. "What about me?"

He shakes his head. "Ms. Jones, Ben's not the only one who suffered trauma here. What are you doing for yourself?"

"Ha." She wipes her eyes again. "Sir, I'm a single mother. With two kids. I haven't got time for trauma."

"Ah," he says again, and she laughs through the tears. He looks at her quizzically.

"Sorry," she says. "You sound like someone I used to know. He was a therapist, actually. Do they teach you to do that 'ah' thing in psychology school?"

He smiles at her. "There's even an exam." His face grows serious again. "Ms. Jones, have you considered that your reluctance to pursue therapy may be part of the reason it hasn't helped Ben?"

"What?"

"Just a thought. If you don't believe in it or make time for it, then why should he?"

She feels her cheeks getting hotter. "So this is my fault?"

"No. It's not a matter of fault. It's a matter of getting the help you both need." He writes something on a piece of paper and slides it across the desk. "This is the name of a therapist we recommend." He stands up to let her know the meeting is over. His voice is gentle as he says, "I can't make you get help. For yourself or for Ben. But, Ms. Jones, there's only so much slack we can cut him."

"I know," she says in a small voice. She stands up and takes the paper off the desk. "Thanks, Mr. Burnham. I'll do what I can."

He nods. "That's all any of us can do. And, Ms. Jones? If you need to talk again, my door's open."

She feels the tears coming again and nods her thanks. *This is more than I've cried in years*, she thinks. *I really need to get my shit together.*

# SEVEN

"I'm afraid we've wasted your time, Mr. Keller."

The lady from human resources says it in a way that really means he's wasting hers. She looks at him over her glasses and frowns.

Keller knows what's coming next. "I can explain the felony conviction." He'd considered lying about the question when he saw it on the application, but he figured they'd catch it in the background check anyway.

She sighs and puts down the application she's been holding. "I'm afraid that won't help. The policy is quite explicit. We can't allow convicted felons to work around our students." She smiles apologetically, and it's clear she doesn't mean that either. "No exceptions."

"Mrs. Harrington," he says, "I pled down an auto theft charge because there were extenuating circumstances. There's nothing in my record that says I'd do anything to harm a child."

She shakes her head. "No exceptions," she repeats. "It's a liability concern."

Meaning it's less about child safety than it is about covering your ass, Keller thinks, but doesn't say. He stands up. "Okay. Thanks for your time."

She just nods and turns to her computer.

The halls of the high school are empty; all the students are in class. As Keller turns a corner, he sees Marie coming down the hall toward him. She smiles as they draw closer. "Let's see your hall pass, Mister."

He smiles back. "Sorry, Officer. My dog ate it. Does this mean I have to go to the principal's office?"

That makes her laugh. He likes her laugh, and the fact that she seems to have gotten over her earlier annoyance with him is the best thing that's happened to him so far today.

"How'd the interview go?"

He shrugs. "Didn't get it. My record, you know."

She frowns. "Damn it. Didn't they give you a chance to explain?"

He shakes his head. "No exceptions," he mimics the HR lady.

"You want me to talk to them?"

"No. Wouldn't do any good. Besides, admit it. It would be awkward having me around."

"Maybe," she admits, then smiles. "But I'd get over it."

"You want to come over later?" he asks, a little too casually.

She shakes her head. "Can't. I'm taking Ben home." She sighs. "We need to have another talk. Oh! Can you pick Francis up? And, like, take him to the park or something while I talk to Ben?"

"Okay. That bad, huh?"

She grimaces. "No more than usual. Thanks, Jack."

"Don't mention it."

# EIGHT

"Stop staring," Meadow says.

Ben doesn't answer. Meadow doesn't know if it's because of the earbuds jammed into his ear canals or because he's fixated on the girl in the head scarf. Either way, it's annoying to be ignored by your best friend. She wads her gum wrapper into a tight silver ball and flicks it at his head. The projectile hangs up in his thick black hair and she doesn't think he notices at first. Then he brushes at it, picks it out of his hair, and looks at it stupidly for a moment until he turns to her. He reaches up and takes the bud out of his left ear. She can hear the faint tinny roar of the Swedish death metal he likes so much. "What?" he says.

"Stop staring at that girl," Meadow says. "You look like a stalker."

He reaches down to his phone and kills the music. "I'm not staring." He smiles slyly at her. "What, you jealous?"

She sighs. "Uh, hello?" She points to herself. "Not into dudes, remember?" She looks over at the girl in the head scarf, sitting alone at a table across the courtyard. Groups of teenagers are gathered in knots around the open space between the school buildings, each of the cliques hanging together: the stoners, the jocks, the theater kids, and so on. She and Ben form a clique all their own. "You should go talk to her. She's really pretty."

"You think so?"

"Well, if big dark eyes, cheekbones like a model's, and full lips are your idea of pretty…"

He follows her gaze, biting his lip nervously. "You think she's so hot, maybe you should hit on her."

She shoves him for the lame joke, but without anger. "I'm not saying go hit on her, dumbass. Just go strike up a conversation."

"About what?"

Meadow clutches her head in both hands, fingers digging lightly into the scalp below the closely-cut hair which she's recently dyed pink. "Oh. My. God. Do I have to do everything?" She lets her head go and looks at him with fond exasperation. "Just talk. 'Hey. How's it going? Nice weather we're having.' You know, like a normal person."

"I haven't been a normal person for a long time," Ben mutters.

The look on his face makes Meadow reach out and give his arm a gentle squeeze. "Me either. But that's why we're partners, right, Sundance?"

He smiles at the private nickname they've shared since they caught the old movie together late one night on TCM. "Right, Butch."

She grabs his arm and awkwardly urges him to his feet. "So, go. Talk to her. Bridge cultural barriers and shit."

Ben moves slowly at first, like a man being marched to the firing squad. As he approaches, however, Meadow sees his mother, Officer Jones, bearing down on him from across the school courtyard. "Ah, shit," she mutters under her breath. She doesn't really dislike Officer Jones, but she knows that Ben and his mom have had a rocky relationship lately. It's another one of the things they bond over. Meadow watches as Ben's mother stops him in the center of the courtyard. Ben's head is bowed, and she can tell he's furious at having to talk to his mother in front of all his classmates. Meadow notices the girl in the head scarf has raised her head from her book and is looking on curiously as well. The conversation over, Ben heads back to where Meadow is sitting. "What's wrong?" she asks as Ben snatches up his backpack and jacket.

"I have to go." He doesn't look at her.

"Okay. Talk later?"

21

He just nods and walks off. Meadow shakes her head. She looks over again at the girl in the head scarf. She knows the girl—Allie something—is having her own troubles with Brandon and the group she calls the "goon squad." A sudden impulse makes her pick up her backpack and walk over to the picnic table where the girl sits alone.

She looks up and smiles uncertainly as Meadow takes a seat across from her. "Hello."

"Hi," Meadow says. "Whatcha reading?"

With the same tentative smile, the girl shows Meadow the cover.

Meadow rolls her eyes. "Christ. *The Great Gatsby*."

The girl blinks in confusion. "You don't like it?"

"A total hymn to white male privilege," Meadow states confidently. "It's garbage."

The girl looks down at the text. "Maybe that's why I'm having trouble getting interested."

"Trust me, honey, it's not you. It's the book." She sticks out a hand. "I'm Meadow."

The girl takes it. "Alia. Alia Khoury."

"Nice to meet you. So, you're new?"

Alia nods. "We just moved here. From Pittsburgh. For my father's work." There's something odd, almost robotic, in the way she says it, as if it's been rehearsed rather than lived. Meadow files that away for future consideration. "Tough to make friends in a new place."

Alia pulls back slightly, eyes narrowing, and Meadow curses to herself. *Damn it, you're so clumsy sometimes*, an inner voice rages at her. She fights that voice down, and feels a little stab of pride for doing so. "Anyway. I saw you checking Ben out." At Alia's puzzled look, Meadow rushes in to clarify. "Ben Jones. The tall dark-haired guy who just left."

Alia's eyes widen in a look of horror. "Oh. Him. I…I'm so sorry. I…wasn't checking him out. Really. I didn't know you and he were… you know…"

"No, no, no. We're not like that. He's a friend."

"Okay." Alia still looks confused.

"So, what I wanted to say is, he'd really like to meet you. And I could, you know, arrange that."

Alia looks at her, head inclined slightly. "And why would you do that?"

"Like I said. He's a friend. And, you know..." She takes a deep breath. "I want him to be happy."

Alia shakes her head. "But not with you."

"No."

"Ahh." Realization dawns across Alia's face. "So, you are... I mean, you like..."

"Girls?" Meadow sighs. "I know you've probably heard that. But, fact is, I'm not really into girls either."

"I don't understand."

"Yeah, me either. Let's just call me weird and leave it at that. So let's not talk about me. Let's talk about Ben."

For the first time, Alia laughs. It nettles Meadow a little. "What's so funny?"

"You've read about the Bechdel test?"

"The one where two women in a book or movie are supposed to talk about something other than a man?"

Alia nods, still smiling.

"Okay, first," Meadow says, "this isn't a movie. And second, if we're going to be friends, we're going to talk about a lot of shit other than boys. But here and now, I want to talk about my friend Ben."

"So, we're going to be friends, then?"

This time it's Meadow's turn to smile. "Guess so."

Alia nods. "Then I'd like it if you'd introduce me to your friend Ben."

"Okay, great. See you around, then?"

"See you around."

Meadow's feeling cheerful as she walks away. Today's good deed is done. Then she spots Brandon Ochs and one of his gang heading her way. *Fuck*. She hates doing it, but she alters her path to make a beeline for the ladies' room inside. As she gets inside and hopefully just out of their sight, she breaks into a run and slips inside the restroom door just as she hears the door to the courtyard bang open. She goes into a stall, shuts that door, and locks it. When she was a freshman, the school had removed the stall doors "for security" because they were concerned students might be smoking weed in the stalls. Thankfully, a parental protest and the threat of lawsuits backed them down. In a long-practiced move, she perches on a toilet and draws her knees up so no one can see her legs. She doesn't think Brandon and his slack-jawed henchman will dare brave the barrier of the girls' room door, but he's perfectly capable of sending his bitch girlfriend inside to drag her out. She's actually more afraid of Amber than she is of her boyfriend. Brandon will push, humiliate, maybe even smack someone around to get his jollies. Some of the looks Amber gives her have Meadow convinced the blond girl could literally kill her. She stays there, carefully hidden, barely daring to breathe, for at least forty-five minutes. There's no way Brandon has the attention span to wait that long. One or two girls come in, do whatever they came in for, and leave. No one calls her or rattles the stall door. Meadow still doesn't move. When she's sure he's gone, she climbs down, takes a deep breath, and opens the door. No one. She walks as quietly to the bathroom door as she can and peeks out. The halls are empty. Classes have started, but she decides she's had enough of this place for the day. She walks out, brushing her tears away with the back of her hand.

# NINE

Of all the places he's ever been in his life, Keller finds this one the most unlikely: waiting in a line of cars outside an elementary school to pick up his son. It's something Keller's own father had never been there to do, and he's determined to be a better man in every way than the man who abandoned him for most of his life, then came back a year ago bringing only more violence and heartbreak. The cars inch forward, stopping and starting, the sound of children shouting on the playground overriding the radio Keller's turned down low. He sees Francis standing in a group of other children, under the watchful eyes of a middle-aged black woman who Keller knows as one of the teacher assistants. The woman sees Keller's truck, bends down, and says something to the boy. He looks down the line and nods solemnly. Marie assures him that Francis is a normal, happy boy, but he's never been anything but solemn in Keller's presence. "Give him time," Marie tells him. "He'll warm up." Keller wants to ask when, but he knows there's no answer. So he hangs in, does what needs to be done, and waits.

Keller pulls the car to the curb, leans over, and opens the door. "Afternoon, Mr. Keller," the assistant calls as Francis climbs in, tossing his backpack onto the floor at his feet.

"Afternoon, Mrs. Newby." He smiles back before turning to Francis. "Buckle up." The boy looks straight ahead, not answering. Keller looks up at Mrs. Newby, who shrugs.

25

"Rough day," she mouths at him. "Buckle up now, Frank." Only then does the boy fumble for the seat belt and fasten across his body, sighing audibly as if it's a major imposition. Mrs. Newby shuts the door and Keller pulls off.

"Bad day?" he says.

Francis shrugs. "It was okay."

"Doesn't seem like it was okay."

Keller recalls how Mrs. Newby addressed him. "So you're going by Frank now?"

The boy doesn't answer right away. Then he mutters something that Keller doesn't hear. "What was that?"

"I said," the boy's voice rises with irritation, "Francis is a stupid name. It's a girl's name."

Keller gets it now. "So, someone giving you sh—giving you grief over Francis?"

No answer again. "It's a good name," Keller says. "It was your grandfather's name. But even he went by Frank. When he grew up."

"They called him Francis at the funeral," the boy says in a small voice. "I didn't know who they were talking about."

Keller looks over. The boy is staring straight ahead, his face expressionless.

"You miss your grandfather a lot, don't you?" Keller asks.

The boy nods.

Keller nods back. "I get that. He was a good man. And he loved your mom like crazy."

Francis turns to Keller. His voice is even, without malice, but the words cut Keller as deeply as a curse. "He said you never brought my mom anything but trouble and pain."

They're almost to Marie's house by then, and they make the rest of the trip in silence, Keller trying to figure out a better rejoinder than "He may have been right."

Marie's house sits on the top of a hill in the middle of forty acres of farmland that hasn't been tilled in years, since the last occupant passed away and his children were too involved in their lives away to come back and work it. Some of the fields have grown up, on the way to returning to woodlands, but the acre or so of grass around the house at the end of the long dirt driveway is cut short. The driveway slopes down to where the house sits on a flat space, the land falling away on a long slope behind the house.

Marie's car has just pulled up when they arrive; Keller sees both doors opening. Ben's on the opposite side from Keller and he can only see Marie, but she's clearly agitated; she leaps from the car and shouts something to him as he walks to the front door with swift, angry steps. Too late, Keller remembers he was supposed to keep Francis away for a time so Ben and Marie could talk. "Ben," Francis says, his voice fraught with alarm. As Keller pulls to a stop behind Marie, the boy grabs his backpack and leaps from the car. He runs past where Marie is standing, passing her without a glance as if she isn't there. Keller gets out and walks up beside her as she stands in the open door of the car. She clenches her fist and slams it down on the car roof. Keller sees Francis catch up with Ben. The older boy turns and smiles down at his half-brother. He crouches down and says something to him. Then Ben looks over and sees Keller standing with his mother. His face freezes. He stands up, says something to Francis, and takes his hand. The two of them go inside the small farmhouse.

"I take it things didn't go well," Keller said. "Sorry. I was supposed to keep him away longer."

Marie turns to him, and he can see the tears brimming in her eyes. He aches to reach out and take her in his arms, but Francis's words are still lacerating him: *you never brought my mom anything but trouble and pain.* So he stands next to her, arms held awkwardly by his sides.

"God," Marie is saying. "He is so infuriating. He's so much like his father…" She stops and gets hold of herself, ducking back into the car to snag a tissue out of the center console. "How'd things go with you and Francis?"

"About the same."

She sighs. "He's having some problems adjusting, Jack. And I take the blame. I kept him away from you too long."

27

"He says your dad told him I'd never brought you anything but pain."

She looks stricken. "Jack, that's…it's not true."

"True or not," he says, "that's what Francis believes. Oh, he wants to go by Frank now."

She steps back slightly, eyes narrowing. "What are you saying?"

"Sounds like some kids are picking on him for being called Francis. He thinks Frank will make him sound less like a girl."

"Okay, fine. But you know what I mean. What are you saying about Francis?"

Keller shakes his head and looks at the door of the house behind the deep front porch. His son is on the other side of that door, but he might as well be on the other side of the moon. "I shouldn't have come here."

She closes her eyes, and her next words come out through clenched teeth. "God damn it, Jack, I do *not need this* right now, too."

"I know. We'll talk later. You go deal with Ben and Frank."

She opens her eyes and shakes her head. "Frank. It makes him sound so grown up. I'm not sure I'm ready for that."

"Who is?" Keller starts back to his car, then turns around. "I'm not leaving. Not yet. But maybe you should consider that your dad was right."

As Keller gets back in his car, another voice from the past comes to him. *You bring death,* the voice had told him, *and Hell follows with you.* He watches Marie go into the house. When he closes his eyes, he has a vision of the house in flames, the smell of blood and burned flesh in his nostrils. *Burning, they're burning…* He closes his eyes, breathes deeply. Over the years, he's learned to deal more effectively with the flashbacks. *In.* He draws a long, slow breath, not stopping until his lungs are full to bursting. *Out.* He lets the air out slowly, under his conscious control. The effort and the concentration push the images of flames in the desert night and the memory of the smell of burning flesh from his mind. When he's able to breathe normally again, Keller gets in his car and leaves.

# TEN

As Keller pulls into his driveway, he sees a familiar light blue compact car parked in front of the door. A sandy-haired man in a pair of blue jeans and a green polo shirt is stepping away from his door. Keller stops the car and gets out. "Afternoon, Reverend."

The man approaches, an apologetic smile on his unlined, handsome face. "Afternoon, Jack. And like I told you, you can call me Ed." He sticks out his hand.

Keller shakes the hand. It's a good handshake, firm but not overbearing. "I was going to bring the rent by later."

"I know." Ed MacDonald nods. "I was just leaving you a note to let you know I'm going to be at the church all afternoon and that you can bring it up there." He nods to the simple white building that sits across a neatly mowed field from Keller's rented house. That house is a small two-bedroom stone structure, built in the early 1900s by a homesick Scot who'd missed the stone houses of the Highlands. It had been the old country church's parsonage before MacDonald and his family had their third child. Now they live in town and Keller rents the place for a couple hundred a month and doing simple chores around the church.

"Come on inside," Keller says. "I'll get the rent for you." He pulls the note from the door and goes inside, MacDonald following in his wake. The minister takes a seat in the house's tiny living room as Keller goes into the back bedroom to fetch the cash. He pulls a metal lockbox out of a closet and dips into the stash of currency that's part of his father's legacy. The money had been in a safe deposit box in Florida, and Keller tries not to think too much about where it may have come from. He's been trying to put the past behind him. But if today's proved anything, it's that the past has a way of following close behind, whether you want it to or not.

Keller walks back into the living room and hands MacDonald the cash. The minister puts it in his pocket.

"Not going to count it?" Keller asks.

MacDonald smiles. "You wouldn't try to shortchange a preacher, would you?"

Keller shrugs. "You never know."

MacDonald inclines his head curiously. "Everything okay, Jack?"

"Yeah. Fine."

MacDonald doesn't appear convinced. "Okay. Sorry. It's just that you seem a little troubled."

"It's nothing."

"If you say so." MacDonald turns to leave, then turns back as he gets to the door. "By the way, we're having our Wednesday night prayer meeting tonight at seven. You know you're always invited."

"Thanks for the invitation," Keller says, "but I've never been much of a praying man."

"Uh-huh." MacDonald smiles. "And how's that working?" Without waiting for an answer, he turns and walks out.

Keller shakes his head. The man's relentless in trying to get him through those church doors, but Keller can't bring himself to dislike him. Relentlessness has always been one of his own character traits, after all.

# ELEVEN

The man who trudges out of the debarkation area at Raleigh-Durham airport is tall, overweight, and grumpy looking. His most striking feature is a thick mane of silver hair brushed back from a jowly, light-brown face. He's dragging a roller-bag behind him that looks as if it was dropped out of the airplane immediately before landing. He stops and looks around, searching. Waller raises the hand-lettered paper sign up higher, hoping to attract the man's attention. AL-MANSOUR, the sign says.

The man Waller knows as Mohammed Al-Mansour has spotted the sign and is striding towards him. Waller lowers the sign and puts out his hand. "Mr. Al-Mansour? Patrick Waller."

The man hesitates. Waller sees that he's sweating, even in the frigid air conditioning. Waller stands, still smiling, hand still out, until Al-Mansour grudgingly takes it for a perfunctory shake. "Is the car ready?"

Waller nods. "Yes, sir. My associate is bringing it around. We'll take you to a motel near the property." He smiles again, apologetically this time. "I'm afraid the accommodations may not be what you're used to."

"Change them," Al-Mansour barks. "If this truly is the man I've been looking for, he will have people watching nearby hotels. I'm willing to drive a little further to preserve security."

*You mean you're willing to have us drive you further*, Waller thinks as Al-Mansour stomps toward the baggage claim, dragging his battered roller bag behind him like a sea anchor. Waller's not crazy about the imperious tone, but he recognizes it from his days back in the Sandbox. This guy was Iraqi military, a colonel at least. Maybe even a general. From the sound of things, Warehouse Man, the guy they'd been surveilling, may have even been part of the same cabal. A more vicious pack of backstabbing assholes hadn't been seen in that part of the world since the glory days of the Ottoman Empire. A thought occurs to him. "Sir," he calls out, trotting to catch up. "We were staying in that same motel. Do you think—"

"No," Al-Mansour interrupts with the air of someone who regards interrupting subordinates as a God-given right. "He would be looking for...people like me."

"Yes, sir." Now Waller knows why they were hired. He's betting Al-Mansour had tried to track the target using his own people and they'd been made. A couple of white guys, with guns, in this area, though...even if they looked military, the area was full of current and former soldiers from nearby Fort Bragg. Waller does appreciate the deviousness. But it also makes him wonder if Tench isn't right. Al-Mansour is using them. What would be wrong about using him back?

# TWELVE

Keller puts the last dish from his dinner away and contemplates another quiet evening at home. He's been working his way through the collection of worn paperbacks left behind by MacDonald. The minister's taste leans towards classic adventure tales: some Alastair Maclean, some Louis L'Amour, even some Edgar Rice Burroughs with racy Frank Frazetta cover illustrations that MacDonald probably had to hide when parishioners dropped by. He's settling onto his worn couch when he hears the knock on the front door. As he goes to answer, he looks up at the shotgun he's stowed on a pair of brackets above the doorway. The weapon is always loaded, a round of double-ought buckshot in the chamber. Logic tells him he's safe now. All his enemies have been left behind him, and most in the ground. Since he's a convicted felon now, that shotgun, as well as the half dozen other weapons scattered around the small house, could land him back in prison if the cops found them. But they help him sleep at night.

The man standing in the doorway when he opens it is a head shorter than Keller. His face is middle-aged, but his slicked-back hair and neatly trimmed mustache are still dark, perhaps a little darker than is strictly possible in nature. He's dressed a pair of light brown polyester slacks, a bit tight around the middle, and a short-sleeved dress shirt. His skin is light brown, and Keller can't tell at first if he's Middle Eastern or Hispanic. When he speaks, however, it's with an accent Keller hasn't heard in years, the pseudo-British accent of the educated Arab.

"Mr. Jack Keller?" the man asks, blinking at him through horn-rimmed glasses.

"I'm Jack Keller. How can I help you?"

The man holds out a tentative hand. "My name is Adnan Khoury. I am the father of Bassim and Alia Khoury."

Keller shakes the man's hand. It's a handshake firmer than the man's timid appearance would seem to indicate. There's something off about the man, something Keller can't quite put his finger on. But he seems harmless enough. Keller steps aside. "Come on in."

Khoury steps in, looking around at the small space, taking in the worn furniture and the dim lighting. His expression doesn't change, but Keller feels the judgment. It irritates him. "What can I do for you, Mr. Khoury?"

The man looks at him, his chin raised slightly, almost defiantly. Keller can tell that his is costing him something. "I want to thank you," Khoury says, "for helping my son and my daughter today."

"Ah," Keller says. Khoury seems more pissed off than grateful, but Keller decides to take the words at face value. For now. "You're welcome. It was no trouble." Khoury doesn't speak, just continues to look around. "Um," Keller says, nonplussed. "Would you like something to drink? I think I have tea." It's in the back of the cupboard, left by MacDonald and his family, and Keller has no idea if it's still any good, but he needs to say something, and he recalls from his short time in Iraq that the locals sucked down tea by the gallon.

"No." Khoury's answer is so abrupt that Keller's annoyed again, even after Khoury adds, "Thank you." Again, it's as if the words are being dragged out of him. He turns to Keller. "Mr. Keller, I would like to offer you employment."

Keller blinks in surprise. "Excuse me?"

Khoury sighs. "Perhaps I will have that tea."

# THIRTEEN

The three of them meet in Al-Mansour's room at a Red Roof Inn just off I-40 in Durham. It's a good hour's drive to the mission site, but the boss seems to think that's necessary for security, and he's paying. Waller's acceptance of the situation is strained by the fact that while Al-Mansour has a room of his own, he doesn't want to spring for separate rooms for him and Tench. It's only a problem because somewhere between the last mission he and Tench did together and this one, Tench has begun snoring. It's making Waller irritable.

Waller and Tench are seated at the small table by the window in a pair of cheap, uncomfortable motel chairs. Al-Mansour is on the king bed, lying comfortably with a file folder balanced on his ample belly. He closes the folder and peers at them over a pair of gold half-glasses. "So. We move to Phase Two."

*Finally*, Waller thinks. Over a long career that's led him from the Army to private military contract work, he's gotten used to living like a mushroom: kept in the dark and fed bullshit. But he's never learned to like it. "Yes, sir," he says.

Tench nods. "We're all ears, sir."

Al-Mansour shifts his weight. "This man, this fellow who goes by the name of Khoury," he almost spits the last word, "he has something that belongs to me."

Even out of the corner of his eye, Waller can see Tench's smug, triumphant look at him. He can only hope Al-Mansour is too wrapped up in his own story to see it as well. "It might help if we knew exactly what that was, sir. So we know what we're looking for, and can recognize it when we see it."

Al-Mansour shakes his head. "You won't find it on your own. He won't have it hidden anywhere near him. Not on his person. Not in his home. He's too clever for that."

Tench speaks up. "Maybe in that warehouse where he works?"

Al-Mansour ponders that, then nods reluctantly. "Unlikely, but still possible. If it's there, though, it will be well hidden."

"So," Tench says. "The quickest way to recovering your property is to get Khoury, or whatever his real name is, to tell us where it is." He smiles coldly. "And it's not information he's liable to give up willingly."

Waller can tell where this conversation is going. He's been in on a dozen like it. This is the first time it's made him feel weary and vaguely sick. *I'm feeling my age.*

Al-Mansour is nodding with approval at Tench. "Just so."

"Okay," Waller says. "We pick Khoury up. Sweat him. Make him want to give it up. Whatever it is."

"No," Tench says. Waller looks at him, surprised at the assertiveness in his tone. In all the time he's worked with Tench, the man, for all his bellyaching, has always been a follower. "We could do that. But it's like I said, right? He's not going to give up quickly. Not after this much time."

Al-Mansour is nodding again. "I think we are, as you say, on the same page of music. And speaking of time, there is another factor that makes time important."

Waller and Tench look at each other. "Do tell."

Al-Mansour sighs. "Mr. Khoury and his family have some... friends."

*Of course they do,* Waller thinks. "Sir," he says, "we're new to this situation. So we need to know everything that's going on here. We need to know all the players."

Al-Mansour nods reluctantly. "Your Central Intelligence Agency has someone detailed to protect Mr. Khoury."

Waller resists the temptation to bury his head in his hands. "That is definitely a factor, sir."

"One we should have been told from the start," Tench says. "Sir," he adds grudgingly.

Waller decides to concentrate on the immediate. "How many someones are we talking about here, sir?"

Al-Mansour makes a disparaging noise. "One agent. He moves the Khourys from place to place. I can't believe he's anyone of any importance." He leans forward, eyes bright. "So here is my plan. We take out this agent. His name that he is using now is Wilson, by the way. As I said, I do not believe this is a priority. It will take some time for the Agency to send a replacement. In that time, we persuade Mr. Khoury to divulge the location of my property."

"And how do we do that?" Waller asks, although he already knows the answer.

Tench answers for him. "We put pressure on him through the thing he cares about most. His family."

Al-Mansour nods. "Exactly." He cocks his head inquisitively at Waller. "I'm sensing that you have a problem with this, Mr. Waller."

Waller smiles tightly at him. "No, sir. But you have to agree, we're doing more now than simple intelligence gathering."

"You want more money."

Waller nods. "It's only fair, sir." *I sell my soul*, he thinks, *but it's not cheap.*

# FOURTEEN

Khoury takes a sip of the tea Keller's prepared, then puts the cup on the coffee table. He doesn't pick it up again. It takes a few moments before he speaks. "It has not been easy for us here."

Keller doesn't answer. He's seated in the rocker across from the couch, the only other seat in the room. He holds a cold can of Red Stripe beer in his hand. Khoury had given the can a disapproving glance as Keller sat down, but Keller's tired of those looks. If his disapproval drives Khoury to get to the point faster, that's fine. If it drives him out of the house, that's fine, too.

Khoury goes on. "We have had to move around several times. For my work."

"What work do you do?"

"I am in management," Khoury says. The vagueness is another red flag, but Keller lets him go on. "I work long hours. I cannot take my son and my daughter to school. So they have to ride the bus." He looks at the table. "And that is when they are bullied. That, and after."

Keller is finally beginning to understand. The man's not just angry. He's ashamed. "What about Mrs. Khoury?" he asks.

"My wife passed away. Back in Iraq."

"I'm sorry to hear it," Keller says. "But what can I do?"

"You were a soldier, is that correct?"

Keller's eyes narrow. "And how would you know that?"

Khoury shrugs. "Something in the way you carry yourself." He smiles thinly. "Also, I asked a few questions. Am I correct, though?"

38

"Yeah. But that was a long time ago. And, well, I wasn't very good at it."

Khoury raises his eyes to Keller's. "I would like for you to take my children to school. Make sure they get there safely. Meet them at the end of the school day. Get them home, and make sure they are safe until I return."

Keller can't believe what he's hearing. "Wait a minute. You want to hire me to babysit?"

"No. This would be in the nature of security."

"A bodyguard." Keller shakes his head. "Mr. Khoury, isn't this kind of an extreme reaction to school bullying?"

"I will pay you five hundred dollars a week," Khoury says.

"Mr. Khoury—" Keller begins, but Khoury speaks over him.

"Seven hundred and fifty dollars."

Keller folds his arms across his chest and leans back to regard Khoury silently. Then he speaks. "Mr. Khoury, are you sure all you are worried about is a few redneck kids hassling your son and daughter?"

Khoury meets his eyes, and for a moment, the mild-mannered, nerdy manager is gone. Those eyes are eyes he's seen before, flat and hard and merciless. "I don't know what else you might be talking about. But I will do what it takes to protect my children. Anything it takes."

Keller drains the rest of his beer and stands up. "I can respect that. But I know you're lying to me." He cuts off Khoury's rejoinder. "But you know what? I'll take your job. You want to know why?" He doesn't wait for an answer. "One, because I came here to see my son, but he's got a problem seeing me. That's nothing that concerns you, but it does leave me with some time on my hands. Two, well..." He fixes Khoury's eyes with his own. "I saw your daughter today at school. She was facing down three guys, each one of them about thirty pounds heavier than her. She was doing it to protect her little brother."

Khoury looks down at the table. "She is a girl. Bassim should have—"

Keller interrupts again, enjoying the way that makes Khoury visibly clench his jaw. "Oh, I give the boy respect as well. She kept having to pull him back from charging into an ass kicking. You've got some good kids, Mr. Khoury. Tough. Fearless. I like that. And I don't like bullies. Whoever they might be." He holds out his hand. "We have a deal?"

Khoury stands up. That look in his eyes is gone, hidden behind the middle manager facade. But now Keller knows that facade for what it is. "We have a deal." He takes Keller's hand, gives it a quick shake.

When he tries to pull away, Keller squeezes tight, holding the hand in his own. "It would help," he says, "if you come clean with me. Tell me what else you're worried about. Think about it." He releases Khoury's hand.

For a moment, that hard look is back, then it disappears behind the mask again. "Thank you, Mister Keller. Can you start tomorrow?"

"Sure. I'll be there at seven thirty."

Khoury merely nods and leaves.

Keller takes a seat in his easy chair and picks up one of the paperbacks, a Louis L'Amour adventure called *Last of the Breed*. After a few minutes of trying to concentrate, he puts the book down. "What the fuck did I just do?" he says aloud. He just took a job working for someone who he knows is lying to him. A job that's almost certainly more dangerous than dealing with a bunch of high school bullies. The look in Khoury's eyes tells him there's more going on than he knows. It's then that he realizes why he said yes.

Because that feeling, the feeling that the only thing he's certain of is that there's more danger than meets the eye…that feels more like being home than anything he's felt here.

# FIFTEEN

"You did *what*?" Alia tries very hard to avoid being disrespectful to her father, but she can't keep the disbelief and outrage from her voice.

The three of them—Alia, Bassim and their father—are seated around the kitchen table. Father had called them downstairs from their rooms after he returned from the errand he said he had to run after supper.

Their father remains calm. "This is for your safety. I heard about you being threatened by mean boys at school."

"So you hired us a nanny?" They've been speaking Arabic until now, but Alia switches to English. It seems more suited to her anger. "Could you possibly humiliate us more?"

She glances over at Bassim. His dark eyes move back and forth uncertainly between her and her father, like a spectator at a tennis match. She feels sick to her stomach. Bassim hates it when they argue, she knows. But she can't contain her anger at being treated as if she were a child. "I can't believe you did this."

Bassim speaks up. "Hey, it's not like we're in love with riding the bus. Maybe we can sleep a little later."

Their father turns to him, his tone icy. "Trust you to think of sleep. If you were a man, and willing to protect your sister—"

"Leave him alone!" Alia flares, too late. She sees Bassim's face crumple with shame, both from her father's words and the fact that his older sister has to defend him. He gets up and leaves the room. Alia whirls on her father. "Why do you have to pick on him? What was he supposed to do? Get beaten up?"

"To protect his family?" he snaps back. "Better than being a coward."

In her rage, she blindly reaches out for the thing that will hurt him most. "Like you? Running from town to town? Moving us every time you see a shadow?" She shifts back to Arabic for maximum impact. "Who's the real coward, Father?"

For a moment, she fears she's gone too far. His face freezes and there's a look in his eyes she's only seen a few times before, a cold, dead look like the eyes of a hawk. But when he speaks, his voice is calm and modulated. "You won't be riding the bus tomorrow," he says. "Mr. Keller will pick you up at seven thirty."

"And who is this Mr. Keller?" She tries to keep the trembling out of her voice. That look in her father's eyes never fails to unsettle her.

"You met him today. He stopped those boys from bothering you."

She shakes her head. "And you trust your children with his man you just met?"

"I know men like him," he says. "I've known them all my life. They will die for you. They will take a bullet for you." He smiles in a way that frightens her more than that look. In times like this, she wonders if she really knows her father at all. "Actually," he says, "it's what they're good for."

# SIXTEEN

Keller's dozing on the couch, his book splayed out on his chest when he's awakened by the sound of a car pulling up outside and the shine of headlights through the open windows. He sits up, instantly alert, and checks the time on the wall clock across the room. Ten minutes past midnight. He tenses. In his experience, visitors after midnight rarely bring good news.

He's at the door before he hears the knock, the shotgun taken down from above the door and leaning against the wall in the entranceway. He looks out of the tiny leaded glass window in the old wooden door and relaxes. He opens the door. "Hey," he says to Marie.

"Hey," she says. Her eyes are tired and a little red, as if she's been crying, but not recently. "Can I come in?"

"Sure." He steps back and lets her in. She's dressed in a light-yellow sundress, and he catches a subtle whiff of perfume as she passes. He's never known her to wear perfume, but he can't say he dislikes it. "You want something to drink?" he asks.

She looks around at the living room, and he wonders for a moment if she's heard him. Then she turns to him, her eyes meeting his, then skittering away. She's nervous about something. "Sure."

"Tea? Water? I've got a couple of beers left."

She nods. "A beer would be good."

He fetches a pair of Red Stripes from the kitchen. When he re-enters the living room, she's perched on the edge of the couch. He hands her the already opened beer, hesitates, then sits next to her.

"What's up?"

She takes a sip of beer, then turns to him. "I'm sorry I was kind of short with you today."

"It's okay." He shrugs. "You have a lot going on."

"Are you really thinking about leaving?"

"Well," he begins, but she stops him with a hand on his arm.

"I don't want you to leave," she says. She puts the beer on the coffee table, and before he can react, she leans over and kisses him, hard, so hard it rocks him back a little. He fumbles his beer onto the coffee table, not caring if it falls on the carpet, and kisses her back, caressing her hair. The touch of her lips, the feel of her hair between his fingers, brings all of the feelings he's ever had for her rushing back in a torrent. He takes a deep breath, drinking in the scent of her like a man coming in from the wilderness. The two of them stand, still kissing, hands moving over each other's bodies. They begin a clumsy stumble toward the bedroom, Keller guiding Marie with gentle pressure. She pulls his shirt up and over his head as the pass through the door, causing him to stumble into the doorjamb. That gets them both laughing as they fall together into bed.

***

Afterwards, they're lying side by side, breathing hard and covered with sweat.

"Wow," she whispers, her voice hoarse. She props herself up on one elbow and smiles. "I wondered if it would be as good as it was before."

He smiles back. "And?"

She leans over to kiss him. "Better. Probably because we're not running for our lives."

He chuckles. "I thought that added spice."

She sits up and swings her legs over the bed. "I gave up spicy food, too. It all ties together." He reaches out to stroke her back. She grabs his hand and kisses it. "Be right back."

While she's in the bathroom, he lies back and closes his eyes. *I'm glad I'm not leaving*, he thinks. *I want to stay. She wants me to stay.*

She comes back in and stretches out beside him, still smiling.

Keller takes her into his arms and looks in her eyes. They're everything he remembers, the brilliant blue of a sunny winter sky. Her eyelids are narrowed, her lips slightly parted with renewed desire. Keller wants nothing better than to draw those lips back to his, to lose himself in those eyes again.

"I'm staying," he says. "I took a job."

"That's awesome." She snuggles against him, stroking his chest.

He caresses her hair. "Maybe I should have told you before."

"Well," she chuckles, "we were a little busy."

"Yeah. But…"

She looks up at him. "But what?"

"I don't know. It's not important."

She pulls away slightly and sits up. "Tell me what you're thinking."

He sits up as well. "I mean, would it have made a difference if you'd known I was staying? Would you still have…?"

Her eyes narrow. "Wait a minute. Are you wondering if the only reason I came here to be with you was to try to get you to stay?"

He feels the moment slipping away and begins to realize how big a mistake he's made. "I just wanted to make sure."

"To make…sure." She shakes her head. "To make sure of what? That I wasn't using my body to try to manipulate you? To *hook* you?"

"No," he protests. "That wasn't it."

"Yeah. That's exactly it." She gets up. He reaches out to stop her, but she's already out of his grasp. Without another word, she picks up her clothes and silently puts them back on. When she's pulled the sundress back on, she looks at him. Her eyes are brimming with tears.

"I know a lot has happened since we were together. I know you were in love with someone else. I know you lost her. And I know all of this because you were honest with me." She takes a deep, shuddering breath before going on. "I was just hoping you had enough love left for me to realize I'm honest, too."

"I…" Keller says, but she yanks the door open and disappears into the night. "God damn it," he mutters.

# SEVENTEEN

Keller arises early the next morning after a night of uneasy dreams. He performs a quick workout: pushups, sit-ups, triceps dips between a pair of kitchen chairs, and finally a few chin-ups on the bar he's placed in the doorway of the second bedroom. When he's done, he takes a deep breath, satisfied that he hasn't fallen too far out of shape. He takes a moment to clear the fast food bags and newspapers out of his truck before driving to the Khoury house.

Alia and her brother are standing outside, waiting. The girl is dressed in a below-the-knee navy skirt, white blouse, and her ever-present head scarf. Bassim's wearing jeans and a T-shirt that says DISTURBED. Keller assumes that's a band. Both have backpacks on their shoulders. He gets out and meets them halfway up the walk. "Good morning." He smiles at them.

The girl is icily polite. "Good morning, Mr. Keller." She walks past him without another word.

Keller looks at Bassim. The young man shrugs. "She's not crazy about this idea," he says in a low voice. Then he looks past Keller. "Nice truck."

"Thanks." They climb in, with Bassim taking the front seat and Alia taking the back seat of the crew cab. She's placed her backpack at her feet and stares straight ahead, not speaking. Keller starts to say something, then lets it go. She'll either warm up or she won't.

As he starts the truck and puts it in gear, Bassim leans forward and

46

punches the power button on the radio. "You mind?"

"No," Keller says. "But how about you ask first next time?"

A country station out of Raleigh is blaring a song about a girl in a truck. Bassim grimaces. "Sorry. You mind if I change the station?"

"Doesn't matter to me," Keller says.

Bassim punches the buttons, scanning through station after station, stopping on each one for only a second before pronouncing his verdict and moving on. "Sucks. Sucks. Really sucks."

"Bassim!" Alia speaks up from the backseat. "Language!"

"Bite me, sis," the boy says without heat. He gives an exasperated sigh and snaps the radio off. "The stations around here blow donkey dick, man."

"Bassim!"

Keller gives him a sardonic smile. "I'll inform the management of your complaint."

Bassim laughs. "No, really. How do you stand it?"

Keller shrugs. "I don't listen to the radio much. Not anymore." While he was doing his prison time in Arizona, he'd had a cellmate named Mendez who'd celebrated earning the privilege of having a radio by playing the thing twenty-four seven, set to the station that played "all today's hits, all day long." The second happiest day of Keller's incarceration was when Mendez's term was up and he left, taking his radio with him. The usual din of prison life had sounded like sweet silence after that.

Bassim is speaking, breaking into the memories. "Pittsburgh has some pretty kick-ass stations."

"You miss the place?"

"Yeah." He sighs. "I was just starting to figure it out. Make some friends. Now..." He looks out the window at the fields rolling by, and his voice turns bitter. "Here we are. In this shithole."

"Bassim!" the girl says again. "That's enough! Do you want me to tell Father?"

Bassim looks at Keller. "Hey, Mr. Keller, does your job include keeping me from smacking my sister in the head?"

"It wasn't specifically discussed. But I'm fairly sure that's part of the job description."

"Well, shit." The boy sinks into his seat with a theatrically exaggerated posture of despair.

Keller grins and goes on. "I also think I'm supposed to keep her from whacking you upside the head. But if you keep trying to get under her skin like you've been doing, I'm not sure I can hold her back."

The boy is all wounded innocence. "Me? What did I do?"

"The language, for one. You know it gets a rise out of her, but you keep doing it. What's that called again?"

"Trolling." Alia speaks up from the backseat. Keller glances back. A smile plays at the corners of her lips.

"Right," Keller says. "Bassim, stop trolling your sister."

Bassim's face turns sorrowful. *This kid should be an actor*, Keller thinks.

"Mr. Keller. You probably shouldn't try to be cool. It doesn't suit you."

Keller matches the look as best he can. "I'll keep it in mind." That makes Bassim laugh and Alia look away. Keller's sure she's hiding her own smile.

They arrive at the school, where a line of cars is moving slowly through a circular driveway in front of the glass doors of the main building. Marie is standing by the curb, watchful eyes on the traffic. Keller sees her freeze as she catches sight of his truck. "Shit," he mutters under his breath, then glances at Alia. "Sorry."

She's been concentrating on making sure everything she needs is in her bookbag and looks up. "For what?"

"Nothing." They've pulled up to the front. Marie is frowning at Jack as Bassim opens the door. "I'll be here at three o'clock," Keller tells them. He reaches above the visor and hands them each an index card. "That's my cell number. If you get held up, let me know. Or, you know, if you need anything."

Bassim nods and takes the card before sliding off the seat and out of the truck. "Hey," he greets Marie, then bolts past her.

Alia looks at the card, then places it in an outside pocket of her bag. "Thank you for the ride, Mr. Keller. But I still don't need a nanny." With as much dignity as she can muster, she gets down from the truck, nods to Marie, and walks into the school.

Marie positions herself inside the door, eyes narrowed. "What the hell, Jack?"

"I'm sorry about last night. I—"

"This is the job you took?" She shakes her head in disbelief.

He nods. "It's a weird situation. And we need to talk. About the safety of those kids."

Her posture stiffens. "The Khourys? What about them?"

The people waiting behind them are beginning to honk their horns. Any delay risks making them late for work. "I'll call you," Keller says. "And again, I'm sorry about—"

"Just go." Marie slams the door and motions him angrily to move forward. There's nothing he can do but comply.

# EIGHTEEN

On the way home, Keller stops at a local diner. After buying a newspaper from one of the racks outside and taking a seat in one of the booths, he orders coffee and the farmer's special breakfast. The coffee is strong enough to peel the enamel off his teeth, but that's the way Keller likes it. He's only taken a few sips and opened his paper when a man slides into the seat across from him. He's smiling. Keller doesn't return it. He puts the paper down and looks the man over. He's in his mid-thirties, dressed in a dark off-the-rack suit. He has thinning red hair and a friendly, open expression on his pale face that Keller immediately mistrusts. "Can I help you with something?" he asks.

The red-haired man's smile never wavers. "I hate to just barge in like this."

"And yet, here we are."

The man acts as if he doesn't notice the tone. "It's kind of an urgent matter. About some mutual acquaintances we share."

*Here we go.* He wonders if this will be the truth or another layer of bullshit. Probably some combination of both. "Let me guess. You're talking about the Khourys."

The man nods and sticks out his hand. "My name's Ted Wilson."

Keller doesn't take the hand. "I doubt it. But it'll do for the moment. Who are you with, Mr. Wilson?"

Wilson's smile doesn't waver as he withdraws the hand. "I don't blame you for being suspicious. Given what you've been through recently."

"I suppose the fact that you've checked my history is supposed to rattle me. Consider me rattled. Now either answer my question or get the fuck out of this booth and let me read my paper."

The middle-aged waitress has arrived with Keller's plate of eggs, pancakes, and link sausages. She scowls at the profanity as she sets it down. She looks at Wilson and it's clear she doesn't approve of him either. "You want something, sir?"

"I will have some of that excellent coffee of yours," Wilson smiles.

"Get him a to-go cup," Keller adds. "He's not staying."

She looks alarmed. "We don't want any trouble in here, you two."

"There won't be any," Wilson says. "Promise."

The waitress is clearly unconvinced, but she moves off.

Wilson turns back to Keller. "In answer to your question, I'm with Homeland Security."

"Uh-huh."

"And the Khoury family...well, they're kind of a special case."

"Do tell."

Wilson lowers his voice. "What I'm about to tell you is highly classified."

"Meaning you're about to feed me a line of complete bullshit. There's no way you'd tell me anything really classified. If I ever did have any kind of clearance, it's long gone. And you would know that."

Wilson sighs. He's no longer smiling. "I was told you'd be difficult."

"You were told right." Keller takes a bite of his eggs.

"There's more to this situation than you know."

Keller laughs. "Well, that's been the story of my life so far, hasn't it?" He puts down his fork. "Let me tell you what I do know that I've managed to figure out on my own. You're probably not actually DHS, but you're *some* kind of spook. Adnan Khoury's an asset of some kind. Someone you need to keep under wraps. But you have to keep moving him. His kids tell me they just moved here from Pittsburgh, and it sounded like they left in a hurry. So, I'm thinking Mr. Khoury, or whatever his real name is, has someone mightily pissed off. Probably someone in the Iraqi community recognized him, or tipped someone off from back home. How am I doing so far?"

Wilson doesn't answer, but from the way his face has gone blank, Keller assumes he's scored at least a couple of points. He takes a bite of sausage and stops to savor it. The sausage is produced locally, and that and the coffee are the main reasons Keller keeps coming back to this diner. The waitress brings the coffee in a to-go cup and places it in front of Wilson before hurrying away. Keller waits until she's out of earshot before going on. "So, what did Mr. Khoury, or whoever he is, do to piss someone off back in the old country?"

Wilson takes a moment to answer. When he does, his voice is flat and emotionless. "He was a translator. He helped out our troops on a lot of—"

"More bullshit." Keller shakes his head. "Come on, Wilson. I didn't just fall off the turnip truck. The way that guy acts, he was used to getting his way. He's not getting it anymore, and it's driving him nuts. I'm thinking he was someone important. An officer, or some kind of government official. Tell me, what does a former Iraqi grand poo-bah have to do that he had to go to us for protection?"

All of Wilson's former veneer of affability is gone. "All I can tell you, Mr. Keller, is that you need to stay away from the Khoury family. We have their security in hand."

"Apparently, the dad doesn't feel that way. That's why he hired me. I guess I'm not the only one who's difficult."

"He needs to trust us," Wilson mutters.

"But he doesn't. And you know what? That actually makes me like the guy a little better." Keller puts down his fork. "Look, Wilson, I know you don't like me horning in, and I get it. I don't like you lying to me, but I get that, too. It's what you people do. But there's no need for us to butt heads. All I care about is the safety of those two kids. Now, we can help each other out. Or not. But I took on a job, and I'm going to do it. You can help me do it better by leveling with me and telling me who's after that family. I can find that out myself eventually. It's not that I'm some kind of Sherlock Holmes, by the way. It's just that you people are so goddamn bad at keeping secrets."

The last jibe makes Wilson's face go red with anger. "I'm giving you a last warning, Keller," he says. "Stay out of this."

"And I'm telling you for the last time. No." Keller goes back to his meal. Wilson stands up, takes a couple of bills out of his pocket, and tosses them on the table before striding off.

The waitress comes back with a pot of coffee and refills Keller's cup without being asked. "Wow. You really pissed that guy off."

Keller smiles at her. "It's a gift."

She chuckles. "You know him?"

"Just met him. You?"

She grimaces. "He's been coming in for a couple weeks. Lousy tipper."

"Figures. He's staying around here, then?"

She shrugs. "Must be."

"You see what he's driving?"

She looks at him with narrowed eyes. "Why do you want to know? You're not going after him, are you?"

Keller shakes his head. "Nah. But if he's coming after me, I'd like to see him coming."

"You think that might happen?" She looks alarmed. "He doesn't look like someone who'd do that."

"Probably not," Keller smiles. "But you can't be too careful."

"He some kind of trouble?"

"Some kind, yeah. Not sure what, though."

She looks around as if to check that no one's listening, then leans over. "I seen him leaving in a little blue car. One of those foreign things."

"Kia? Hyundai?"

She frowns in thought. "The first one, I think. But the thing I noticed is, it had a rental sticker on it."

Keller nods. "Good to know. Thanks."

"Seriously, hon," she says, her brow still furrowed with concern. "I don't want to see no one get hurt."

"Neither do I."

"Okay," she says, but she's still looking doubtful as she walks off to tend to her other tables. Keller finishes his meal and leaves a five dollar tip on a nine dollar and seventy-four cent check. Then he heads off to check the parking lots of the local motels for a blue rental Kia.

# NINETEEN

"I don't know about this," Waller says. This time he's behind the wheel of the truck. Tench is in the passenger seat, playing some game on his phone. The beeps and boops of the game aren't doing anything to soothe Waller's nerves. They're still a way out from their target, rolling down a narrow country road. The game makes an electronic variant on the sad trombone noise, and Tench growls in frustration before looking up. "What's the trouble?"

"We've worked for The Company before," Waller says, using the slang term they always used to use to refer to the Central Intelligence Agency. "They've been a pretty good client, actually."

Tench snorts. "They hung us out to dry in Croatia. Or have you forgotten?" Before Waller can answer, Tench bulls ahead. "You're not seeing the big picture, bro. Sure, we may ruffle a few feathers. But this is our chance to make serious bank. I'm talking retirement money. I don't know about you, but I'm gettin' too old for this shit."

Waller checks the GPS as they reach a four-way crossroads. "It better be retirement money." He hangs a left. "Because if we do this, we're burned. For good. We'll be lucky to get hired to guard latrines in Alaska."

"Fortune favors the bold, my man. Who dares, wins. Et cetera, et cetera…"

"Oh, for God's sake, will you shut the hell up?"

Tench smiles and returns to his game. Waller realizes he's not the only one who enjoys pushing his partner's buttons. He sighs as they drive on, headed for the kill.

# TWENTY

Keller has a few hours before he has to pick up the Khourys. He spends them cruising the parking lots of local motels, looking for a blue Kia. Or Hyundai. Or any small foreign car with a rental sticker. It's not a big town, and there aren't that many places to choose from. He gets a hit on the fourth place he tries. A baby blue Hyundai Elantra with an Enterprise Rent-a-Car sticker on it, parked outside a room at a mom-and-pop motor court that's definitely seen better days. "Not exactly James Bond," Keller says to himself. He pulls the truck over to a corner of the parking lot and watches the room. He doesn't particularly care if Ted Wilson notices that he's being watched. In fact, Keller realizes, he'd prefer that. Let Wilson be off balance for a change. He sits and waits for someone to come out of the room and confirm he's got the right place.

# TWENTY-ONE

Inside room 107 of the run-down hotel, Ted Blair, also known as Ted Wilson, finishes his encrypted e-mail, bounces it through a half-dozen proxy servers, and waits for the tone that lets him know it's been received back at Langley after being shunted halfway around the world. When he hears the tone, he closes his laptop and sighs. It's taken him three tries to send his report through the dodgy wi-fi of this cheap motel. Hell, Islamabad had had more dependable internet service than this hick town. But then again, it had been legal for him to operate in Islamabad, at least legal under American law. Everything about this operation has been either skirting the edge of legality or blithely driving right over the cliff. He doesn't know why his boss is so eager to coddle Fadhil Al-Masri, the man now living under the name of Adnan Khoury, but he's apparently willing to break a number of laws to do it. And after what could very well have been a career ending screw-up in Islamabad, Blair is willing to take those steps to stay in the game. He doesn't like Al-Masri very much, and he knows the feeling is mutual. But his immediate superior, at least, thinks he's an asset worth preserving, and Blair owes that woman everything.

Except now, Al-Masri's gone off the reservation, again, and hired his own bodyguard. Keller. Blair has to admit Keller's got an impressive history of getting in and out of trouble. And his estranged father had apparently forged some sort of dark legend of his own in the Cold War days and the chaos that came after. But however talented an amateur Keller may be, he's still an amateur, and Blair has no patience for amateurs.

He stands up and stretches. He considers waiting for the reply from Langley about what to do about the Keller situation, but he's getting antsy in this tiny motel room. Maybe if he has another talk with Al-Masri, the man will see reason and let him do his job without outside interference. He scoops his keys off the dresser and walks outside. As he's unlocking the rental car, he hears the honking of a horn from across the parking lot. He looks up to see a pickup truck approaching. Reflexively, he opens the door and reaches for the pistol he's hidden between the door and the driver's seat. As he comes up, gun in hand, he sees the driver of the truck passing by slowly. It's Keller. The man actually waves at him as he drives past. He speeds up and squeals his tires as he exits the parking lot. Blair has to fight down the temptation to open fire on the cocky son of a bitch. He takes a deep breath and puts the gun down, carefully sliding it beneath the seat. *Okay, the guy made you. You underestimated him, and he made you. Now what?* When he's feeling calm again, he decides to stick to his original plan. Talk to Al-Masri. Try to persuade him to cut Keller loose. He gets in the car and pulls away from the motel, not noticing the other pickup truck that falls in behind him.

# TWENTY-TWO

"He's headed for Khoury's house," Waller says.

Tench is attaching a suppressor to his favorite pistol, an HK45 tactical. "Good. So are we." He looks up. "We're coming to the bridge. Get ready."

They're traveling down a two-lane country road, with thick stands of pine trees on either side. They've been down this road at least a dozen times, and they know there's a narrow bridge coming up that spans the Deep River, one of the tributaries that come together to form the Cape Fear River. The small rental driven by their target is a quarter mile ahead, the target still oblivious to their presence. Tench looks over at Waller. "You going to make your move, bro?"

Waller speaks between gritted teeth. "Wait for it."

Tench frowns, wondering if his partner is getting cold feet. Maybe the mention of The Company has spooked him. He's about to speak up again when Waller stomps on the accelerator and the truck leaps forward, engine straining.

"Hang on," Waller says.

# TWENTY-THREE

Blair's not looking in his rearview mirror as the truck that's been behind him for the last few miles has accelerated, and it's only the suddenly increased volume of the engine that tips him off. That delay costs him. He glances back just in time to see the front of the larger vehicle draw even with his left rear quarter panel, then even with the door. He tries to speed up, too late to make any difference. The impact as the truck swerves into him shoves his small car to one side and nearly off the road. A plume of dust shoots up as his right tires kick up dirt and gravel. He's fighting the wheel, trying to force his way back onto the hard road, but the white truck swerves into him again, inexorably pushing him off to the side. He only has time to growl a curse under his breath before he looks back to the windshield and sees the bridge abutment just ahead. He brakes as hard as he can, but he's too close. With a sickening crunch of rending metal and a spray of broken glass, the car slams into the abutment.

# TWENTY-FOUR

Waller pulls the truck to a stop on the bridge, then backs up, next to the blue compact. Tench is out and moving towards the mangled pile of metal and broken glass before the truck is fully stopped. The target is slumped forward, but still moving. Tench raises his pistol in a two-handed grip and continues advancing, waiting for the point-blank shot. The first shot that rings out, however, doesn't come from his own weapon, but from inside the car. The target, injured and dazed as he is, has managed to raise his own pistol and get off a shot that whines past Tench's left ear. "Motherfucker," Tench snarls, and opens fire, the reports muffled by the suppressor to the point where all that can be heard is the action cycling on the semi-automatic. The target's head slews to one side, then his body slumps over. Tench doesn't lower his gun until he's standing by the car and can visually confirm the hole in the side of the driver's head. Without taking his eyes off the body, he motions behind him to Waller. In a moment, Waller passes him, carrying a large clay flower pot in each hand. Each pot is filled three-quarters full with a light gray powder. A long, twisted black fuse is standing up in the powder. Waller puts one of the pots on top of the car, towards the back, above the fuel tank. The other one goes on the roof above the body of the driver. Waller pulls out a cigarette lighter and lights first one fuse, then the other, as Tench begins backing away. Tench can't believe his eyes when he sees the body in the truck begin to stir. "Bro," he calls out, "I don't think he's dead."

"Too bad for him," Waller says grimly. "'Cause this shit's gonna hurt." Tench raises his gun to finish off the target, but by then the fuses have caught and Waller's running past him as fast as he can. Tench has no choice but to turn and follow. The truck's moving again before Tench can even get his passenger door fully closed. He looks back to see a figure moving inside the car. Then the homemade thermite inside the flowerpots catches fire and blossoms into twin balls of white-orange flame. The chemical reaction of the burning aluminum powder creates a cascade of molten iron that begins to cut through the thin metal of the vehicle as if it were paper. Tench turns away, nodding with satisfaction. If the son of a bitch wasn't dead before, he surely is now. He hears a dull thump and looks back again. The hot stream of metal has reached the gas tank, igniting the fuel within, and all he can see is a pillar of smoke and flame as they drive away. If experience is any guide, Tench knows there won't be much left of either driver or vehicle to identify. He turns to Waller. "We still need to get rid of this truck. We got dents all down one side that I don't think we can cover up with Bondo."

Waller doesn't take his eyes off the road or acknowledge the lame joke. "I know."

"You got something lined up?"

Waller just nods. "On it. Once we pick up the other targets. We just bought ourselves a little time."

Tench smiles. He'd been worrying that the other man might be getting a little wobbly, but his performance at the bridge was reassuring. That's good. This next part is bound to get ugly.

# TWENTY-FIVE

Alia and Bassim are waiting for him in the designated spot in front when Keller swings in. Marie's not out front today; the other SRO, a big, beefy, square-jawed ex-deputy who Keller thinks is named Rogers, is out front directing traffic. Keller's only met Rogers a couple of times, but he seems like a solid guy. He pulls the truck door open and peers at Keller, his brow wrinkling with puzzlement. "Jack, right?"

"Yeah," Keller answers. "I'm here to pick up the Khourys." He looks past Rogers to where the two are standing, looking uncertainly at each other.

Rogers's frown deepens. "You on the pickup list?"

"I should be. Their dad hired me to make sure they get to and from school okay."

Rogers shakes his head. "I didn't see the update." He cocks his head at Keller. "You're Jones's friend, right?"

"Yeah." Keller's not totally sure of that status right now, but he'll gamble on it.

Rogers nods. "Okay." He steps aside and leans the passenger seat forward to let Alia clamber in.

She nods to Rogers, then to Keller, and takes her seat in the crew cab with all the dignity of a princess climbing into her carriage, looking straight ahead. Keller represses a smile. She clearly still hates the situation, but she's not going to whine or complain anymore.

Rogers puts the seat back and Bassim climbs in. "'Sup," he says, jerking his chin at Keller with such exaggerated insouciance that Keller laughs out loud.

"'Sup," he replies. Bassim grins as they pull away.

Keller's not used to making conversation with children, but he reaches for the only subject that he can think of. "So, how was school?"

"Sucked," Bassim says cheerfully. "Sucked big ol' donkey balls."

Keller glances back at Alia to check how she reacts. She doesn't. Keller nods. She's learning. Best way to deal with someone trying to needle you is to ignore them. "How about you?" Keller calls back.

"It was fine." She's not warming up, but she's unfailingly polite. Until she turns to him and asks sweetly, "So you are Officer Jones's friend?"

Keller feels as if he's stepped into a minefield. "Yeah. You could say that."

"I heard you're her baby daddy." Bassim smirks, and suddenly Keller doesn't like him as much as he did a minute ago. He slows down, then pulls the truck over to the side of the road. Bassim looks alarmed, and even Alia has a worry line between her brows, a crack in her icy facade. Keller takes a deep breath. He's not here to frighten children. "Look, guys," he says with all the calm he can muster. "Whatever history Officer Jones and I have, that's our business. But if you really need to give someone a hard time about it, give it to me. Every day. All day if you like. But leave her alone, okay? It's a tough situation, and she's got a tough job. I don't want it getting any harder." He looks from one of them to the other. "Okay?"

Bassim is looking down, embarrassed, but Alia is nodding. When she speaks, her voice is soft. "You care a lot about her."

Keller looks her in the eye. "Yeah. I do."

"Well, okay," Bassim says, looking up with a smile. "As long as we can give *you* shit about it."

Keller smiles back. "Deal." But the smile fades. "But don't push me."

Bassim looks alarmed again, until Keller grins. "Gotcha."

Bassim shakes his head and laughs, a little nervously. "You're a fucking riot, Jack."

"Bassim," Alia says.

Keller silences her with a wave. "You don't ever need to worry, Bassim."

"Buzzy," the boy says.

Keller leans back in surprise. "What?"

Bassim nods. "I've decided I need a more American name. Buzzy's close to my real name, and it sounds pretty American, doesn't it?"

"Well, yeah," Keller says. "But..."

"Bassim!" Alia snaps, her eyes wide and mouth twisted in outrage. "You will not be...be...*Buzzy*! What are you—"

He grins at her. "Gotcha."

She looks at him in shock for a moment, then makes a sound that's a combination of a sigh and a growl, slumps back into her seat with crossed arms and turns to look out the window.

Keller scowls at Bassim. "What did I tell you about trolling your sister?"

"That it's fun?"

Keller shakes his head. "You and I are going to have a long talk, kid." He starts the truck and pulls back onto the road. Alia's slumped furiously in the backseat, while Bassim is looking absurdly pleased with himself. Despite it all, Keller's really starting to like these two.

# TWENTY-SIX

Waller and Tench arrive at the Khoury house, a one-level mid-century modern with lots of glass and odd angles, sitting on a big, sandy, wooded lot. It's a little before the time when they've determined the bus drops the kids off. The corner where they're dropped off is about fifty yards from the property, and the plan is to wait till the bus leaves, then scoop the children up and take them to the place in the country they've rented. Al-Mansour had groused about the cost, but eventually succumbed to the logic of needing someplace isolated to do whatever needed to be done. Waller has a cooler behind the seat of the truck, with a jug of chloroform and several rags pre-soaked with the stuff. "What can I say?" He'd shrugged when Tench had suggested syringes of paralytic drugs. "I'm a fan of the classics." In addition, he'd argued, drugs required precise dosages and could take minutes to take effect. This acquisition requires a fast grab and takedown. Waller had also nixed the use of the flashbang grenades they'd brought along. Too noisy, he'd said. Too likely to attract the neighbors.

Tench checks his watch. "Any minute now."

Waller nods. He chambers a round in his Beretta 9 mm, acquired in a Fayetteville pawn shop under one of a dozen false sets of papers. He doesn't think the pistol will be necessary, but he's always taken a suspenders-and-belt attitude towards this kind of operation. It never hurts to be prepared, because there's always something going wrong.

Like today. It's not a bus that pulls up to the corner down the road, it's a big black pickup that pulls into the Khoury's driveway. And it's not the skinny boy or the tall girl who get out first, it's a tall, rangy guy with long blond hair.

"Who the hell is that guy?" Tench mutters.

Waller shakes his head. "I don't know. He looks familiar for some reason."

"Guess they're not riding the bus." Tench lets out an exasperated sigh. "So I guess we have to take out this jackleg now."

The blond man is saying something to the kids, a smile on his face. Then he glances their way and the smile vanishes. He turns slightly, and a shock of recognition runs through Waller. "No. Fucking. Way."

# TWENTY-SEVEN

Keller pulls the truck into the driveway, laughing at Bassim's imitation of Mr. Lynch, the science teacher. He stops and sets the parking brake. "Okay, guys. Go on in. I'm going to look around a bit."

"For what?" Alia looks at him curiously.

"Just getting the lay of the land." He opens the door and steps down. If he's going to do a proper job of guarding, he needs to reconnoiter. As his boots touch ground, he notices the white Ford truck parked down the road. His smile at Bassim's joke fades. "Guys," he says. "Get in the house."

Alia is the first to pick up on the change in tone. "What's wrong?" Then she notices the truck as well. "Bassim. Get inside."

"What?" the boy says. "What's going…?"

"Now!" Alia snaps.

"Jesus. Okay." Bassim starts toward the house, slouching insolently until he too catches sight of the truck and notices Keller and Alia's fixation on it. "Jack?" he says uncertainly.

"Move," Keller snaps. He looks beside him to see Alia standing there. "You too, kid."

Alia's voice is steady. "My father has a pistol. In his bedside table. Do you need it?"

Keller almost laughs, not in derision, but in amazement. "Thanks. Brought my own. But…" He stops.

"What?" The girl is still staring at the truck.

68

"You know how to use that gun?"

"Is it hard?"

Keller nearly groans. "Get inside. We'll talk about that later."

She lifts her chin defiantly, but Keller can see it trembling. "I'm not afraid."

"I know. That's why you're in my goddamn way. Now get your ass inside."

She stares at him, looking as if she's about to cry—from fear or anger, he can't tell. Then she turns and runs back to the house. She leaves her bookbag behind her on the ground. Keller doesn't take his eyes off the white truck. He backs up toward his own vehicle, fumbles the door open, and reaches below the seat for the .45 caliber Colt 1911 he's stashed there. Before he can get it out, however, the white truck starts up and pulls away. Keller looks, but he can't make out the face behind the wheel. He holds the big gun down by his leg as he watches the truck take a right at the intersection. He takes a deep breath, marveling at how good he feels. He recalls another voice from his past. *You need to run after people and kick down doors and take out the bad guys. You need to put yourself in the line of fire. You don't feel alive unless you're doing that.* It had all been true, and it's cost him every love he ever had. He bows his head and sighs. The wind is picking up, and he hears the distant roll of thunder. He looks up, savoring the cool breeze on his skin.

Then he hears the gunshot from inside the house.

# TWENTY-EIGHT

"You mind telling me that that was about?" Tench demands.

Waller's staring straight ahead through the windshield. "That guy? The guy who was driving the Khoury kids home? I'm ninety-nine percent sure that was Jack Keller."

"Who?"

Waller reaches into a pocket, pulls out a pack of Marlboros. "You ever hear of Arlen Riddle? Did a lot of work down south of the border. They called him the Hellhound."

Tench nods. "He dropped off the radar a while back."

"He didn't drop off anything. Jack Keller killed him." Waller shakes a cigarette out of the pack, puts it between his lips, and lights it. "You ever do any work for Jerico Zavalo? Cartel guy. Liked to put his opponents into a vat of acid. "

"Heard of him. Never worked for him. He was supposed to be really crazy." Tench is looking uneasy.

"Keller did him, too. Shot the hell out of his bodyguards, then stuck Zavalo's head in a vat of his own acid. Kept pulling him out while he was still alive to listen to him scream, then stuck his head back in until he died. At least that's what I heard."

Tench snorts. "You believe that bullshit?"

Waller ignores him. "Remember back in Afghanistan? Early days, when we were still in uniform? There was a contractor named DeGroot. From South Africa."

70

The name makes Tench even more uncomfortable. "Interrogator. Liked to go beyond enhanced, right into slice and dice. A total bastard." He shakes his head. "You're telling me…"

"Keller killed him, too. You remember Danny Patrick? Mark Holley?"

Tench smiles. "Markey-D. That was one crazy son of a bitch. Whatever happened to him?"

"Dead," Waller says. "They teamed up with DeGroot. So Keller killed them. And then he flat out murdered DeGroot while he was on his knees begging for his life."

Tench shakes his head. "You make this Keller guy sound like he's some kind of Terminator."

"No," Waller tosses his cigarette on the ground and grinds it out with the heel of his boot. "Look, I know most of this stuff is bullshit. Legend. But if a third of it is real, we're gonna need more guys."

"No." Tench's smile is pure malice. "We just need to shoot the motherfucker in the back." He frowns. "So how did you recognize this guy anyway?"

"After Riddle got his ticket punched, the guy who hired him put out a contract. An open one. Big. Seven figures. He sent out pictures of this Keller."

"Let me guess. No one dared to claim it."

Waller shakes his head. "No one had time. The guy who put it out got a subpoena from a Congressional committee. He ate his own gun."

"So no payday, no contract. Sounds like Keller got lucky."

"Yeah."

"Well," Tench smiles, "we're pretty good at making people's luck run out."

# TWENTY-NINE

Keller slams into the house, holding the big Colt out in front of him, scanning for targets. "*Alia!*" he bellows. "*Bassim!*"

"In here," Alia calls back. "The bedroom."

Keller moves quickly and quietly, his weapon at the ready. He enters the bedroom. Alia is sitting on the bed, staring at something on the floor. Her hands are shaking. Keller glances down and sees a small black handgun lying on the carpet a few feet away from her. "Are you hurt?" he says. Before she can answer, he senses movement to his left and whirls, his finger on the trigger.

Bassim yelps and backs up so quickly that he smacks into the wall and knocks a picture frame down. The boy throws his hands up. "Don't kill me! Please!" His voice is so high it's almost a squeak.

"We're all right," Alia says, her voice shaking as badly as her hands. "There's no one else here. Please put the gun down."

Keller lowers the weapon and looks over to the gun on the floor. "So. You went and got your father's gun. And you didn't know what you were doing, so..." He walks over and picks up the gun. That's when he sees the neat round hole in the door of the clothes closet. He sighs and looks at the pistol. It's a nine-millimeter Makarov, made in Russia, used by some Iraqi army units. Probably Khoury's service weapon.

"It was me," Bassim speaks up. "I'm the one who did it."

Keller looks him in the eye. "Really?"

72

Bassim nods, then looks away.

"No." Alia stands up. "It was me. I got the gun out."

Keller fights down the urge to grab the girl and shake her. "Kid," he says in as even a voice as he can manage, "what in the hell were you thinking?"

She looks back at him with that defiant look he's come to expect. "I was thinking there were two of them and one of you. And that if they got by you, I might have to defend my brother and myself. Do you want me to apologize for that?"

Keller stares at her, then shakes his head. "No. I don't want you to apologize. But I do want you to tell me what's going on. Who are those guys? Why are they watching you?"

She's still standing, but Keller can see the tears in her eyes. "I don't know," she says softly. "I've never seen them." She sits back down on the bed.

Keller looks at Bassim, who shrugs. "I don't know them either. But I do know—"

"Bassim!" she snaps. "No more."

"Ah, come on, Alia. Jack's right. He's trying to help us, and he's got to know what's going on if he's gonna do that." He turns back to Keller. "Truth is, we don't really know everything. We don't even know a lot. But we do know a couple of things." He glances at his sister, who's looking at the floor sullenly. "Our father was a policeman. In Iraq. Before the last war. We think he ended up doing something with your government."

"Our government," Alia mutters. "We're citizens."

"Whatever. But I think whatever he did, it pissed someone off back home." He darts another look at Alia, but the expected admonition about language doesn't come.

"Any idea who?"

"Terrorists," Alia says, and looks up at Keller. "It must have been terrorists. And now they want to kill us."

Keller frowns. He hadn't been in the second Iraq War, only the first one. But what he'd heard from people who had been there, the pre-war government had been a snake pit, and the post-war one the same, just with different snakes. There are any number of factions that could bear grudges. But not all of them would get you Agency protection. He lets it go for the moment. "What about this guy Wilson?"

Bassim looks puzzled, then comprehension dawns on his face. "Red-haired guy? Always acts like he's trying to sell you a car?"

As tense as he is, the description is so apt that Keller has to chuckle. "Yeah. That's the one."

Bassim shakes his head. "He shows up whenever Dad thinks he's seen someone from back home."

"And then we move," Alia says. "To get away. And to be protected from the terrorists."

Bassim goes over to the bed, sits down and puts a protective arm around his sister. He looks at the hole in the closet door and then back at Keller. "Look, don't tell my dad about this, okay? The gun, I mean."

"I'm not going to tell him," Keller says. He looks at Alia. "You are."

She looks alarmed. "Me?"

"Kid, when your dad finds a bullet hole in his closet door, takes out his pistol, and sees it's been fired, what do you think is going to happen? Best thing you can do is fess up, because if he has to drag it out of you or your brother, it's just going to be a hundred times worse. Trust me."

"Can we?" Alia looks up. "Trust you?"

Keller nods. "Yeah, Alia. You can trust me. Both of you."

"Then will you do me a favor?" she asks.

"Depends on what it is."

"Stop calling me 'kid.'"

Keller smiles. "Okay." He looks at the clock on the bedside table. "Your dad gets home at, what? Five thirty? Six?"

"Between five thirty and six," Alia says.

"Okay. I'll stay here till then. And then your father and I are going to have a talk. In the meantime, you guys got homework?"

The two teenagers look at each other, then nod to Keller. "Get to work, then," he says. Without another word, they get up and leave.

Keller carries the pistol into the kitchen and sits at the table to look it over. It's well cared for, cleaned and oiled, and there'd apparently been a round in the chamber. Khoury had been ready for trouble, and more than just the kind posed by some schoolyard bullies. Keller's going to find out just where that trouble was coming from.

# THIRTY

"Jesus." The smell coming off the wreck nearly makes Brock Fletcher gag as he gets out of his unmarked car. There's the pleasant smell of charred wood underneath, overlaid by the sharp tang of burned metal. What really assaults the nose, however, is the cloying stench of roasted flesh.

"Here." Fletcher's partner, Lauch Cameron, tosses him a green-capped bottle of Vick's VapoRub.

"Thanks." Fletcher opens the bottle and rubs a little of the pungent goo under his nostrils. The fumes open his sinuses right up, but mask the worst of the smell. Fletcher puts the bottle in his pocket and approaches the wreck. The ambulance crew on the scene hangs back, not all that eager to move this particular body. Beneath the old and crumbling concrete bridge, the stream flows sluggishly.

Fletcher's investigated a lot of wreck scenes, but he's never seen a vehicle so totally consumed. There's nothing left but a twisted and blackened metal skeleton, like a crude outline of a car drawn in charcoal. In the center is what's left of the driver, a stick figure with its limbs drawn up in the familiar pugilist position, the contraction of burned muscles bringing the arms up and curling the hands into tight fists, as if the corpse had futilely tried to fight the flames with bare hands. Fletcher stops and puts his hands on his hips. "Burned hot."

"Yep." Cameron stands beside him and looks it over. "Pretty damn hot."

"Too hot, maybe?"

"Maybe." Cameron pulls on a pair of black nitrile gloves. He leans in, looking the charred corpse up and down, then takes hold of one of the window posts of the vehicle. It breaks off in his hand. He steps back to where Fletcher's standing. "Can't get a VIN number," he says, referring to the unique vehicle identification number assigned to every automobile and truck. "Plate's burned right off."

Fletcher just grunts. At that moment, there's a rustle in the bushes behind them and a skinny young man in a deputy's uniform steps out. He takes stock of the two detectives standing there and swallows nervously. The nametag on the pocket of his uniform shirt reads CHILDRESS.

"You done losing your lunch back there, Childress?" Fletcher says without anger or malice. He'd lost it on his first bad call-out back in the day, a drowning who'd taken a week to wash up on the shore of the Cape Fear.

Despite the mild tone, Childress still looks like a child who's just been slapped for spilling the syrup. "Yes, sir," he mumbles. "Sorry, sir."

Fletcher pulls the little bottle of Vick's out of his pocket and passes it to the young man. "Rub some under your nose. Cuts the smell." Childress hesitates, then unscrews the cap. He takes a little too much of the stuff, and when he rubs it on his upper lip, the pungent fumes send him into a fit of sneezing. Cameron turns away, trying to hide his laughter. When Childress seems to recover, Fletcher speaks again. "So, Deputy, what happened here?"

The young man still has tears in his eyes, and his voice is still choked, but he gets the words out. "Looks like he wasn't paying attention. Got going too fast, ran into the bridge abutment."

"And caught fire," Fletcher says. "Burned the whole thing up."

"Well, yeah. I mean, yes sir." Childress looks back and forth between Fletcher and Cameron, as if he's expecting a prank to be sprung.

Cameron speaks up. "Cars often burst into flames when they hit something? In real life, I mean, not the movies."

Childress frowns. "You know, this is the first time I seen that happen." His eyes widen. "You think maybe this wasn't an accident? Like, maybe a bomb or something?"

"I don't know what to think, Deputy Childress," Fletcher says. "And you're just now figuring out that neither do you. Am I right?"

Cameron has taken out his cell phone and is using the camera to snap photographs of the scene.

Childress nods. "Yes, sir. So, what do we do?"

"Well, you call Billy Sims at A-1 Auto Salvage. Tell him to get his flatbed out here and haul this to the impound. Tell him to be extra careful."

Childress looks doubtful. "Garrett's Auto Body is next in the rotation."

"Fuck the rotation. Garrett'll tear that thing apart getting it to impound. While you call…who, now?"

"Billy Sims," Childress replies dutifully.

Fletcher nods. "I'll be calling someone who owes me a favor. I want to know why that vehicle burned the way it did."

Childress nods. "You really think this is a homicide, sir?"

Fletcher doesn't answer right away, he just looks at the burned-up car. "Where'd you go to high school, Childress?"

Childress is clearly puzzled by the question. "West Harnett Senior High. Sir."

Fletcher nods in approval. "You ever have Mr. Duncan for chemistry?"

"No, sir. I think he retired before I got there."

"Too bad. He said something that's stuck with me for a lot of years. Would you like to know what that is?"

Childress's expression says he's not sure if he does, but he says, "Yes, sir," anyway.

"He used to say that most discoveries didn't begin with someone yelling, 'Eureka!' They began with someone going, 'Huh. That's weird.' You know what I'm saying?"

Childress still looks puzzled. Then he smiles and nods. "Yes, sir. Keep an eye out for the weird stuff."

Fletcher nods back. "Exactly." He motions to the ambulance crew. "This one goes to the medical examiner," he calls out. "And try not to break him."

# THIRTY-ONE

The man Keller knows as Adnan Khoury walks through the front door at 5:47 p.m., looking like any tired dad after a hard day's work. Keller is seated in the living room, on the couch, reading his Louis L'Amour book. Khoury's pistol is on the coffee table in front of the couch. Khoury stops and stares for a moment, then frowns. "What is that doing here?"

"Hang on just a minute, if you would. Sir." Keller raises his voice. "Hey, guys. Dad's home. Come on down."

"What is this about?" Khoury demands. "What is going on?"

Keller gives him a tight, professional smile, the smile of a non-commissioned officer politely bullying a lieutenant, or, if he's feeling particularly bold, a captain. It's one he hasn't used in ages, and he's a little surprised by how naturally it comes to him. "Just a moment, sir. We need to get everyone together."

Khoury just stands there gawking, as shocked by the quiet assumption of command as if Keller had just grown horns. Alia and Bassim come down the stairs, with Bassim in the lead. Both look as if they'd rather be anywhere else.

"Have a seat, guys," Keller says. He moves to one end of the couch. "You too, sir." They comply, with Khoury taking the easy chair Keller deliberately left vacant and the children sitting on the couch closest to their father. It's obvious that Khoury's about to lose his temper. Keller moves quickly to maintain the leadership. "Sir. There was an incident earlier."

Khoury's rising irritation dissipates, replaced by fear. "What?"

"Two men. In a pickup truck. They were clearly watching the house." He looks at Alia and Bassim. "And your children."

Khoury looks shaken, as Keller hoped he would. "Who?"

"I don't know, sir." Keller deliberately lets his professional demeanor slip a notch. "I was hoping you could tell me. I think I surprised them. They pulled off."

Khoury looks at his children, sitting on the couch, eyes down. "Bassim. Alia. Go to your rooms."

The two turn to Keller. "With respect, sir," he says, speaking as carefully as he can, "they have something to tell you. Before we talk."

Khoury glances at them impatiently. "What, then? Out with it!" His harsh bark makes Bassim flinch, but Alia raises her eyes and thrusts out her chin in the way Keller's getting to admire.

"I saw the men, Father. I went and got your pistol. But I didn't know how to fire it. It went off."

Khoury looks as if he's been hit from behind with a brick. "What?"

"No one was hurt," Keller says. "As you can tell."

"There's a hole in your closet door," Bassim volunteers. "I think I can fix it. With some spackle, or something."

"Be quiet, Bassim," Khoury snaps, and Keller hates the way the boy seems to fold in on himself from the harsh words.

"I think it's time for us to have our talk now, sir," he says.

Alia stands up. "I'll make dinner." She looks at her brother. "Come on, Bassim." The two of them exit the room. Khoury watches them go and mutters something under his breath.

Keller concentrates on the issue at hand. "So, Mr. Khoury. Why don't you tell me the truth? For once, I mean."

Khoury looks at him sourly. "I see you've dropped the 'sir.'"

"That was for your children. I don't want to do anything to make them disrespect you. But I need you to stop playing games with me. I need to know who's really after you if I'm going to protect you and your family."

"Can you describe them? These men you saw?"

"White guys. Mutt and Jeff team." Khoury looks confused at that, so Keller fills in the reference. "One big, one smaller. Short hair. Looked military. But not completely."

Khoury's eyes narrow. "Contractors?"

"Yeah. That would be my guess."

Khoury sits back in his chair, looking stricken. "That is…a new development."

Keller leans forward, speaking in a low, intense voice, trying not to be heard in the kitchen. "Damn it. Sir. I'm trying to keep you safe. Stop being so cryptic."

Khoury glances toward the kitchen, then pitches his voice low so as not to be heard from there. "All right. I must trust you."

"That would be good, yeah."

Khoury hesitates, then he begins. "You have to understand. There are still some people in my country who regard me as a traitor."

"Why?"

Khoury looks at Keller. "When your country invaded mine, everyone in my government tried to deny what was happening. We were going to repulse the invaders."

"The mother of all battles," Keller said. "I remember."

Khoury nods. "Well, some of us saw what was coming. We… provided information to the Americans." He takes a deep breath and lets it out. "We collaborated. To save ourselves and our families."

Keller thinks about that. "So, these people who are after you. They're people pissed at you because you sold out Saddam?"

Khoury looks down as if ashamed. "Yes."

"Bullshit."

Khoury looks up, angry again. "What did you say to me?"

"Spare me," Keller snaps. "The people who supported Saddam ended up either in some overseas exile or at the end of a rope. They're definitely not living and working here. Try again, Mr. Khoury."

Khoury stares at Keller for along moment, eyes hard. "Fine," he says. This time, he doesn't break eye contact. "There is a large sum of money involved."

Keller nods. "Now we're getting somewhere."

# THIRTY-TWO

"Wow," Meadow says. "Sounds like the singer's throwing up in a trash can."

"I like it," Ben says defensively. He's sitting back against the headboard and she's lying back, her head in his lap. The miniature stereo nestled on his bookshelves is blasting his latest metal obsession.

"I like it, too." Francis looks up from the floor, where he's building something complicated with his Legos.

"You tell her, buddy." Ben smiles at him.

Meadow blows them both a raspberry. She looks up at Ben. "So, you going to call her?" She can feel him tense.

"Yeah," he says.

"Do it now." She sits up and smiles at him. "It's the perfect time."

"I don't know." He looks down. "She might be eating dinner."

"Buk. Buk. Bu*caw!*" She flaps her arms in a clumsy imitation of a chicken.

Francis laughs with delight. "Bu*caw*," he echoes, flapping his arms, but widely, more like a seagull.

Meadow laughs and slips down off the bed to sit cross-legged beside Francis. "Whatcha building, buddy?" As Francis begins a long and detailed explanation, Meadow looks at Ben and puts her index finger to her ear, pinky by her chin. "Call her," she mouths.

Ben sighs. There's no escaping Meadow when she has a bug up her ass like this. He takes out his phone and dials the number she's given him for Alia Khoury.

# THIRTY-THREE

Alia has just put the harissa, a stew made of leftover chicken and coarsely ground wheat, on the stove when her phone chirps. She glances at it, recognizes the number Meadow gave her earlier, and smiles. Then she casts a worried glance at Bassim, who's slicing bread on the counter. She ducks out the door of the kitchen and bows her head as she answers. "Hello?"

"Hey. Ah. Alia?"

"Hi, Ben." She tries to make her voice sound as welcoming as possible without sounding too eager. "How are you?"

"Um. Fine." There's a long and painful silence. "So," Ben says finally. "We need to pick a team for the science fair. Have you joined up with anyone yet?"

*Like that's going to happen.* "No. Not yet."

"So..." Ben begins, then stops. Alia waits. Finally, Ben speaks. "Meadow—you know her as Melissa—and I. We've teamed up. We need a third. Would you like to, you know..."

She jumps in. "Yes, Ben. I'd love to join you two."

"Awesome." Ben sounds so relieved that Alia stifles a laugh. This awkward-but-cute thing, she thinks, could get old fast. But for the moment, she's willing to go along with it. After all, what other friends does she have? "Shall we meet after Chemistry class? I have a free period then."

"Yeah. Okay. Um. See you then."

"See you then." She ends the call and shakes her head.

Bassim interrupts her thoughts by popping into the hallway where Alia's fled for privacy. "Sooooo," he says brightly. "Who was that on the phone?"

She drops back into Arabic. "Shut up, Bassim."

"Was it Ben? I bet it was Ben."

"I swear," she grates, still speaking in Arabic, "one of these days, I am going to strangle you."

He puffs himself up and shakes his finger at her like one of the imams back home. "You must not swear," he says in a pompous voice, "it is un-Islamic."

Despite herself, she laughs. "Come on. We need to get dinner on the table."

# THIRTY-FOUR

"Oooh," Meadow says. "So suave." She pronounces it "swave," but with a smile in her voice.

"Shut up," Ben mumbles.

"Ben's got a girlfriend, Ben's got a girlfriend," Francis sings out.

Meadow picks up a Lego and tosses it at him, laughing and careful to miss. "You stay out of this, Pintsize."

Francis laughs and dodges away, even though the little plastic block is nowhere near his head. "Ben's got a—"

He's interrupted as the door opens and Marie sticks her head in. "Boys, dinner's on the table." She notices Meadow on the bed. "Oh. Hello, Melissa."

"Mom, can *Meadow* stay for dinner?" Ben leans on the name the girl prefers.

"Yeah, Mom," Francis speaks up.

Marie frowns. "I only made enough pork chops for us. Sorry."

"That's no problem," Meadow says. "I'm a vegetarian."

"She can have my vegetables," Francis offers.

Marie sighs. "Okay. Sure. But, Francis, you will be eating your own veggies."

"Aww…"

But Marie's gone.

"I don't think she likes me very much," Meadow observes.

"She will," Francis says. "Once she gets to know you." He sounds so full of confidence, so like a little adult, that Ben and Meadow both laugh.

"C'mon, little man," Ben says. "Let's go eat."

# THIRTY-FIVE

"So," Keller says. "A lot of USAID money went missing. Almost a billion. In cash. I remember reading about that. And there are people who took it who think you took it from them."

Khoury nods. "That sums it up." He looks around, gesturing at the modest house where he and his family live. "But look. Do I look like a man who's sitting on a billion dollars?"

Keller shrugs. "Who knows? Whitey Bulger was caught living in a shitty condo in California."

"Who?"

"Never mind. I still think you're lying. But we're getting closer to the truth." Keller stands up, walks to the living room window, and raises the mini-blinds to have a look outside. "And the CIA keeps moving you from place to place."

Khoury's face darkens. "I am not moving again. I am sick of running."

"Okay. Fine. I get that. I've done some running, too." He smiles thinly. "It didn't suit me. So I'll do what I can to help."

Khoury eyes him suspiciously. "I suppose you will want more money."

"No, I'm good. I'm glad for the pay, mind you. But you know what? I like those kids of yours."

The frown deepens. "You do?"

"Yeah. Alia? She was scared out of her wits this afternoon. But went and got that gun because she was ready to do anything to protect

86

herself and her brother. And then she looked me in the eye and dared me to tell her she was wrong. That little girl's a warrior, Mr. Khoury."

Khoury mutters something in Arabic.

"What?" Keller says.

Khoury looks at him. "I said she is like her mother in that way."

Keller nods. "And Bassim? He's scared too, but he's got guts. He tried to stand up for his sister and take the blame. He's going to be a tough one himself, if you don't beat him down."

Khoury steps back, eyes narrowing in anger. "I do not beat my children."

"Not what I meant. Figure of speech. Maybe it doesn't translate well. But don't..." He stops and sighs. "It's not up to me to tell you how to raise your children, Mr. Khoury. But just know this. They're good kids. Strong. Kind. You can be proud of them. Both of them."

For a moment, it looks again as if Khoury's iron facade is going to crack again. But he recovers himself and just nods. "Thank you. I am."

"So, even though I'm pretty sure you're still lying to me, I'm going to do whatever I can to protect Alia and Bassim. You need to know, Mr. Khoury, that the only thing keeping me from throwing you under the first bus that comes along is I know what it would do to those children. They think you hung the moon. But don't mistake me, Mr. Khoury. If it comes down to a choice between them and you? That bus is waiting."

Khoury looks at him and nods. Keller can't help but notice the way he thrusts his chin out in defiance is an exact copy of Alia's gesture. Or, more likely, she's learned it from him. "I would expect nothing less. I would do anything to save my children. Anything."

"I may just hold you to that."

"And what about your children, Mr. Keller?"

Keller's almost to the front door, but the words stop him in his tracks. He turns to look at Khoury. "What about them?" he says in a low, deadly voice.

"I'm just saying, Mr. Keller. There are bad people involved. Some of them are very bad indeed."

"You're saying they'd threaten my family."

Khoury shrugs. "It's possible."

"Then all the more reason those people need to die."

Khoury laughs scornfully, but for a moment, there's a flash of uncertainty in his eyes, the look of a man wondering if the bars between him and the beast in the cage are quite strong enough. "You think you can deal with anything, don't you? I tell you, these are evil men. Relentless. They will stop at nothing."

"Good to know. But you need to know that neither will I." He puts a hand on the doorknob. "I'm going back to my house, Mr. Khoury. You've given me some things to think about, and I need to make some phone calls. But I'll be back. Sir. If you need any help in the meantime, you know where to find me." Before Khoury can answer, he's out the door and walking to his truck.

He has his phone out before he's halfway there, punching the first number on his speed dial. The call goes straight to voicemail and he grits his teeth. "Marie," he says when the outgoing message ends. "It's Jack. I need to talk to you. As soon as possible. Call me." He hesitates a moment before adding, "Please." He hangs up before standing by the door of his truck. He looks up at the stars in the night sky, cold and impersonal as they look back down on him. He feels the adrenaline singing its high, sweet, keening song in his blood, feels the soft spring winds blowing on his skin. He knows that it's a bad sign that moments like this, where he knows he's heading for an inevitable violent collision, are still the moments when he feels most alive. It's even more wrong to feel that way with his own son and the woman he loves possibly in the line of fire. But he can't help it. Whatever this situation is—and he knows he still doesn't have the whole story—he's deep into it now. And he won't back down.

As he thinks about the task before him, however, Keller realizes the difficulties he's facing. There are too many soft targets here. Alia. Bassim. Add in Francis, and Ben, and even Marie, and the number of people he has to cover, to try to keep safe, becomes overwhelming. He's only seen two threats so far, but who knows how many more people his still shadowy opposition may be able to put in the field. He knows he can count on Marie, especially where her children are concerned, but he still needs allies.

"Fuck," he says out loud. "Wilson." He'd blown Wilson off at the diner, but in a situation where he needs every gun, he really can't afford to turn away possible help. He'll just have to see if he can make the man his ally and see what resources he can bring.

# THIRTY-SIX

With the beginnings of a plan in his mind, Keller gets in the truck and drives to the hotel where he'd seen Wilson earlier. The little blue car isn't there. Keller frowns and parks in front of the unit he'd seen the Agency man coming out of. There are no lights behind the curtains. Maybe he's checked out. There's still a light on in the office and a VACANCY sign in the window.

A set of what look and sound like sleigh bells hanging from the door announce Keller's presence as he enters. He can hear the sound of a television playing from a back room as he steps up to the Formica counter. There's another bell on the counter, but Keller holds off on that one. After a short pause in which Keller hears the TV being turned down, a short, round black man with a receding hairline and a clip-on tie emerges from the back room. His plastic name badge identifies him as REGGIE. GUEST SERVICES.

"Help you?" he says, looking Keller up and down suspiciously.

"I'm looking for Ted Wilson," Keller says, putting on what he hopes is his most ingratiating smile. "He still registered? I think he was in room 107."

Reggie of Guest Services frowns. "You police? You don't look like police."

"No, no," Keller says, "I'm just—"

"Guest register's private. Unless you're the police."

"Fine," Keller says. "But can I leave him a message?"

"Didn't say he was here."

90

"I know. But if he is still a guest here, you could get a message to him, right? Speaking hypothetically."

The man snorts. "Hypothetically? Ain't no hypothetically. He here or he ain't."

Keller resists the temptation to grab Reggie of Guest Services by the neck and throttle him. "Let me just leave a number. And if Mr. Wilson is here, give it to him. Okay?"

Reggie thinks about it for a moment, then nods grudgingly. "Ain't sayin' if he's here or not. But if I see him, I'll give him the number."

"Thanks," Keller says. "You got a piece of paper and something to write with?"

Reggie looks at him as if he'd asked for an assignation with his wife and daughter. Then he sighs heavily and reaches under the counter for a pad and a cheap pen.

Keller writes his name and number on the top sheet, rips it off, and hands it to Reggie. "Thanks."

"Ain't nothin' to thank me for. I din't say he was here."

"Right," Keller says. "Well, you have a good evening."

"Have a blessed day," Reggie says, then ambles back to his TV program.

Keller goes back out to his truck. He sits for a moment, then pulls out his phone. No calls. He dials Marie's number again.

# THIRTY-SEVEN

Al-Mansour is on the bed again, leaned back against the headboard, propped up with all of the pillows from both beds behind him. He's dressed in what looks like the same bowling shirt and a pair of baggy shorts. He looks like an old man on a beach trip, but Waller wonders if he's moved from the bed since the last time they saw him.

"So," Al-Mansour is saying, his face an expressionless mask. "You have removed the problem of Mr. Wilson. And now you tell me there is a new problem. One requiring more resources. Do I have this right?"

The suspicion in his voice rankles Waller. "We're not making it up, if that's what you're insinuating. Sir."

Al-Mansour regards him for a moment, still not changing expression, before turning to Tench. "And your opinion?"

Tench shrugs. "There was a guy there. Armed. I saw the gun. But it was only one guy."

"Hmph." Al-Mansour folds his plump hands across his ample belly and looks down at his feet, clad in huarache sandals. He doesn't speak.

In the silence, Tench gives Waller an annoyed look. He doesn't want to bring anyone else in. He'd have to co-opt them into whatever scheme he's cooking up to double cross Al-Mansour, and conspiracies are harder to pull off the more people you bring in.

Finally, Al-Mansour speaks. "What exactly do you know about this man? This Keller?"

Waller is starting to sweat a little. "I haven't looked at a dossier or anything. What I know is mostly what I've heard through the

92

grapevine."

"Campfire stories," Tench says scornfully. "Boogeymen."

Al-Mansour looks baffled. He clearly doesn't get any of the idioms.

"Rumors and gossip," Tench adds helpfully.

"Maybe," Waller admits. "But some of it might be real. And if even half of it is, then this Keller is a very dangerous man. I can do some looking around. Some research."

"There's no time," Tench argues, and Waller grits his teeth to see Al-Mansour nodding his head in agreement. "Look, no matter how bad-ass this guy is, he's one man. And if we don't try to take him face to face, it doesn't matter how tough he is."

"You can do this?" Al-Mansour asks.

Tench smiles. "I have just the thing."

Al-Mansour nods. "Then do what you need to do."

After they leave the room, Al-Mansour sighs. He'd had his misgivings about these hired guns from the beginning. They weren't of the Faithful. He's not a particularly religious man himself, but he understands the power of faith when it comes to manipulating warriors. These Americans only fight for money, and while it's easy to find men who'll kill for money, it's never as easy to find men who'll die for it. He'd seen in Waller's face a fear of death that he knows no amount of money can overcome. He doesn't know who this Keller is, but Waller is no coward. While he may think too much for a foot soldier, he's not a man to run from shadows. This Keller, whoever he is, must be a serious opponent, requiring a serious response.

Al-Mansour takes a deep breath. It's time to take the step he's been putting off, the one he now knows he should have taken from the beginning. To be honest, the Chechens scare him. But when they're bought, they stay bought. And once they take on a mission, they won't stop. For anything. He picks the phone up off the bed and dials.

# THIRTY-EIGHT

It's a pleasant enough dinner, largely because Francis's constant chatter keeps everyone smiling and doesn't give Ben much chance to snap at his mother for her constant stares at Meadow. The girl is polite, almost excruciatingly so, but Ben doesn't see that making much inroad into his mother's concerns about his best friend. He's about to break in and say something when Marie's cell phone buzzes. She sighs, gets up, and walks to the kitchen counter. She sighs again when she looks at the screen. "Sorry," she mumbles as she goes to the door, "I have to take this." As she walks out, Ben hears her say "Jack..."

"It's him," Ben says. "Keller."

Meadow takes a bite of her green beans. "What do you have against that guy, anyway?"

Ben shakes his head. "He's a fu—" He glances over at his half-brother. "He's a psycho. He's nothing but trouble."

Francis nods. "That's what Grandpa said."

Meadow inclines her head quizzically. "But from the way you tell it, he saved your life." She smiles and puts a hand on his. "I can't say I hate him for that."

Ben looks down and shakes his head. "You don't get it." He closes his eyes and suddenly, without warning, it comes over him again. He's back on that hillside, the smell of smoke in his nostrils, the sounds of gunshots as the man he'd looked up to, thought of as his protector, shoots a man kneeling in front of him in cold blood. And laughs. He hears that laugh in his nightmares.

94

"Ben," Meadow's voice is tight with alarm. "You're shaking. Open your eyes. Please."

Ben takes a series of deep breaths, like the therapists have taught him, and waits for the tide of adrenaline to break and roll back before he opens his eyes. "I'm okay."

"You need your medicine?"

He shakes his head. Neither his mother nor Meadow know it, but he hasn't been taking the pills his latest doctor prescribed. They make his head hurt and give him a restless jittery feeling that makes it hard to focus. "I'm fine."

"You haven't been taking it, have you?" she grimaces. "Ben, you need to—"

"You need to drop it." He pushes his plate away, knowing his anger is irrational, but not able to help himself. "I'm not hungry anymore."

"I'm sorry," she says quietly. "I only worry because I care about you."

"I already have one mom." He gets up and walks away from the table. He knows he's hurt Meadow. It's not the first time. When he calms down, he knows he'll hate himself. But she won't hate him. She never does. She's a good person. Unlike him. He knows he's not worthy of her, or Francis, or even his mother. He wishes he were dead. It's not the first time for that, either. He goes into his room and closes the door behind him. After making sure the door is locked, he takes a deep breath and goes down on his knees, beside his bed. He reaches under the bed and gropes until he finds the wooden box. It's about a foot and a half square, made of unfinished wood, picked up at a yard sale by his mother so long ago he can't remember and stuck in a closet until he found something to put in it. He drags the box out and opens it.

The .38 caliber revolver takes up almost all the space in the crude wooden box. Ben takes it out, hefting it and appreciating the weight in his hand. The grip is worn, but it feels molded to his hand. He turns the gun to look at the bullets nestled in the cylinder, each one a promise of oblivion. Those blunt, abruptly curved assurances of release beckon him for a long time, until he finally sighs and nestles the pistol back down into the wooden box. *Gutless*, his inner voice jeers at him. *Coward.*

*For now*, he thinks to himself. *For now.*

# THIRTY-NINE

Marie walks back into the kitchen, putting her phone back on the counter. "Where's Ben?" she asks.

"I think he went to his room." Melissa, who insists on being called Meadow, is looking at her plate. Her voice is shaking, as if she's trying not to cry.

"What happened?" Marie says. "What's going on?"

It's Francis who answers. "Ben got mad again." He looks like he's about to cry as well.

*God damn it*, Marie thinks. She wants to go to Ben's room, pound on the door, pick him up by the shoulders and shake all this angst and drama and self-pity out of him. Then she immediately feels ashamed. She knows her son has real problems. Her anger is born of frustration, the feeling that no matter what she does, it doesn't seem to help. *It's just so exhausting. I'm so tired of being tired.* "Okay. Best thing to do right now is give him time to cool off." She's annoyed when Melissa/Meadow nods in agreement. *I don't need your permission, hon.* But she keeps that to herself as well. "I need to go out for a little while anyway. Melissa, would you like a ride home?" She doesn't miss the look of dread on the girl's face. She knows there's a reason she spends so much of her time over here. But she's got her own damaged kids to deal with.

"Thank you, ma'am," Melissa says. "I'll get my stuff."

"Okay." Marie turns to Francis. "I won't be long. Make sure you get washed up before bed. Tell Ben to help you if you need it. And the two of you can clean up and get the dishes put away, okay?" Francis just nods and looks at his plate. She crosses the room and leans down to hug him from behind. "I love you, Francis," she murmurs into the top of his head.

His voice is slightly muffled. "Frank."

"Okay. I love you, Frank." She breaks the hug and steps back.

"I love you, too, Mom."

Melissa's standing in the doorway. "Ready."

They make the drive in silence, Melissa looking out the window. When they arrive at the double-wide trailer where she lives, there are no lights on. Marie hears the girl sigh with relief. She looks almost cheerful as she turns back toward her. "Thanks, Officer Jones."

"You're welcome."

Melissa pauses a moment. "Ben's a good guy," she says. "And I know you really care about him. And I know he doesn't show it all that well, but…he loves you a lot, too."

Marie feels a lump in her throat. "I know you care about him, too." She laughs. "Maybe that's why I'm having trouble dealing with you."

The girl's eyes narrow. "Because of the way I am?"

"No. Because I'm his mom. I'm supposed to be the one he comes to when he's hurt."

Melissa opens the door and gets halfway out. Then she turns back and nods. "You know, I think I get that." She smiles. "Good night, Officer Jones."

"Good night. Meadow."

Meadow's smile widens. As she exits the car, Marie calls to her. "Meadow." The girl sticks her head back in. "If there's any kind of trouble," Marie says. She gestures at the darkened trailer. "Anything you need to tell me about, you know I'll listen. And I'll help."

Meadow nods. "I know." She looks at the trailer, then back at Marie. "And thanks. But there's nothing, you know, illegal going on. No one's beating me or, you know. It's just kind of shitty all the time."

"Because of the way you are."

Meadow nods. In the dimness of the car's interior light, Marie can see the tears in her eyes. "Because of the way I am."

"Well," Marie says. "That sucks."

"Yeah."

"But look, Meadow. If you need a safe place to be...our door's always open."

"Really?"

"Yeah. Really."

Meadow nods gratefully. "Thanks again, Officer."

Marie smiles. "We don't have to be so formal outside of school. You can call me Ms. Jones."

Meadow laughs. "Good night, Ms. Jones."

"Good night." Marie watches until she's certain the girl is safe inside the trailer. Then she heads off to meet Keller.

# FORTY

"Trust you," Marie says, "to find a roadhouse with a name like the Stumbling Pig."

Keller smiles and takes a drink from his bottle of Red Stripe. "Thought you might like it."

The place is a dive, with most of the illumination provided by neon beer signs, stools that waver and wiggle as if they're about to collapse and yet somehow never do, and a tattooed bartender with a ZZ Top beard who looks mean enough to bend iron bars between his teeth. Marie can't help but like it.

"You want anything?" Keller asks as Marie takes a set on one of the rickety stools.

Marie considers. "I don't suppose they have a Pinot Grigio."

"I'm guessing no." He raises a finger and the bartender saunters down to see what he wants. "Another beer for my friend here."

"Okay." The bartender looks at Marie. "What you need?"

"Red Stripe."

"Ain't got it."

"Bud Light."

"Got it." He reaches in the cooler and hands over a beer. Then he takes a seat on his stool, crosses his arms, and regards the bar with a baleful stare.

"Come on," Keller says, "let's get a table."

They find one in a booth around the corner from the blaring jukebox, which gives them a little privacy. "Look," Keller says, "to begin with, I'm sorry for what I said. About you wanting to keep me here. That was a shitty thing to say."

Marie takes a sip of her beer. "It was."

"I know. And I'm sorry. But there's a bigger problem here."

"How do you mean?" she says.

"After the incident you saw, Alia and Bassim Khoury's father hired me to protect them."

Marie shakes her head. "From what?"

"That's the big question, isn't it?" Keller asks. "At first, you'd think it was from that redneck dude—Brandon, his name was? And his buddies. But does that make sense to you?"

*Like hiring someone to burn the house down because you saw a cockroach.* "No," she says.

"So." Keller leans forward. Marie can't help but notice the eager look on his face. "Today, I saw these other guys. Two of them. Watching the Khoury kids. And me."

Marie puts down her beer. "Wait. What?"

Keller nods. "Yeah. I never saw them before, but I know that look. Military contractors."

"Mercenaries," Marie breathes. Then she pulls back. This is nuts. "Are you sure?"

Keller nods. "I know. Seems really off the wall, right? But the same day, this guy sits down with me at Webster's."

"The diner?"

Keller nods. "He says his name is Wilson. Says he's with the government. Tells me they've got the security of the Khourys under control. I should just stand down."

Marie shakes her head and laughs ruefully. "Obviously, he never met you."

Keller chuckles as well. "Then I talk to Alia and her brother Bassim, and they tell me some wild tale about how Daddy's pissed off the terrorists and those are the ones who are after them."

Marie takes a drink of her beer. "I don't suppose you've been to the local police about this."

Keller shrugs. "What am I going to say? There's an international terrorist conspiracy brewing in Harnett County? The CIA's protecting an Iraqi asset here and I'm not sure they're up to it? You're the only person here who knows me well enough to know that I'm not nuts." He takes a drink and laughs bitterly. "Or at least that my story isn't nuts, even if I am." He looks at Marie. "Look. I know it all sounds bizarre. But if anything happens, I want you to be ready."

"Thanks. But, Jack, you know if there's a credible threat, I have to report it."

Keller nods. "I understand."

Marie shakes her head. "No. I don't think you do. If I report a terror threat as credible, the whole school system shuts down. Across the county. Kids stay home. Working moms have to either scramble to find someone to look after their kids or stay home and risk losing their jobs. Makeup days have to be scheduled, some of them on Saturdays and vacation days. People get really, really unhappy about that, and those people yell at the school board, and then the school board yells at my boss, who yells at me. I'm willing to be yelled at. It's happened before. But you'd better be dead damn sure there's a threat, Jack. Are you?"

Keller stares down at the table. "Yeah. I am."

Marie looks hard at him for a long moment. "Okay, then." She looks across the room and sees something that makes her whisper, "Fuck. My. Life."

Keller looks up. "What?"

Marie sighs. "Over there in the booth under the Stevie Ray Vaughn concert poster. Look familiar?"

Keller looks. "Well. Speak of the devil."

"Brandon Ochs." Marie says it like a curse. "And two of his dumb little buddies."

Keller nods. "None of them of legal age to be in here."

"Nope."

"You're not on duty, right?" Keller sees her look, raises his hands placatingly. "Sorry."

She sighs, drains off the last of her beer, and stands up. Keller does the same. She shakes her head at him. "This is my job, Jack. Not yours."

"Three on one. And we don't know how drunk any of these knuckleheads are. You're going to want backup."

He's right, but it doesn't make her any happier. "Stay back. Let me do the talking."

Keller nods. "Got it."

Brandon is the first one who sees her coming. His lip curls in his customary sneer until he sees Keller walking a step behind her, moving out to flank her on her right shoulder.

"Hey, Brandon." Marie's tone is as friendly as if they were in the lunchroom. Her next words are a good bit sharper. "I'm thinking that's not just Coke Zero in that glass."

The boy looks defiant. "You ain't got no jurisdiction here, Jones." The two other young men seated around the table nod as if he's made a point.

Marie raises an eyebrow. "Well, look at you, all lawyerly and shit. You going to teach me about jurisdiction? I mean, I've only been in law enforcement for seventeen years, but I can't wait to hear legal arguments from a goddamn eleventh grader." He looks as if he's ready to say something, but she silences him with an upraised hand. "This is going to go one of two ways. You can all set those drinks down and walk out that door, nice and quiet. Or I can tell the bartender you're all underage and jeopardizing his business." She looks over at the bartender, who's now scowling at the scene being played out.

Brandon looks down at his drink, then looks around at his followers. They don't meet his eyes. He mutters something under his breath.

"I'm sorry," Marie says. "What was that?"

He looks up at her, eyes blazing. "I said, fucking bitch."

Keller starts toward him, but she blocks him with an outstretched arm, smiling broadly. "Oh, sweetie," she says to Brandon. "You say that like it's a *bad* thing."

Brandon drops his eyes and he and his cohorts start to shuffle out.

"Oh, one more thing," Marie adds. They stop, glowering at her. Her smile widens. "I'm going to need whatever fake IDs you used to get served here."

They look at each other, then back at her. "We didn't—" one of Brandon's nameless followers begins.

Marie cuts him off. "You just need to know that if any of you is using someone else's ID, that's identity theft. Class H felony. And if it's a made-up identity? Oh, boys, you don't want any part of that. That's the sort of stuff Homeland Security gets really interested in. So, save yourself a lot of trouble. Lay those cards on the table, fellows."

The group looks down at the floor, then, as one, they reach into their back pockets, pull out their wallets, and silently lay a series of laminated plastic cards on the table. Marie nods. "Good boys. Now you can go." They file out, not looking at either Marie or Keller. She scoops the cards up off the table and shuffles through them.

"Hey." The tattooed bartender appears at Keller's shoulder. "What's going on?"

Marie hands him the stack of fake IDs. "Caught some boys drinking in here underage. You might want to be more careful in the future."

He frowns. "You a cop? You don't look like a cop."

"I get that a lot. Just keep an eye out, okay?"

The bartender nods and walks back to the bar, shuffling the fake IDs and muttering to himself.

"Damn," she hears Keller say.

She turns to him, sees the smile on his face. "What?"

He hesitates, then says, "I've really missed you."

She feels a lump in her throat again, then remembers what he's told her about the time he's spent apart from her, the time she's spent loving other people. "I've missed you, too," she says carefully, "but I have to get back." She smiles in a way she hopes is convincing. "Usual home drama."

"Sure," Keller says. "We'll talk soon."

"Yeah. Soon."

# FORTY-ONE

Alia wakes up in the middle of the night, staring up at the ceiling like a hundred other nights before. She doesn't know what awakened her, but she knows from experience it'll be a long time before she gets back to sleep. She sighs and sits up. The house is silent. She's always felt a special fondness for this time of night, when she has the house to herself. She pulls a long white robe around her and stalks softly through the house, enjoying the feeling, as if she was a spirit gliding to and fro among the living. She eventually ends up at the sliding glass door to the backyard. She hesitates for a moment, then pulls the door open, slowly so as to minimize the noise, and steps into the fenced-in enclosure. At the far end, there's a makeshift barbecue grill, made of stacked cinder-blocks. When they moved in, it was unused, overgrown with creeper vine and kudzu. Now, all the vegetation has been cleared off, but the grill has still never been used. Alia sits down in one of the cheap plastic chairs that were in the back yard when they moved in and regards the cinder-block structure.

She'd awakened one night, shortly after they'd moved in, and heard the sounds of digging in the back yard. She'd peered out the window of her bedroom, but couldn't make out the pale figure in the backyard. It was only when she'd gone to the back door that she recognized her father, dressed in a white t-shirt, sweating and straining as he dug a hole next to the scattered blocks of the barbecue grill. She'd watched for a long time as he excavated a hole amongst the disorganized piles, then put the blocks back in place. She'd felt herself too young at the time to ask him what he'd been doing. But now, as she feels danger closing in from every side, she thinks she knows.

# FORTY-TWO

"Fucking bitch." Brandon is pacing back and forth behind his truck. The pair of boys who've stayed with him since the bar look at each other nervously. "Fucking bitch."

They're pulled up at a spot on the bank of the river, a gravel lot where a half dozen other cars and trucks are pulled in, little knots of people congregated around each vehicle. Mostly they keep to themselves, but now and then a figure will move from one group to the other, conduct some business, then go back to his own clique. The faint sounds of southern rock, country, and heavy metal meet and mingle in the spaces between.

"Hey, Brandon," Pete, one of the followers, says. "Let's just go home, bro. This night's fucked."

Brandon stares at them through eyes rendered small and blood-red by whiskey and the smoke he scored from one of the other cars a half hour ago. "Fine, motherfucker. Go on home."

"You're our ride, man," the other follower, a lanky, buck-toothed boy everyone knows as Bunny, points out.

Brandon laughs, a harsh cough without any humor in it. "Guess y'all are the ones fucked, then, ain't ya?" He spots a truck pulling into the gravel lot and laughs again. "Night's lookin' up, boys." Without looking back, he heads over to greet the new arrival.

By the time Brandon makes his stumbling way across the lot, the driver of the truck is out, leaning against the left rear quarter panel. He's a skinny dude in a wife-beater that may have been white at some point but which has now been badly and repeatedly washed into a sad and nondescript gray. He looks at Brandon through heavy lidded eyes. "Whassup, young blood?"

Brandon is too wasted for subtlety. "I need a pistol, cuz."

The man by the truck looks around. "Jesus, Bran, keep your fuckin' voice down."

"Sorry, Jake," Brandon says with no perceptible decrease in volume.

Jake rolls his eyes. "Fer Chrissakes. How goddamn wasted are you?" Before Brandon can answer, Jake motions to the front of the truck. "Come on, man. Talk to me. In private."

Brandon follows Jake around the front of the truck, tottering a little on the edge of the embankment that leads down to the river. Jake turns and delivers a stinging slap that rocks Brandon's head to one side. When he looks back at Jake, Brandon's eyes are a little more focused, but still flaming red. He smiles with a little blood on his teeth. "Shit. Can't you hit no harder than that? Daddy'd knock me down by now."

"Your daddy hits you 'cause he's an asshole," Jake snaps. "I'm just tryin' to wake your drunk ass up."

Brandon nods. "Okay. I'm awake. Now sell me a gun."

Jake sighs with exasperation. "And why you need a gun?"

"That's my business, ain't it?" He flinches as his cousin Jake raises his hand for another slap.

"It's my business," Jake says, his hand still raised and poised but his voice incongruously reasonable, "if you're gonna use this pistol, which I may or may not have, in some sort of half-bright criminal enterprise that might get traced back to me."

"It ain't comin' back to you, cuz," Brandon says.

"Imagine how much better that makes me feel. Now, why you want a gun?"

Brandon grits his teeth and looks away. "Son of a bitch disrespected me." He doesn't want to say that the person he's really ashamed of being disrespected by is a woman.

Jake shakes his head. "So, you want to shoot him, that it? You're gonna risk the death penalty 'cause you got your feelin's hurt?"

As he starts to walk away, Brandon remembers the confrontation at school and blurts out "They threatened me, too."

Jake stops and turns around. "Well, that's different, ain't it?" He leans his head back and regards his cousin through narrowed eyes. "You ain't lyin' to me, are you?"

Brandon shakes his head. The beer, poured on top of the liquor from the bar, combined with the weed he's just smoked, has his head spinning. He feels like he's about to throw up and doesn't trust himself to speak. He leans against the truck, closes his eyes, and braces himself with one hand until the spinning stops. When he opens them again, Jake is standing there with a cloth bundle in his hands. He's frowning.

"You okay?"

"I'm fine," Brandon mumbles.

Jake doesn't look convinced, but he unwraps the bundle to reveal a short-barreled black handgun. "Ruger 9 mil," he announces. "One magazine loaded. You want more ammo, I can get that, too." As Brandon reaches for the gun, Jake pulls away. "There are some conditions."

Brandon squints at him. "What conditions?"

"If you have to use this, you get rid of it. Immediately. Bring it back to me if you have to. I know how to make guns disappear."

"What, you don't trust me?"

"I seen that look in your eyes," Jake says. "Like a kid at Christmas. This is a pistol, cuz, not a new toy. If you have to use it, it turns into evidence. That's how motherfuckers get caught."

"I got it." Brandon licks his lips. "How much?"

"Two hundred." Jake grins. "Family discount." When Brandon looks hesitant, Jake shrugs and begins folding the cloth back around the pistol.

"Wait." Brandon reaches into his pocket and pulls out his wallet. He counts some bills into Jake's outstretched hand.

When he's out of bills, Jake looks at him, sighs, and returns a couple of bills to him. "You gave me too much," he says. "Whyn't you let me hang on to this till tomorrow, when you're not totally fried?"

Brandon shakes his head. "I paid for it. Give it here."

Reluctantly, Jake hands the pistol over. "Go home," he says. "And sleep it off. You try to use this tonight, you're gonna shoot your dick off."

Brandon doesn't answer, just turns and walks away, a slight stagger in his gait. But by the time he makes it back to his worried friends, he's whistling. "So, Pete," he says. "You know where the bitch lives, right?"

# FORTY-THREE

Marie awakens to the sound of shouting outside her house. She sits bolt upright in bed, instantly awake. She hears an unintelligible yelling outside, then a sound she never wants to hear anywhere near her or her children again, the sound of a gunshot.

She leaps out of bed and crosses the room in a second, taking her service weapon from the lockbox on top of her dresser. Another shot, and she hears the shattering of glass in her front windows. She pulls back the slide and chambers a round just as her bedroom door opens.

Francis is standing there, his blonde hair a bright spot in the dimness. "Mom?" his voice is quivering with fear.

She rushes to him and crouches down, throwing an arm around him, then moves him behind her. "Go get behind the bed, baby," she whispers. "Stay there till I come get you."

"Why?" She can hear the tears in his voice.

"Do as I say," she hisses, and shoves him toward the bed. He falls on his ass and begins to cry harder. Another figure appears in the doorway.

"What's going on?"

She swings the gun around in a two-handed grip pointed at the shadowy outline. It leaps backward.

"Jesus, Mom!"

She lowers the pistol. "Get in here," she orders Ben in a low, urgent voice. "Get your brother. Get behind the bed."

"Mom," Francis wails, loud enough to make Marie grit her teeth.

110

Ben reaches down and scoops him up under one arm, carrying him to the space between wall and bed. "It's okay, buddy," he says. "Shhh. It's okay." He deposits the boy in the narrow space, then slides across the bed toward her.

"What are you doing?" she demands.

He rolls off the bed onto the floor and holds up the cell phone he's grabbed from the bedside table. "Calling 9-1-1."

She nods as he begins punching in the numbers. "Good. Stay here." She moves in a crouch out of the bedroom, gun extended before her, straining to hear if anyone's trying to breach the front door. She hears another shot, then a whoop of drunken laughter.

"Take that, bitch!" a voice yells, and it's a voice she knows too well.

"Brandon," she snarls. "Now you're at my fucking house?" She straightens up and moves to the door, caution giving way to outrage and fury. The sound of a big engine comes through the door. She yanks it open, ready to do murder, but all she sees is the taillights of a jacked up white pickup disappearing down her long driveway. She steps out onto the porch of the farmhouse, weapon at the ready, as the truck disappears into the night, the thumping bass of some kind of rap music slowly diminishing as they get away.

# FORTY-FOUR

Keller pulls his truck into the tiny gravel pad that serves as a driveway to his cottage. He sits in the quiet for a moment, listening to the slow tick of cooling metal, and rubs his eyes. The day has left him both exhausted and too wired to sleep. It's a feeling he's all too familiar with. He glances across the field separating his house from the church. Might as well get some work done. He exits the truck and trudges down the narrow gravel path separating the old parsonage from its church. Halfway to his destination, he stops, places his hands at the small of his back, and stretches to work out the stiffness he feels there. The arch of his back makes him look up at the stars, glittering and uncaring. After holding the stretch for a moment, he resumes his walk to the church. He knows the door won't be locked. A plaque in the churchyard tells the story of a man found dead on the steps after a snowstorm in 1898 and the resolution of the church elders to never again lock the sanctuary doors to anyone in need. It's a nice story, but Keller has gotten MacDonald to admit that there has been some vandalism and some acts of outright desecration as a result. But, the preacher has been quick to point out, one of the vandals, while cleaning up the obscene graffiti he'd scrawled in his own feces on the sanctuary walls after being caught and put on probation, decided to commit his life to Christ and is now a valued member of the congregation. Despite himself, Keller hopes that story is true. Redemption is something he'd very much like to believe in.

The big oak doors creak as Keller enters. He snaps on the lights in

112

the sanctuary and locates the vacuum cleaner in a closet off the foyer. He plugs the machine in and begins the process of cleaning. It's not a large church, but getting into all the nooks and crannies and narrow spaces between the pews is time-consuming. But that's exactly what Keller needs at this point: to consume time with as little thought as possible.

He's worked his way from the back of the church almost to the worn rug before the communion rail when he notices the figure seated in the next to last pew. *Shit*, he thinks, *how did I not notice*? He kills the vacuum cleaner and waits until its high-pitched whine cycles down before calling out. "Can I help you?"

The person doesn't answer at first, just looks around the simple interior as if they're seeing the cathedral of Notre-Dame for the first time.

Keller frowns and walks up the aisle. "I said, can I help you?"

"Perhaps." The person in the pew slides down and out and heads up the red-carpeted center aisle, stumping toward Keller on a dark wooden cane. As they draw closer together, Keller sees that the visitor is a middle-aged woman, no more than five feet tall. Her hair is cut short and curls around her face, black streaked with silver-gray. Her face is lined and friendly.

"I don't think there are any services until tomorrow night's prayer meeting," Keller says. There's an uneasy feeling he can't explain. "Reverend MacDonald will be here in the morning, if you need to talk to him."

"Good. Good," the woman says absently, still looking around. Then she turns her focus on Keller. "But it's you I'd like to talk to," she says, "Mr. Keller."

Keller shoves the vacuum cleaner to one side and faces the short woman. "So talk."

She looks amused. "You look as if you're getting ready for a fight, Mr. Keller." She chuckles. "Do I look as if I'm eager to fight?"

Keller realizes that he's dropped into a slight crouch, arms by his side, as if confronting a threat. He's still not willing to concede that she isn't, but he relaxes slightly. The woman chuckles again and slides into a pew about halfway down the aisle. She takes a seat in the middle and pats the cushion next to her. "Come. Sit." Keller hesitates, then takes a seat just out of reach. That makes the woman shake her head in amusement and look down. After a moment, she speaks. "I'm looking for Ted Wilson. I understand you've been looking for him as well."

Keller's getting annoyed. "And you are...?"

She smiles. "You can call me Iris. It's as good a name as any."

"Well, Iris," Keller says, "I went looking for Mr. Wilson. He wasn't at his hotel."

Her face turns serious. "I know you went looking for Mr. Wilson. I also know you'd had a confrontation with him earlier. At the diner."

"So," Keller says, "he's been reporting back to you. You're his control, then?"

"Let's just call him a protege of mine. I'm concerned."

"Concerned why?"

"He hasn't reported in."

"I'd say if you came all the way down here from Langley, or DC, or wherever you're out of, that's more than just some concern."

The previous jolly attitude is starting to slip. "Wilson said you're an annoying bastard."

Keller smiles. "I appreciate the endorsement. But the fact that he's dropped off the radar gives me some concerns, too. About the Khourys. Isn't that our main goal? Protecting your asset? And his family?"

The scowl remains. "You need to leave this to us, Mister Keller."

"That's what Wilson said, Iris. And now he's MIA. Seems to me you're not in a position to refuse help." He stands up. "Because unless I miss my guess, ma'am, there's no other help coming."

She stares at him, all pretense of friendliness gone. "What do you mean?"

Keller shakes his head. "I should have figured this out sooner when I saw there was only one guy detailed to the Khourys. An asset that valuable would need a team at least. Then the one guy disappears, and the person who comes down to look after the situation is his boss?"

Keller leans over, puts his hands on the pew and looks her in the eye. "This is off the books, isn't it? You and Wilson were freelancing. Trying to find that missing USAID money without the Agency finding out. So you could get it for yourself. Tell me, are those two contractors I spotted at the Khoury house yours?"

It takes almost a full second for her to hide her shock before her face goes completely blank.

"Not yours, then. So, there's another player here. Would you have any idea who that might be?"

As Keller speaks, the woman who calls herself Iris has risen from the pew and shouldered her way past Keller. Cane thumping, she makes her way up the aisle toward the back of the church.

He calls after her as she reaches the back doors. "All I care about is the safety of…" But she's gone.

Keller shakes his head. Then he puts the vacuum away, turns the lights off, and goes home.

# FORTY-FIVE

"Are you sure?"

The sheriff's deputy sent to respond to the shots fired call is beginning to piss Marie off. He's acting as if he's interviewing some civilian. "Yes, Deputy," she looks at the nameplate over his pocket, "Gresham. I'm sure. Brandon Ochs. O-C-H-S."

"And you know this how?"

"Because I hear his voice every goddamn day, Deputy," Marie snaps. "I'm the SRO at his school. I just faced him down for underage drinking and chased him off at a local bar. I figure that gives him motive. All you have to do is find out about his movements since then and you've got your opportunity. Hey, are you listening to me, Deputy?"

Gresham has his head turned to one side, muttering into the mobile microphone clipped to his lapel. He finishes his conversation and turns back to Marie with a professional smile. "We'll check this out, ma'am."

"Yeah," Marie mutters. "You do that." She wonders what will happen tomorrow if Brandon Ochs shows up. It would probably be a firing offense, she muses, if she ripped the little bastard's head off. She sighs, knowing that the right thing to do is to turn this over to her boss and her partner. But she's not quite there yet. Hopefully in the morning.

"Motherfucker." The voice beside her makes her jump. She turns to see Ben beside her, looking at the departing deputy with rage in his eyes.

116

"It's okay." She tries to speak as soothingly as possible, despite her own anger at the cavalier way the cops seem to be treating this. "The sheriff's department will deal with this. Once it works its way up the chain of command."

"Bullshit." The flat declaration sets off all the alarm bells Marie's come to dread. She sees the widened eyes, the flared nostrils, the clenched jaw that reminds Marie so much of his late father, and she puts a hand on his shoulder. "Ben. Take a breath. We'll talk about this in the morning."

He turns to her, gives her a bright smile that's terrifying in its insincerity. "Sure, Mom. Tomorrow." He turns and walks back to the house.

# FORTY-SIX

Inside the house, in his bedroom, Ben reaches under the bed and draws out the rough wooden box. Now he knows what the gun nestled inside is for. He takes it out, checks the revolver again to make sure the weapon is fully loaded. He looks at his school backpack, leaning against a wall across the room. Taking a deep breath, he stuffs the gun down deep into the backpack.

*Tomorrow, motherfucker,* he thinks. It's always been a frightening feeling, this rage that seems ready sometimes to take him over. But now, it's found a focus. There's a reason for it, and that's to protect his mom and his little brother. That makes the anger feel righteous. Ben closes his eyes. He's back on that hillside, the scent of smoke and blood and fear an acrid reek in his nose. But this time it's him holding the gun as his tormentor kneels unarmed before him. It's his finger on the trigger.

It's his own laughter ringing in his ears.

Ben opens his eyes, sucking in a deep, shuddering breath. The feeling's intoxicating. He wonders if that's what Keller felt. He wonders if that's how it will feel when he pulls the trigger on Brandon Ochs.

# FORTY-SEVEN

Mohammed Al-Mansour is dozing on the bed when the soft knock comes on the door. He opens his eyes, a feeling of dread coming over him. He wonders if he's made the right decision, even as he realizes the question is now moot. The Chechens are here. He gets up and opens the door.

The woman standing in the doorway is tall, just a little under two meters. Her dark hair falls in waves to her shoulders, and she has the strong features of a fashion model. She smiles at him. "Sheikh Al-Mansour?"

She's so lovely, he instinctively nods and starts to smile back. The smile dies as he sees the other two women standing behind her in the walkway outside the motel room. Like her, they're tall, dark-haired, and striking, but they gaze at him with the blank-eyed rapaciousness of predatory birds. He takes an instinctive step back.

The leader smiles and takes the opportunity to enter the motel room, followed by the other two. "I am Natalya," the first woman says in Arabic. "My sisters are Liza," she points at one who's taking a seat in the room's one easy chair, "and Marina," she points to the other sister, who leans against the dresser, arms folded across her chest. He notices that Liza has a prominent scar running from the corner of her left eye down to the corner of her jaw. There's something strange about Marina's mouth that he can't quite put his finger on. Natalya speaks up and pulls his attention away. "I speak for the family. Tell us your problem."

119

He explains as succinctly as he can, telling her and her silent sisters about the money he and Fadhil Al-Masri conspired to siphon off from the Americans, how Al-Masri, now known as Adnan Khoury, took off with both shares, how the CIA, or someone he thought was CIA, had been protecting Al-Masri/Khoury, but now he's begun to doubt that America is actually protecting them. He hesitates before admitting his doubts about hiring the Americans, but plunges ahead when he decides they need to know everything.

Natalya listens until he's done, then shakes her head sadly. "You're right. You should have come to us first. These *giaour*," she uses the Chechen for unbeliever, "are weak. They can't be trusted. But you can trust us. We are of the Faithful." She looks at him appraisingly. "Can we trust you?"

He bristles a bit at being questioned that way by a woman, but nods.

She smiles. "Good." She nods at Marina. "Because my sisters, Marina in particular, don't have much trust in men. And they tend to be…unforgiving of men who betray them."

Marina straightens up and leans over to look intently into Al-Mansour's face with those dead, blank eyes. He can see the pale white tracery of scars around her mouth.

"You see," Natalya says, "Marina trusted a man once. A Russian soldier. He promised he'd protect her in the war that was raging in our land." She shakes her head. "But he was false. Like many men are false. He took her one night to the barracks where his men were. He gave her to them. When they grew tired of her screaming, they had the company medical officer sew her mouth shut. She was sixteen. She hasn't spoken since."

Al-Mansour swallows. "Infidels," he whispers. "Savages."

Marina straightens up, steps back to lean against the dresser again. Al-Mansour breathes more easily.

"No doubt," Natalya says. "But after that, she does not respond well to men who do not deal with us in good faith. Do you, sister?"

Marina's answer is to produce a quickly shining butterfly knife that vanishes almost before his eyes can register it. "She is very fast with the knife," Natalya says. "But she can also be very slow and careful when enacting payment. Back home, our fighters captured the Russian who'd betrayed her. They let her have him. He was begging for death for three days before she ended him, and then it was only because the unit had to move on." Natalya gives Al-Mansour a smile that chills his blood. "If these Americans you are concerned with betray you, my sisters and I will be glad to teach them a lesson. No extra charge."

Al-Mansour is shaken, but he keeps his voice steady as he says, "Thank you. I will keep that in mind."

Natalya's smile widens as she realizes she's made her point and gained the upper hand in the negotiation. In her world, the one who wins the deal is not the one who can walk away, but the one who can inflict the most agony and fear. "Let's talk payment, then."

# FORTY-EIGHT

The auto salvage yard seems to stretch for miles, endless rows of crumpled, dented, and utterly destroyed vehicles as far as the eye can see. The sun's barely up, and Fletcher's yawning and resorting often to the cup of coffee provided by his old friend and Army buddy Billy Sims, who owns the place. Billy, who's got a titanium hip and about sixty pounds more that he should be carrying on his five-foot-five frame, waddles over to stand beside Fletcher and stares at the burned-out frame of the vehicle Fletcher had towed there.

"I don't know if you thought you were doin' me a favor," Billy says, "but you weren't. Ain't no way I can sell any part of this wreck."

"I know." Fletcher takes a sip of the coffee. It tastes like something Billy might have drained from one of the fractured radiators in the vehicles surrounding them, but he doesn't complain. "You're doing me a favor. And you know the county's good for it."

Billy just sighs. "Yeah. Eventually." He looks up the aisle formed by the lines of vehicles and frowns. "Who's that?"

Fletcher looks. "That's who I've been waiting for."

The man approaching is as short as Billy, but so skinny as to seem almost anorexic. He's dressed in a standard Army Combat Uniform and boots. The nametag over his pocket says BROWNE.

"Rob." Fletcher greets the new arrival. "Thanks for coming."

The man just nods and looks at the destroyed vehicle. His eyes narrow and he inclines his head curiously. "This the one?"

"Yeah," Fletcher says.

122

Browne walks over and stands next to the car, hands on hips. He looks it up and down before leaning over and sniffing, delicately, like a cat. Whistling absentmindedly through his teeth, he walks around the burned hulk, bending down from time to time to examine something more closely.

"Who the hell is this guy?" Billy Sims whispers.

"Explosives expert, out of Fort Bragg. I've used him in a couple of arson investigations."

Browne finishes his inspection and walks over to where Fletcher and Sims are standing. "You want me to tell you what you already know?" he says.

"I know what I suspect," Fletcher replies. "I don't know anything. Yet. But something tells me I'm about to."

Browne nods. "That's not regular burn damage. That's a demolition."

Sims looks disgusted. "God damn it."

Fletcher ignores him. "How do you mean?"

"For one thing," Browne says, "whatever burned that vehicle burned hot. Way hotter than the gas in the tank. I'm thinking maybe thermite."

"Why?" Fletcher says.

"Walk over here." Browne walks to the vehicle with Fletcher right behind him. "See?" Browne points. "There. And there."

Fletcher shakes his head. "I see. But I don't understand."

Browne sighs. "The burn pattern. You've got two places where it looks like something extremely hot was placed on the vehicle and burned straight down through it. One right over the gas tank, and one over the engine block. I'd have to do a chemical analysis to be sure, but thermite's the best guess. It's cheap, you can make it yourself with the right ingredients, and it'll do the job."

"What job?" Fletcher asks.

Browne looks impatient at Fletcher's apparent obtuseness. "Destroying evidence."

Fletcher nods. "Okay. Thanks."

"God damn it," Sims says again.

Fletcher glances at him. "What's your problem?"

"So now I'm holding evidence for you." He gestures at the burned-out car. "I wasn't going to get doodly-squat for that wreck anyway, and now I'm not gonna get anything."

Fletcher looks puzzled. "You'll get storage fees, right?"

Sims looks disgusted. "Yeah. When the sheriff's department has the money. I'm still waiting on my money from some of those DWI confiscations of piece of shit cars I can't sell. In case you didn't notice, Fletch, this is what I do for a living."

"Come on, Billy, you know I'll—hang on." Fletcher's cell phone is blaring its electronic tone in his pocket. Fletcher hates the ringtone, but doesn't know how to change it. He pulls the phone from his pocket and looks at the screen. It's Cameron. "Yeah."

"We just got a call from the M.E.," Cameron says.

"And?"

"Two bullets in the body we pulled out of the wreck."

Fletcher sighs. He wonders what it's like to enjoy being right. "Okay. I'm at the junkyard. Looks like someone burned the car up to try to destroy evidence. Open it as a homicide."

"God *damn* it," Billy says as he stomps off.

# FORTY-NINE

Marie's working the drop-off line again as Keller pulls up with Alia and Bassim. But this time, the other SRO, Rogers, is behind her. He's watching the line like a hawk, his hand on his holstered sidearm. Keller notices a sheriff's cruiser pulled up in the faculty lot, and a pair of deputies in full tac gear standing beside it. Alia and Bassim notice at the same time.

"What's going on?" Bassim says.

"I don't know. Sit tight." Keller pulls the truck up to the drop-off point and rolls the passenger side window down. "What's happening?" he calls to Marie. As she steps over to the window, he can see the dark circles under her eyes and the exhaustion in them. "Nothing, Jack," she says in a hoarse voice.

"Marie," Keller says, "tell me."

She opens the door. "Come on, guys. Let's get going."

Alia and Bassim look at Keller, who nods. "I'll be back at the usual time."

Reluctantly, they climb down from the cab.

Rogers nods to them as they walk quickly past. He doesn't take his hand off his gun.

Marie turns back to Keller. "Someone shot at my house last night." She takes a deep breath. "I think it was Brandon Ochs." Keller sits back, eyes narrowing. She notices the look and speaks quickly. "You need to let us handle this, Jack."

He has to take several deep breaths before he can speak. Cars behind him are beginning to honk their horns. "How's Francis?" he finally says quietly. "And Ben?"

"Frank's shook up, but I think he'll be okay. Ben..." She looks back at the school as if searching for him. "I don't know, Jack. He's completely closed off. He's polite. He's agreeable. And that scares the shit out of me." Another horn honks. Marie steps back and closes the door. "You need to get moving."

Keller nods and puts the truck in gear.

"And let us handle this!" he hears her call as he pulls away.

# FIFTY

"Oh my God," Meadow says. "Are you okay? Is Frank okay?"

Ben just nods.

"Oh my God. Oh my God. I can't believe that asshole...are you sure it was Brandon?"

Ben shakes his head. "I didn't hear him. Just the shots. The breaking glass. I heard my mom telling the deputies she thought it was Brandon. That's why there's extra security."

She looks across the lot at the sheriff's deputies posted down. "I'm surprised they didn't do a lockdown."

"I think they talked about it." Ben's eyes are distant, his tone distracted.

Meadow puts her hand on his arm. "I don't think you're okay."

He shakes the hand off. "I'm fine."

Meadow's feeling of alarm rises. "Let's get out of here. Let's ditch school and hang out by the river. Come on. If anyone needs a mental health break, it's you today."

Ben shakes his head. "I've got something I need to deal with."

"Brandon?"

Ben says nothing.

"Ben. What are you thinking of doing?"

He looks at her as if noticing her for the first time. "Nothing. But maybe we shouldn't hang around with each other today." He takes a deep breath. "Or maybe not at all anymore."

She steps back, her eyes wide with shock. "Okay, now you're really freaking me out."

He glances at his backpack, then picks it up and slings it on one shoulder. "Just stay away from me. Leave me alone." He gives her a hard look. "You fucking freak."

Tears spring to her eyes. "You don't mean that. I know you better than that."

He doesn't answer, just walks away.

"Ben!" she calls after him, her voice breaking.

He doesn't look back.

# FIFTY-ONE

Brandon pulls up to Jake's old farmhouse. He feels like shit that's been hammered flat, doubled over, then hammered flat again. His buzz from last night is nearly gone, and the adrenaline rush from shooting up the bitch cop's house has long deserted him. He sits in the pickup for a moment, trying not to fall asleep over the wheel. Maybe Jake will let him crash here for the day. He's sure as hell not going to school.

Jake comes to the door and leans against the frame, watching him. He's got a beer in one hand that he takes a pull from as he stands there. Brandon doesn't like the look on his face. Slowly, moving like an old man, Brandon gets out of his truck. He holds the pistol down by his side. "Hey."

"Hey." Jake still doesn't move.

"I brought the gun back, like you said."

Jake nods. "Bring it here."

Brandon crosses the packed dirt of the yard, yawning as he walks. He holds the gun out, grasping it by the barrel. Jake takes it in his free hand, still with no expression on his face. He reaches behind him to place the weapon inside the house. "Your mama called."

Brandon blinks stupidly at him. "She did?"

"Yeah. Deputies came by the house looking for you." Before Brandon can process that, Jake's hand comes around and smacks him across the face, harder than last night.

Brandon's head whips around with the blow. "Hey," is all he has time to say before the backhand comes back and knocks him to the ground.

"You dumb son of a bitch," Jakes snarls down at him. "You shot at a fuckin' *cop*? A *female* cop?"

Brandon tries and fails to keep the whine out of his voice. "She ain't a real cop. She's just a—" He flinches away as Jake aims a kick at his midsection. The kick misses by an inch.

Jake stops, breathing hard, and studies Brandon on the ground. "You told me somebody threatened you."

Brandon gets slowly to his feet. "Someone did. But I think that was her boyfriend."

"So instead of shooting at the boyfriend, you shoot at the fucking *cop*." Jake shakes his head in disgust. "Did she actually see you?"

"No. I don't think so. I mean, it was dark. I was in the truck. I wasn't driving, though."

"Oh, good, there were witnesses. This shit just gets better and better. Which of your dipshit friends was with you?"

Brandon looks down and mumbles. "I don't wanna say." Jake rears back for another blow and Brandon blurts out, "Bunny. Bunny was drivin'."

"You think he'll keep his mouth shut?"

Brandon nods, with more confidence than he feels.

"Good," Jake says. "Well, get ahold of him. Tell him to keep quiet, or he'll answer to me. I gotta get rid of this gun you suddenly turned into evidence, and didn't even make a fuckin' dime off of it. Do you feel even just a little bit stupid?"

"Yeah," Brandon says miserably. "I feel really stupid."

"Well, that's a start. Come on in the house. We gotta get our story straight."

Brandon looks up, feeling hope for the first time. "We do?"

"I don't rat family out to the cops," Jake says, "even if that family member is a dumbass. I'll say you were with me, but we need a timeline. Come on."

Brandon licks his lips. "Any chance I can have one o' those beers? I could use a hair of the dog."

Jake sighs. "Sure. Whatever."

# FIFTY-TWO

"All I know," Reggie Allgood snaps, "is that I was supposed to get relieved three hours ago. So you tell that boy if he ain't in here in a half hour, he best not come in at all." He slams the phone down. "Lazy-ass cracker," he mutters. If he'd have known when he took the manager's job at this motel that part of his duties would include working double shifts because some skeezy white opioid-popping motherfucker couldn't be bothered to stir his ass out of bed in the morning to get to work, he'd have turned the job down. He realizes too late that his ultimatum may have doomed him to work yet another full shift to cover the idiot he just fired. He sighs and stretches, hands at the small of his back, feeling the creak and pop of his spine. "Damn it," he mutters savagely. Then he notices the woman standing in the tiny lobby. He hadn't seen her come in. "Help you?" he says, trying not to snarl.

The short woman in the dark-grey pantsuit smiles. "Rough day already?"

He musters a tired but, he hopes, professional smile in return. "No problem. What can I do for you, ma'am?"

She leans on her cane and looks up at him. "I'm supposed to meet a colleague here. Ted Wilson?"

Reggie frowns. "Mr. Wilson expecting you, ma'am?"

"Actually, no." Her smile never wavers. "But he hasn't checked in with me. I got concerned."

Reggie inclines his head worried. "You his wife?" She looks way too old for Wilson, but you never can tell.

She chuckles. "Oh, heavens no. As I said, I'm a colleague. Can you see if Mr. Wilson's still here?"

"Another one," Reggie mutters, then immediately wants to kick himself. Exhaustion has made him careless. The woman isn't, however; her eyes are sharp and inquisitive as she leans forward.

"Another one? Someone else has been looking for Mr. Wilson?"

"I said too much already," Reggie says. "Sorry. I can't release information about guests. Except to the police. Company policy."

The woman nods. "A good policy. I expect some of your guests really appreciate it."

He stiffens. "What you mean by that?"

"Nothing, nothing," she says soothingly. "Look, let me set your mind at ease." She reaches into her suit coat and pulls out a slim leather wallet. She approaches, flipping the wallet open. He leans forward, studying the credential she's displaying. His eyes widen and he steps back. The woman never stops smiling. "Does that help?"

He nods, suddenly filled with dread. *What's coming down here?* "What do you want to know, ma'am?"

"Well, first off, who else has been asking about Mr. Wilson?"

# FIFTY-THREE

Keller drives blindly, taking random turns with no particular destination, fingers tapping a rapid staccato on the steering wheel.

*That bastard shot at my family.*

The thought keeps ricocheting around in his head, interrupting any rational thought trying to take root there.

"I should let the police handle…"

*That bastard shot at my family.*

"He's just a punk kid…"

*That bastard shot at my family.*

Part of him realizes that family might be a stretch. He's Francis's father, but his relationship with Marie is, at best, up in the air. Ben, he thinks, hates and fears him. Still. The anger is real, and it's tied to the unshakable feeling *that bastard shot at my family.*

Finally, his wanderings take him down a long dirt road that ends at the river. He stops, kills the engine and sits there, watching the sluggish black flow of water as it makes its slow progress to the sea. He thinks of the time not too long ago when he'd dumped a sheaf of papers into that river and watched it sink, a legacy of betrayal and vengeance slipping beneath the dark water. Keller thought he'd put his past behind him at that point, shed his history of anger and the addiction to adrenaline that had led him to ever more reckless and destructive acts, just so he could feel something.

He thought he'd left all that behind. But even now, Ben is suffering for the violence Keller had brought into his life. And Francis. The son he hadn't know about for years. Now that innocent little boy is being targeted, and Keller has no illusions that it's not because he faced that punk down...*that bastard shot at my family.*

He puts the truck in gear and turns it around.

# FIFTY-FOUR

Ben sits on a stone bench against the wall of the school building and scans the courtyard. Brandon Ochs is nowhere to be found. Some of his clique are laughing and joking across the way, but he notices a couple of them aren't looking very happy. His little butt-boy Jerrard, for one, is looking distinctly ill, and more than a little worried. Ben's brows draw together in what he hopes is an intimidating scowl. He stands up, ready to advance across the common space and force Brandon Ochs's bunch of gangster wannabes to cough up his location. At gunpoint if need be. He reaches down and traces the outline of the pistol grip beneath the nylon fabric of his backpack.

"Hello, Ben."

He turns to face the voice, ready to snap at whoever's interrupting his violent reverie.

It's Alia Khoury, taking up a seat on the bench beside him and pulling a brown lunch bag out of her own backpack.

"Hi," he says, his anger sidetracked for the moment by his awkwardness around such a beautiful girl.

She takes a bite of her sandwich and looks around the courtyard. "Have you seen Meadow?"

He shakes his head, then says, "Well, yeah. Earlier."

Something in his tone makes Alia turn her head to look at him curiously. "Is everything all right?"

Something in her wide, innocent dark eyes makes it impossible to lie. "No." He tells her about the visit Brandon Ochs paid to his house last night He tells her about the fear, the helplessness, the rage that's consumed him all day. He can't look at her as he speaks, but when he's done, he sneaks a glance. He's amazed to see her nodding as if she understands. She looks again around the courtyard, her gaze more focused this time. "He's not here. He's hiding out, I think."

"Where?" Ben doesn't want to involve her in this, but her calm calculation steadies him.

She takes another bite of her sandwich, chews it thoughtfully. "We could go over there. Ask his group," her lips twist around the word, "where he is. But I don't think they'll tell us."

"I think I have something that might persuade them," Ben says, and reaches down for the backpack.

Alia stops him with a hand on his. "Ben. Do you have a gun in there?"

"No," he blurts out, "I'm just really happy to see you."

She blinks in confusion. "Well, I'm, um…"

He can feel himself blushing scarlet. "Sorry. It's a reference."

"Ah. Remember, I don't always get those. But…do you? Have a gun, I mean."

He nods. "I'm looking for Brandon."

She nods back. "But he's not here."

He looks across the courtyard at Brandon's cohorts. "I bet they know where he is."

"Perhaps. But if you pull out that gun here, you'll be stopped. You may never find out the answer you need."

He ponders that for a moment. "You're right," he says grudgingly. "So how do we find out?"

Alia finishes her sandwich. "We need to get Meadow's advice. Meadow is the smartest person I know."

"Hey," Ben says, "I'm right here."

Alia smiles at him, then her teasing grin turns to a look of concern as she looks over his shoulder. Ben looks around to see his mother's SRO partner, Rogers, headed his way. Ben's never had any problem with Rogers, who doesn't go out of his way to be either hard or easy on

Ben because of his mother's associations. But the cold and impersonal look on the SRO's face doesn't bode well.

"Ben," he says, "you need to come with me. And bring your backpack."

Ben tries his best to look innocent. "Why? What have I—"

"Don't make this harder than it has to be, son," Rogers says.

Ben feels a rising sense of panic, and with the fear, as always, comes an equally increasing anger. "Don't call me son," he snaps. He reaches down and begins to unzip the pack. If he can just get a hand on the gun...

"Ben, no," he hears. He looks over and sees Meadow standing a few feet away. Her hand is over her mouth and her eyes are wide, almost panicked. He realizes why Rogers is there.

"You bitch," he snarls, close to losing control. "You fucking ratted me out."

"Ben!" Alia's voice, usually so calm and soothing, is harsh, stronger than Ben can remember hearing. He turns to her in shock, and Rogers takes the opportunity to grab his right wrist in a grip so hard it makes Ben gasp. With the other hand, Rogers grabs a strap on the backpack and moves it behind him, out of reach. "What were you reaching for, Ben?" he says softly. "Were you really going to do it?"

Ben can't answer. He just looks down at the brick of the courtyard. Rogers stands up, drawing Ben with him. "Come on, kid. Let's not do this here." As the SRO leads him away, Ben can hear the hubbub rising behind him and he feels the burning heat of embarrassment on his face as he realizes it's all about him. He can also hear the sound of a woman sobbing. He doesn't know if it's Meadow or Alia.

# FIFTY-FIVE

Alia looks around at the crowd in the brick courtyard. Meadow is standing a few feet away, weeping as if her heart is breaking. Most of the crowd is staring and talking among themselves. A couple of Brandon's friends, however, are smiling with even more than their usual maliciousness. She makes a snap decision. "Come on," she says to Meadow, standing up and slinging her own backpack on one shoulder. "We need to go."

Meadow looks up, misery written all over her face. "Wh-what?"

Alia grasps her gently by one arm and bends down to look her in the eye. "This place isn't safe. We need to leave. Now."

"But...Ben..."

"We can't help Ben now. Come with me."

# FIFTY-SIX

Still sniffling, Meadow allows herself to be guided through the swinging doors into the hallway. They're a good way down the hall when she hears the doors to the courtyard bang open. She looks back to see Brandon's girlfriend Amber with a couple of her own female followers coming in, followed by the boys they'd seen earlier from Brandon's posse. They all look pissed off in a way that makes Meadow's heart clench in her chest. Whatever trouble Brandon's in, Meadow realizes, these people are going to take it out on her and Alia. The freaks. The outsiders. The people throughout history who've always been the first to take the punishment when things go wrong.

Alia's been tapping at her cell phone when she hears the sound behind her. She turns to Meadow. "Run. For the front doors."

"They'll catch us," Meadow says.

"I called Jack." The name seems to give her confidence. She picks up her stride.

"Officer Jones's boyfriend?" Meadow can't quite make the connection. "What does he—"

Alia's not listening. She's back on her phone. "Front door. Now."

Meadow looks back. Amber and her small but terrifying phalanx are striding down the hallway after them with grim purpose. *We're not going to make it to the front door. We're fucked.*

# FIFTY-SEVEN

Bassim is in class, half asleep, drowsing his way through the American Revolution, when his ringtone blares, the opening synthesizer riff of Europe's *The Final Countdown*. The lecture stops for a moment, the silence only broken by the tittering of the other students.

"Mr. Khoury," the teacher, a curly-haired, bearded twentysomething man says as sternly as a curly haired twentysomething man can. "Would you like me to get that?"

Bassim checks the screen. "No, sir," he says with a brightness as sincere as the teacher's. "I got this." He puts the phone to his ear, intending to answer in a suave voice. Before he gets a chance, Bassim hears his sister's voice. "Okay," is all he can say in response to the barked order. He looks up at the teacher glowering at him. "Sorry, sir. Family emergency. Got to go."

# FIFTY-EIGHT

A soft chime comes over the intercom, echoing through the hallways. "Condition Red," a voice says. "Condition Red. This is a lockdown. All students, report to the nearest classroom. All teachers, report to the nearest classroom and initiate a Code Red stance. Repeat. This is a lockdown."

"Shit."

Meadow stares at Alia in shock. She's never heard even the mildest curse from the strait-laced Muslim girl. She glances back. Amber and her friends are stopped, gazing around in confusion. A male teacher steps out of a classroom door, says something in a low, urgent voice. Amber looks up the hall, her eyes narrowed in hatred, but she obeys the teacher. When she follows him into the classroom, the group with her goes as well.

"Alia. Melissa." Meadow turns to see Miss Othmar beckoning from a nearby doorway. She's clearly terrified out of her wits, judging from the shaking in her bony knees. "In here," she beckons. "We need to shelter in place."

"Sorry, ma'am," Alia smiles apologetically, "but we have a ride coming."

The teacher blinks in confusion. "But. We're in lockdown."

Alia continues walking down the hall, still smiling. "Yes, ma'am."

The combination of verbal agreement and physical defiance seems to be frying Miss Othmar's brain. "But," she says again.

Meadow bites back a hysterical laugh and waves. "Enjoy the lockdown, y'all." She turns and follows Alia, who's making for the front doors. Behind her, she hears the door slam. "We are in so much fucking trouble," she says.

Alia doesn't break stride. "Yes," she says as they turn the corner toward the front of the school.

Meadow hears the pounding of running feet. She turns and looks down a hallway that leads to the freshman wing of the high school. Bassim is running as fast as he can toward them, almost stumbling over his own feet in his haste. He catches up as the three of them reach the front door. He says something in Arabic to his sister, who replies with a curt phrase in the same language. He turns to Meadow. "Hey," he gasps, breathing hard from exertion.

"Hey." She scans the parking lot. From far away, she can hear the sound of sirens drawing nearer. "So, where's our ride?" she asks.

# FIFTY-NINE

Keller's cruising the county roads, his mind walking that dangerous border between red fury and cold calculation. He needs to know how to find Brandon Ochs's address, but the calculating part knows that any attempt to get that information will set off alarm bells. His fingers tapping on the steering wheel are hitting harder and harder, the prelude to pounding on the wheel and screaming in primal rage, when his phone goes off. He picks it up off the passenger seat and looks at the screen.

ALIA.

Keller's heart feels as if it's skipping beats in his chest. He answers. "Keller."

Alia's voice is calm but urgent. "We need help. Front door of the school. Please."

There's only one answer he can make. "On my way. Sit tight. Is Bassim with you?"

"He will be. And one other."

*One other?* Keller thinks. "Hang on. I'm on the way."

# SIXTY

Marie stares at the gun on the table. She doesn't speak. There are a thousand things she wants to say, to shout, to scream into her son's face, but she stays mute.

"What were you thinking about, Ben?" Rogers is asking her son.

Normally, she likes her fellow resource officer a lot. They've laughed, joked, made plenty of snarky comments about the faculty and staff. But right now, Marie is the mother of the boy Rogers is interrogating, and she's having a hard time not hating her partner.

Ben just shrugs, and Marie has to admit, while she's not anywhere close to hating her son, she's finding it nearly impossible to like him right now. "Answer the man, Ben."

He looks at her, eyes blazing with anger and betrayal. "Fine. You want to know what I was thinking? I was thinking I was going to kill that son of a bitch." He looks at her, eyes brimming with tears. "The one who shot at my mom. And my little brother. If you fuckers want to put me in jail for that, then do it."

"No one's going to jail, Ben." It's Vice Principal Burnham who speaks up from across the office, his voice calm and soothing. He smiles sadly. "I get that you're angry—"

"You don't get shit," Ben mutters.

Burnham goes on as if he hasn't heard. "But we do have a problem with one student killing another. Can you see that?"

Before Ben can answer, the school intercom chimes. "Condition Red. Condition Red. This is a lockdown. All students, report to the nearest classroom. All teachers, report to the nearest classroom and initiate a Code Red stance. Repeat. This is a lockdown."

Burnham closes his eyes wearily. "Of course."

"What?" Marie says.

Burnham shakes his head. "Once the word got to the main office that a gun was found on campus, the lockdown goes into effect. It's automatic."

"Sir," Rogers says, "in a lockdown, the SROs are supposed to be in the halls."

Burnham nods. "To address whatever threat caused the Condition Red. But it seems to me, Officer Rogers, that's already been addressed." He nods at the gun on the desk. "Wouldn't you agree?"

"Maybe, sir. Still. There's a protocol."

"Ah. Yes. Of course. Protocol." He waves toward the door to the office. "Go ahead, Officer Rogers. Check it out. And let me know if there's another problem we need to deal with."

"Yes, sir, thank you, sir." As Rogers exits, Burnham shakes his head and sighs. He turns to Marie. "Do you and Ben need a moment alone? Before the deputies get here?"

Marie grits her teeth. "I should be backing up SRO Rogers, sir."

Burnham nods. "I applaud your dedication," He looks over at Ben, slumped miserably in a chair in front of the desk. "Except the threat, such as it is, is here."

"My son's not a threat. Sir." Marie hates the desperation that she can't seem to keep out of her voice.

Burnham nods toward the pistol on the desk. "That would seem to indicate otherwise." He reaches out and picks up the weapon by the barrel, as gingerly as if he's picking up a rattlesnake by the neck. "I'll just take this someplace safe. Until law enforcement arrives." He walks out, leaving Marie and Ben alone. Ben continues to glare at the empty desktop.

Marie hears him mutter something underneath his breath. "What?" she says.

He looks up, and she feels sick as she sees the rage in his eyes. "I said, you're such a fucking hypocrite."

She shakes her head in confusion. "I don't know what you're talking about."

"Sure you don't." He slumps back down in the chair, unmoving.

"So help me out here, Ben. Tell me what I'm missing. Tell me why I'm such a hypocrite."

He shakes his head. She steps over, puts a hand on either arm of the chair, and leans down until her face is inches away from her son's. "Tell me, god damn it." Her voice is low and intense, but it has the force of a scream.

He looks up at her. "All I was trying to do was stop someone from threatening us. You. Me. Frank. And for that you're going to let them take me to jail. Your precious Jack Keller shot someone down in cold blood. In front of us. To protect us. And you're *fucking him*."

She has to hold tight to the arms of the chair to keep from slapping him in the face. He looks away, blushing furiously at his own boldness. After a long moment, she takes a deep breath and stands up. She walks to the other side of the room and leans her head against the wall, eyes closed. She straightens up and turns to face him. "Ben," she says in a shaky voice, "it's true that Jack Keller is a part of my life. He probably always will be. If for no other reason than he's Francis—Frank's father." She walks over and crouches down beside his chair, looking up into his face. "But, son. I say this from the bottom of my heart. Whatever my feelings for Jack Keller, I would do anything, literally anything in this world, to keep you from being like him."

Ben looks away. Marie stands up, her eyes brimming with tears. She has a sickening, gut-twisting feeling that it may be too late. The damage may already be done, and may be irreversible. She feels a sudden surge of panic as she looks at her watch. *Shit*, she thinks. Whatever happens next, it's going to take a while. And that means she's going to have to call the one man she really doesn't want to talk to right now.

# SIXTY-ONE

Keller sees Alia and Bassim standing by the curb as he pulls up. He doesn't recognize the skinny figure with the close-cut hair standing with them. He assumes this is the "one other" that Alia mentioned. He can't tell if it's a boy or a girl.

Alia yanks the door open before the truck is fully stopped. The three of them scramble in, Alia and the new person in the back, Bassim in the front as usual. "Drive," Alia barks.

Keller bites back the retort that comes to his lips. The girl is clearly holding herself together by sheer force of will, and if taking charge is helping her do it, he'll let her take charge, at least for the moment. He steps on the gas and roars away from the school.

The person in the back leans forward. From the delicate features and the high voice, Keller surmises they're a girl. "Hi," she says in a bright yet shaky voice. "I'm Meadow." She holds out a hand.

Keller takes it. "Pleased to meet you. I'm Jack. So what's going on?"

Alia is slumped in the backseat, her arms folded across her chest. Keller can see her shaking.

"There was a lockdown," Meadow says. "Ben Jones brought a gun to school."

"What?" Keller nearly swerves off the road as he turns to the pair in the back seat.

"Watch the road, please," Alia speaks up.

Keller looks back through the windshield and steadies the truck.

Alia goes on. "Someone shot at his mother last night. Officer Jones."

147

Keller grits his teeth. "I know."

Alia nods. "Of course you do." She shakes her head. "Ben thinks he knows who's responsible." She looks at Keller shrewdly. "And you do, too. Don't you?"

"Brandon Ochs," Bassim offers.

"Yeah," Keller says. "We had a little run-in with him last night. At a bar where he wasn't supposed to be."

"So," Meadow says. "He takes a shot at Officer…at Marie. Ben gets a gun and sets out to do the same. And you, Jack, you knew about Brandon?"

Keller looks at her irritably. "Just who are you again?"

She smiles wearily. "Just a friend. The kind who asks annoying questions. I'll shut up now." She sinks back in the seat.

"Yeah. You do that." He looks in the rearview at Alia. She's chewing nervously at a thumbnail. "Alia. Want me to take you guys home?"

The girl thinks for a minute, then nods.

"Okay," Keller says. A thought occurs to him. "If there's a lockdown, they're going to try to account for everyone. Right?"

Bassim answers. "Yeah. At least that's what I remember when they told us about lockdown."

"Glad someone was paying attention," Meadow says.

"So I guess when I get you home, I need to call and let the school know where three missing students are."

Meadow sighs. "I guess." She leans forward again between the seats, her face bright. "Maybe you should call Officer Jones. I'm sure the two of you have lots to talk about."

"Weren't you supposed to be shutting up?" Keller says.

She gives a mock salute. "Yes, sir."

"Meadow," Alia speaks up. "Enough. Okay? Just not any more right now."

The girl looks chastened as she leans back into the back seat. "Okay. I'm sorry." Her next words are a murmur, almost too low for Keller to make out. "I'm worried about Ben, too."

"I know," Alia whispers back. "I know."

They make the rest of the drive home in silence. As they pull into the driveway, Keller's phone rings. He checks the screen. KHOURY.

"Yes, sir," Keller answers.

"Mr. Keller," Khoury says. "There has been an incident. At the school. They called me."

"Yes, sir. I know. I have your children." He looks at Meadow. "And a guest. We're at your house."

Khoury doesn't answer at first. Then, all he says is, "Good."

"Is that my dad?" Bassim asks.

Keller nods.

"Is he coming home?"

*Good question*, Keller thinks. "Sir. Are you coming home?"

Khoury's voice is impatient. "Do you not have the situation under control?"

Keller shakes his head, hardly able to believe what he's hearing. "Yes, sir. But they're pretty upset."

"I will be home as soon as I can. Until then, do your job."

"Yes, sir," Keller says through gritted teeth. But Khoury's already hung up.

"He's not coming," Bassim says, dejection in his voice.

"He is," Keller reassures him, "as soon as he can."

"He has to work, Bassim," Alia says, but her heart's not in the defense.

"He's a real piece of work, that one," Meadow says from the backseat.

Keller looks at her, ready to tell her to shut up, but one look in her eyes tells him she's as shaken as the other two. Everyone's dealing with this in their own way. "Go on inside," he tells them. "I'll be there in a minute."

Bassim gets out first and holds the seat forward to allow his sister and Meadow to exit the vehicle. Alia puts her arms around her brother's shoulder as they walk to the house.

Meadow lags behind, standing in the door of the truck for a moment. She's dropped the brittle facade, and Keller can see the fear in her eyes. "We're going to be okay, right?"

Keller nods. "Yeah. Everything's going to be fine. Now get inside." The girl looks as though she's about to say something, but then she just nods and runs off after the Khourys. Keller watches the three of them until they're safely inside, then pulls out his phone and dials Marie. The call goes straight to voicemail. "Marie," he says. "It's Jack. Call me as soon as you get the chance." He kills the call and leans back against the seat.

Ben brought a gun to school. Probably to kill Brandon Ochs. Keller hadn't had any kind of plan, just to track down the asshole who'd fired at his son and the woman he still loved. And then what? He didn't know. It wasn't going to be pretty. And if Brandon still had a gun...

Keller closes his eyes, grips the wheel, and leans his head on it. *It never ends.* The harder he tries to get away from the violence that's marked his life for years, the more it seems to find him. Now it's passing down to a new generation like a genetic condition. And it's his fault. Ben had gotten drawn into a world of violent death at an early age. His father dying in front of him from a killer's gun, Keller killing that man, in turn, in front of Ben. He'd done it, picked up the gun and pulled the trigger, to protect the people he loved. It had seemed the only thing to do at the time. But now Ben's doing the same. Picking up the gun. Using it to go after a threat to the people he loves. And risking his future, and his very life, in the process.

*It never ends*, Keller thinks again. *It just never fucking ends.* He sits up, takes a deep breath. There's work to do, unconnected with his revenge. There are still people depending on him. He'll think about all that other shit when he has the time.

He gets out of the truck, walks around to the bed where a large Craftsman tool box sits behind the cab. He opens the box to reveal a Mossberg tactical shotgun nestled into a special compartment he'd built himself into the tool box. He checks to see that there's a round chambered, then walks to the house, gun held down by his side, looking around the yard and vicinity for threats. His doubts and fears threaten to bubble up into his psyche, but he ruthlessly pushes them back down again. It gets easier to do, he's found, as he gets older. And for some reason, probably encroaching age, being able to do that doesn't worry him as much as it used to. Work to do, he thinks. Work to do.

# SIXTY-TWO

*Blair's dead*, Iris Gray thinks. It's the only explanation for this long a silence.

She sits in her rental car, tapping on the steering wheel as she considers what to do. Being down a man hurts a lot worse when it's a two-person operation. Not that poor Ted Blair, aka Wilson, had known that. He'd assumed he still had the full power of the US intelligence apparatus behind him when he was carrying out her orders. She sighs. He'd been a good intelligence officer with a promising career. Then a screwup that wasn't even arguably his fault had gotten a couple of local assets tortured to death in Islamabad. He'd been sidelined after that, with pressure building to force him out. He'd still had talent and dedication, but the burning desire to get back in the game had made him pitifully easy to manipulate. He still hadn't been able to tease out the information as to where the man living under the name of Adnan Khoury had stashed the funds he'd appropriated before he'd fled Iraq. And now, she understood, Al-Mansour had followed him again, and brought some contract muscle along. That implies he's getting ready to exert more direct pressure on the Khourys, probably using the children. She needs to get to them first. But this bodyguard the father has hired, this Keller fellow, is going to be in the way.

Gray wonders if she's made a mistake in not trying to co-opt Keller rather than push him away. But the information Wilson had gathered, supplemented by her own inquiries, convinces her she made the right decision. Keller's a loner, not easily controlled, and suspicious to the point of paranoia. She'd have to spend as much time keeping an eye on him as on the targets. So, not an ally. Not an enemy either yet, thank goodness. She'd read what happened to some of his enemies. There's still time to get him out of the way while she makes her move. It doesn't have to be for long. And suddenly, she knows what she needs to do. She takes out her smart phone and Googles the address of the local sheriff's department. It's less than a mile away. She starts the car.

# SIXTY-THREE

Fletcher's at his desk, writing up a report on an Obtaining Property by False Pretenses case reported by the local Wal-Mart, when his intercom buzzes. "Brock," the young woman at the front desk says, "there's a lady here to see you. Asking about any unsolved homicides."

Fletcher sits back and stares at the phone. "Say what now?"

"She asked if there were any unsolved homicides in the county. I said maybe she needs to talk to you."

He frowns. "Be out in a minute. You seen Sergeant Cameron?"

"He just got back in from that meth bust out near Flat Branch."

"Tell him to join me, okay?"

"Yes, sir."

In a moment, Cameron appears in the doorway to his tiny cubicle. He's still wearing his tactical uniform and his bulletproof vest. "How'd it go?"

Cameron shrugs. "No one home. Lots of empty two-liter bottles, bunch of empty boxes of precursors, but whoever lives there was long gone."

"Think someone tipped them off?"

"Or they got locked up somewhere else. Property owner says they were renters. Hasn't seen them in a week or more, and they hadn't paid rent in two months. Anyway, what's up?"

"Lisa says there's a lady here to see us. Asking about unsolved homicides."

Cameron raises an eyebrow. "Think she's come to confess to our crispy critter?"

"That shit only happens in the movies, Lauch. She's probably a nutcase."

"So you wanted me in on it."

Fletcher grins. "Wouldn't want your life to be without entertainment."

"Gee, thanks."

The short, skinny woman in the lobby doesn't look like the average looney tune, but Fletcher knows you never can tell till they open their mouths. Sometimes even then it takes time. She stands up and regards him solemnly through her thick glasses as he approaches and sticks out a hand. "I'm Detective Sergeant Fletcher." He nods at Cameron standing behind him. "This is Detective Sergeant Cameron."

She takes the offered hand and shakes it. Fletcher's surprised at the firm grip. "My name is Iris Gray," she says. "I'm going to reach into my handbag and pull out a set of credentials. Will that be all right?"

Fletcher tenses as she doesn't wait for the response and reaches inside. He hadn't thought to wear his sidearm in the lobby, and he's in Cameron's line of fire if she comes out shooting. He's relieved when all she produces is a thin leather wallet. The relief fades when she opens it and shows him the card inside. *Well, things just took a turn for the weird.*

The woman sees his discomfort and gives him a thin smile. "Is there someplace private we can talk, Sergeant?"

# SIXTY-FOUR

Keller sees Meadow's eyes widen with shock as he walks into the living room with the shotgun. "Easy, kid," he reassures her. "You're safe here."

"Am I?" she asks. "Am I really? You think guns keep people safe?"

"They do when I'm the one holding them."

She rolls her eyes. "How theatrical."

He puts his annoyance aside. *Work to do.* "Lucky for me I'm not looking for your approval. Where are Alia and Bassim?"

"Bassim's in his room. Alia's washing her face. You know, violence just leads to more violence."

He looks at her, a grim smile on his face. "Sweetheart, I think I know that a lot better than you do."

She bristles. "Don't call me sweetheart."

"Fine," Keller says. "Just let me do my job."

She shakes her head and gestures at the shotgun. "This seems like a real overreaction, even for a bunch of assholes like Brandon Ochs and his little pals."

"You're right. It is. But that's not all that's going on."

She blinks in surprise. "What?"

"I'll let them tell you. If they want. But there's a reason I'm here, and it's not that idiot Brandon. Although if I do get a chance to have a word with him, I'm not going to pass it up."

Alia comes in, deftly wrapping her headscarf back around her face. "Ben wanted to have a word, as you put it. Now look where he is."

"He's a kid," Keller says. "He needs to let adults deal with—"

"He's afraid of you," Meadow blurts. "He told me what happened. When you killed that man. In cold blood."

All conversation stops at that point. Alia stares at Meadow for a moment. "You need to know the whole story," Meadow says defensively.

Alia turns to Keller. "What is she talking about?"

Keller takes a deep breath. Before he can explain, his phone rings. He grits his teeth and fishes it out. The screen says MARIE. "Sorry," he mutters, "I need to take this." He answers. "Hey. How's Ben?"

"Under arrest," Marie says, her voice tense. "This may take a little while. So I need you to pick Francis up again."

He looks around the room. "I'm…kinda working right now."

"I know. You have the Khourys, right?"

"Yeah." He looks at Meadow. "And a guest."

"Short pink hair? Full of opinions? Likes to get in everyone's business?"

Keller has to chuckle. "That's the one."

"That's Meadow. Not her real name, but whatever. Go easy on her. She's a good kid, and she's Ben's best friend." She pauses. "I really need you to get Francis, Jack."

"I know." He looks at the clock. "Three o'clock, right?"

"Plenty of time for you to figure something out."

"Right." His voice softens. "You okay?"

"Yeah. This sucks, but what are you gonna do?"

"What you've got to do. See you later?"

"Yeah. See you later."

Keller breaks the connection.

"How's Ben?" Meadow asks.

Keller looks at her. She may be annoying, but Marie says she's Ben's best friend, and there's no denying the concern in her eyes. "He's under arrest right now. But his mom's with him." He looks over at Alia, standing wide eyed with her hand over her mouth. It occurs to him that "under arrest" are truly terrifying words where she's from. "He's going to be okay," he says. "Really." He only wishes he believes it. "Look," he says, "I need to go pick up Frank at school. Marie's going to be there for a while. You guys will need to come with me."

Alia frowns. "Will there be room in the truck?"

"I guess we'll have to make room," Keller says.

# SIXTY-FIVE

The conference room is tiny, and there are banker's boxes of files from an upcoming drug-murder trial stacked along the wall, but it's got the privacy Gray asked for. They'd initially led her to one of the empty interrogation rooms, but she'd taken one look at the camera high in the corner of the room and shaken her head. Fletcher had given in to her air of authority and the weight provided by the organization on the card.

Homeland Security. Even seventeen years after the terrorist attacks on New York and Washington, it's a name to take seriously. And if the case of that burned body in that vehicle has a terrorist angle, everyone's life is about to get a lot more complicated.

"So, ma'am," Fletcher says as they take their seats. "You were asking about unsolved homicides of people not from here. As it happens, we do have one."

She nods. "White male? Approximately thirty-five years old?"

"Hard to tell, ma'am. The body was badly burned. We think an accelerant may have been used."

For the first time, the woman shows emotion. She closes her eyes as if in pain. It only lasts a moment before she opens them again and her face regains the bland mask she's been wearing since she came in.

"If it's any consolation," Cameron says, "we believe he was dead when the body was burned."

"Slight consolation," she says. Fletcher can't tell what emotion, if any, truly lies behind the words. She sighs. "In any case, I believe he

159

may have been an agent of ours. Someone working under me. Before he lost contact, he was working here under the name of Ted Wilson."

"And now this Wilson's disappeared."

"Yes." She takes a piece of paper out of her handbag and pushes it across the table. "These are people who had contact with Mr. Wilson. Before his disappearance. One in particular seemed to have had a strong disagreement with him. The person who witnessed it is the first name on the paper."

Fletcher picks it up. "I know her. She's a waitress at Webster's diner."

Gray nods. "This person later showed up at Wilson's hotel, asking after him. The second name was the employee who talked to him."

Fletcher turns to Cameron. "Reggie Allgood."

Cameron nods. It's a familiar name to the both of them. The sketchy little hotel's had its share of crimes, mostly drugs and prostitution, and Reggie's usually the one reporting them. "And the third name, I suppose, is our suspect." He squints slightly as he reads the name. "Jack Keller."

# SIXTY-SIX

"So where's the parent?" the gray-haired magistrate asks from behind his plate-glass window.

Marie realizes that since she's still wearing her SRO shirt, he thinks she's one of the charging officers. "I'm his mother."

"Huh." The magistrate turns to the young deputy on the other side of Ben. "Deputy Childress, anything you want to tell me about this?"

Childress shakes his head. "No, sir. Gun's been confiscated, and they just lifted the lockdown. I don't have any problem with releasing the young man to his mother."

"Thank you," Marie says to him in a low voice. The magistrate peers at Ben through his thick glasses, then shakes his head. "I don't know. Bringing a gun to school's pretty dangerous. He oughta know better, especially with his mother bein' an SRO and all."

Marie keeps her voice level. "I can assure you, Your Honor, this isn't going to happen again. Is it, Ben?"

Ben looks down, his shoulders tensing, and Marie's afraid he's going to say something stupid. But he looks back up and simply says, "No, sir. I made a mistake. I'd like to go home now."

"What about the boy's father?"

Marie feels a flash of irritation. If Ben had been standing there with his father, would the man be asked if mother was at home? "He's passed away, sir."

The magistrate doesn't answer right away. Marie realizes he's stretching the moment out, trying to scare Ben. She's seen it dozens of times in her law enforcement career, someone standing beside her, facing an official who had the power to change their lives and who's toying with them, just for the joy of watching them sweat. She's never had a problem with it before. They're just defendants, after all. If they didn't have it coming, she never would have arrested them. Now it's her son standing at that line painted on the concrete floor of the booking room, and she's seeing things in a new light.

"Okay," the magistrate says, and bends to start hunting and pecking on his keyboard. "Custody release to a parent or other responsible adult. Court date's May twenty-ninth for first appearance."

"Thank you, Your Honor," Marie says.

The paperwork done, Childress walks them out of booking and to the street. She turns to him. "Thanks for the help in there."

He smiles. "Not a problem. Call it professional courtesy." His face turns serious. "We got the word on someone taking a shot at you and your family. I want you to know we're beating the bushes for this Ochs guy. We can't let that kind of shit—sorry, that kind of stuff slide." He looks at Ben. "Doesn't mean you can go after him yourself, understand. We can't let that slide, either."

Ben nods, looking down. "No, sir."

Childress smiles. "Not that I might not do exactly the same thing if someone took a shot at my mama." He pats Ben on the shoulder. "But let us handle it, okay, buddy?"

Ben nods again. He doesn't speak or look up.

Childress looks annoyed at the lack of response for a moment, then smiles at Marie. "You have a good day, Officer."

She nods. "You, too." She turns to her son. "Come on, Ben."

# SIXTY-SEVEN

There are a lot of things Ben Jones expects on the ride home. Silence isn't one of them. It hurts more than screaming. When they arrive back at his house, his mother gets out, goes to the trunk, and gets out his backpack—minus, of course, the pistol inside. She hands it to him without a word.

"Mom," he says, his voice cracking. "I'm so sorry."

Her face is like stone. "Go inside. Go to your room. And if you have any other weapons in there, I'd really like it if you brought them to me."

"I don't," he says. "I swear it." The safety razor blade he keeps in the bottom of his father's old shaving kit under the bathroom sink isn't a weapon. Not exactly. More like his final escape hatch. His mother looks as if she's about to say something else, but at that moment, a large black pickup truck pulls into the drive. Ben frowns as he sees Jack Keller behind the wheel. But the frown vanishes as the door opens and his little brother squirms out from behind the driver's seat. Francis runs toward him, his backpack falling to the ground behind him, and Ben stoops to receive the smaller boy into his arms. "Hey, buddy."

"I heard you were in trouble," Francis mumbles into his shoulder. "I was worried."

"I'm fine, Frank," Ben says. "It's okay." He straightens up and sees Meadow standing a few feet away, arms folded across her chest, her eyes wide and filled with tears. He knows he should be furious at her for turning him in. He should have something cutting to say. But at that moment, he needs his best friend. "Hey," he says.

That's all it takes. She rushes to him, arms wide, and embraces him. Francis, momentarily crushed between them, squeaks in protest. Meadow breaks the hug and steps back, her hands still on his shoulders. "I'm sorry, Ben. I really am. I just didn't want you to do something stupid."

"I know." All of the anger, the righteous desire for vengeance, seems to drain away like an outgoing tide. "It's okay." He holds out his arms, and this time, Francis has time to duck out of the way before they hug. Neither of them notices Alia Khoury, who's gotten out of the truck and is standing a few feet away, hands at her sides, looking down at the pavement.

# SIXTY-EIGHT

Jack Keller, however, does notice. He steps over to Alia. "Come on. This is a family thing. Let's get you home." Without speaking, the girl turns and walks back toward the truck, shoulders slumped. Keller looks over at Marie. "Can she stay with you?" He jerks his chin at Meadow, who's still engaged in intense conversation with Ben.

Marie nods. Francis is already wrapped around her legs, seeking comfort.

"I'll call you later," Keller says, and walks to his truck. Alia's inside, looking out the passenger window.

Bassim is in the backseat, trying to offer encouragement, and exhibiting more loyalty than comfort. "To hell with that guy," he's saying. "He's not worth it."

"Bassim," she says wearily. "Please shut up."

For once, the boy takes direction.

They drive back toward the Khoury house in silence. When they pull into the driveway, there's a vehicle parked there, an unmarked SUV with windows tinted darker than allowed for civilians. The two men slouching against the car aren't dressed in any kind of uniform, but from the cheap suits and the way they look at him as he pulls up, they can't be anything but cops. He looks more closely at the SUV. He can just make out the sheriff's department logo and decals that blend into the dark paint job. He's heard about these ghost cars that law enforcement has been using more and more, but this is the first one he's seen.

"Jack." Alia's leaning forward to see out the front. "Who are those men?"

"Police," Keller replies. "Go on in the house. I'll deal with this."

# SIXTY-NINE

"This the place?" Tench is behind the wheel again, Waller in the seat beside him with the binoculars. They're cruising slowly by the little stone house across the field from an old church.

"Records check says it is." Waller gives the place a quick once-over as Tench drives by, then speeds up. "Doesn't look like there's anyone home."

"So how do we handle this?" Tench says. "Lay up and wait for this Keller to get off duty and come home?"

Waller looks out the window and taps on the frame of the open car window as he thinks it over.

"Maybe leave him a surprise for when he comes home?" Tench suggests.

Waller looks over at his partner. "That's not a bad idea. But it's going to require some improvisation."

Tench grins. "That's another one of the things we're good at, isn't it?"

"Pull in," Waller says. "Let me get a quick look at the set up. Doors, windows, stuff like that."

Tench frowns. "We don't want to get seen there."

"Won't be too long," Waller reassures him. He reaches into the glove box and pulls out a flat leather case. He holds it in his lap as Tench pulls into the short driveway of Keller's house. "Keep the motor running," he orders as he slips out the door.

The old locks yield to the picks in his case within a moment, and

Waller slips inside. The front door leads to a shallow foyer with a flagstone floor and coat pegs protruding from one wall. Waller steps through into a living space with a worn couch and easy chair. He turns and looks back at the front door. The interior wall is faced with the same stone as the outside of the cottage. An explosion in that tiny space will do horrific damage. Waller knows instinctively what they need to do. He doesn't bother locking the door behind him as he trots back out to the truck where Tench is waiting impatiently. "I got it," he says as he reaches for the small duffel bag they've stowed behind the driver's seat. "Drive. Come back and pick me up in fifteen minutes."

"You sure? What if Keller gets back in the meantime?"

Waller grins and pulls a Walther pistol out of the bag. "Then I take care of the problem sooner rather than later. And call you for a faster pickup. Now go."

# SEVENTY

"Fletch," Lauch Cameron says as they wait, "you got the same funny feeling about this as I do?"

Fletcher shakes his head. "What am I, a mind reader?"

"Come on. Admit it. This is a little too good to be true, don't you think? We got a mystery, some lady shows up, says, 'Here ya go,' then leaves?" Cameron spits into the grass by the driveway. "It's weird. Ain't you the one who says look for the weird stuff?"

"Yeah. This is hinky as all get out. But the leads that lady gave us panned out." Fletcher holds up a fist, extends his index finger. "One, Keller did have an argument with that Wilson guy. Rachel at the diner confirmed it." His middle finger joins the pointer. "Two. Reggie says a guy fitting Keller's description showed up at the motel looking for him." He raises his ring finger. "Three. We do a quick check and find that this Keller guy has a felony record, plus some interesting history, including a number of homicides no one could seem to make stick." He extends his pinky. "Four. We find a dead guy…"

"Who may or may not be this Ted Wilson…"

"But who turns up about the time this Wilson guy goes missing…"

"According to this lady we never met before. I dunno, Fletch. I just have this feeling we're gettin' steered. And I don't like it."

Fletcher shrugs. "All we're doing is asking some questions. Following some leads. We'll see what shakes out."

"I guess." Cameron straightens up. "Here he comes."

The truck pulls up and sits for a moment, engine still running.

They can see the man whose record and prior mug shots they've been examining looking out at them from the driver's seat. Then the motor dies and the man gets out. He's tall, lean, and to Cameron's practiced eye, as tense as a steel spring. *Maybe there's something to this after all,* he thinks. Innocent people usually aren't this tense around the police. A pretty teenage girl in a headscarf gets out on the passenger side, followed by a skinny boy with a prominent beak of a nose and a shock of curly black hair. They stand on the other side of the truck from Cameron and Fletcher until Keller says something to them in a low voice. They hesitate, then walk toward the house.

Keller steps forward. "Can I help you fellows?"

Fletcher speaks up. "Jackson Keller?"

Keller nods. "That's me. And you are?"

Fletcher puts on an easy smile. "Detective Sergeant Brock Fletcher." He gestures back at Cameron. "This is Sergeant Cameron." Fletcher offers a handshake.

Keller says nothing. He doesn't take the offered hand, doesn't attempt to ask what's going on. His face is totally blank. It's as if he's become a hole in the space of the driveway. Cameron finds it a little unnerving.

Fletcher clears his throat. "Have you got a minute? We're investigating a—"

"No." The word is so flat and decisive that it stuns Fletcher into silence. Cameron's never seen his partner shut down so abruptly before. Usually, even the guilty are eager to talk to them, if only to spin out some easily disproved bullshit that will eventually lead to their downfall. Cameron wonders if they may have chanced upon the only smart criminal in the world.

Fletcher's smile vanishes. "What do you mean, no?"

"I mean, no. I'm not speaking to you. Not without a lawyer."

Fletcher puts his hands out. The smile's back, a little more forced this time. "Whoa, Mr. Keller. What's all this talk about lawyers? No one's getting charged with anything here."

"Good." Keller starts toward the house. "Sorry. I've got work to do."

Fletcher loses the smile again. "What work?"

"Babysitting."

Cameron sees his partner's mouth set in a hard line. "So. You mind if we search your vehicle?"

Keller stops and turns back toward him. "What?"

"I said, do we have consent to search your vehicle?"

Keller's eyes narrow. "Am I under arrest?"

"No, sir," Fletcher replies in the same frosty tone. "But we're conducting a missing persons investigation. And you're obstructing it."

"I'm not obstructing anything."

"You're being evasive." Cameron can already hear the words of the incident report: *Subject was evasive and defensive. Reporting Officer decided to conduct vehicle search for officer safety.* It might not pass muster with the US Supreme Court, but it would almost certainly pass the scrutiny of an elected judge who didn't want to lose the support of law enforcement in the next election. Cameron's still ambivalent about it. But when his partner says, "Lauch. Search the vehicle," Cameron goes, because it's his partner asking. He goes through the passenger compartment, checking the glove box and under the seats. Every few seconds, he steals a look to make sure Keller's not going to try something. He isn't. He's standing there, hands by his sides, staring at Fletcher.

His search of the interior complete, Cameron exits the vehicle and walks around to stand by Fletcher. "Nothing."

Fletcher doesn't take his eyes off Keller. "You check the toolbox in the back?"

Keller speaks up then. "Let me guess. You got a visit from a short lady. Walks with a cane."

That stops Cameron in his tracks.

"Lauch," Fletcher says, "check the toolbox."

Cameron shoots him a worried glance, but he goes. As he climbs into the bed of the truck, he can hear Keller speaking in a low, calm voice.

"I'm working security here. Guarding those kids you just saw. That

170

woman was trying to get me away from them. Why do you think that might be?"

Cameron walks to the plastic Craftsman toolbox that spans the bed of the truck. He undoes the clasps that hold it closed and raises the lid. There's nothing inside.

"Think about it, Fletcher," Keller is saying. "Think about why she might want to leave those children unprotected."

Cameron looks more closely. The bottom of the compartment he can see is too shallow for the apparent depth of the box. He slides his fingertips underneath and pries the bottom up. Nestled in a foam holder, crudely cut to hold the weapon, is a Mossberg pump shotgun. Slots cut around the weapon hold rows of shells. Cameron sighs. He picks the shotgun out of its impromptu hiding place and holds it up.

Fletcher glances over and nods. He turns back to Keller. "They won't be unprotected, Mr. Keller. We'll get a deputy here, and if necessary, Social Services. But right now, you're under arrest for possession of a firearm by a convicted felon." He takes the handcuffs off his utility belt. "Turn around, please."

Keller glances back at the house. "I can't leave them alone."

"The girl looks old enough to look after her brother until the father gets here. Now turn. Around."

For a moment, Cameron thinks Keller's about to make a move. He puts a hand on his sidearm.

Keller looks back and forth between them. His voice is mild as he says, "Can I make a call first?"

Normally, the procedure would be to have the subject make the call from the sheriff's department, but Fletcher glances over at the house. Cameron can see the girl in the headscarf peering through a half-drawn curtain. He can't make out her expression, but he figures she's terrified. He hears Fletcher sigh. "Okay. But make it quick."

"My phone's in the truck. Can I go get it?"

"I'll get it." He steps around Keller, keeping carefully out of Cameron's line of fire. As he walks back to the truck, Cameron gets on his portable radio. "All units, 10-78 to secure a residence at 14017 State

Road 109."

In a moment, Fletcher's back with Keller's phone.

"Thanks," Keller says as he hands it over.

"Reverend," he says when someone picks up on the other end, "it's Jack Keller. I need to ask you a huge favor."

# SEVENTY-ONE

Keller's not surprised when they don't take him straight to booking. This has never been about him having a weapon. He takes his place at the table in the tiny interrogation room, glancing up at the camera he assumes is on. Fletcher takes the seat across from him, and the mostly silent cop, Cameron, leans back against the institutional green wall, hands folded across his chest, just at the edge of Keller's field of vision. He sighs. This is all so predictable. And he has work to do.

"Okay," Fletcher says, opening a portfolio with a set of papers inside of it. "Before we start—"

Keller interrupts him. "I have the right to remain silent. Anything I say can and will be used against me. I have the right to an attorney. Blah, blah, blah. Consider me informed." Fletcher's looking pissed off, but before he can say anything, Keller goes on. "Let me tell you what you're going to say next. You already know the answers to the questions you're asking. You want to hear my side. I need to get out ahead of this if I want your help. It's weighing on me, you can tell. We all need to get on the same page. I can come clean and get it all behind me." He sits back. "Guys, I've been here before. I've heard the questions so many times, I could probably teach the course you two took in interrogating suspects. And I'm not saying shit until I get my—"

Cameron interrupts before he can say the magic word, lawyer. "What do you know about Ted Wilson?"

That stops Keller. "Wilson?" He looks from one cop to the other.

"Wilson's your missing person?"

Fletcher's recovered his calm demeanor. "What do you know about Ted Wilson?"

Keller looks back and forth between the two cops. He knows better than to talk to them. But then, he thinks, there's a lot of things he's done that he's known better than to do. He's known some bad cops, but he's also encountered some decent ones, and these two might just be the kind he wants on his side. God knows he can use allies at this point. He takes a deep breath. "I got a job," he says. "Looking after the Khoury children."

"Seems like a strange job for a convicted felon," Cameron says.

"Maybe. But I got it because I stepped in and kept those kids from getting bullied at school. By a guy you may be looking for. Brandon Ochs."

The two cops look at each other, then back at Keller. Clearly, the whole department's gotten the word to look out for that boy. "You have any idea where Brandon Ochs is?" The eagerness in their eyes convinces Keller to trust these two.

"No. But he also took a shot at my...my son's mother. She's an SRO."

"We know," Cameron says. Fletcher gives him an annoyed look. What was supposed to be an interrogation is getting away from him.

Keller goes for broke. "Look, Officers, you want to get on the same page, let's get on the same page. There's a lot you need to know, because I get the feeling some shit's about to go down in Harnett County, and you need to be ready for it."

# SEVENTY-TWO

When the van pulls up, Bassim's on the couch, earbuds in and eyes closed, listening to his music. Alia's been at the window, watching and worrying. She's tried to call Ben, then her father. Both calls went to voicemail. She paces back and forth, chewing at her thumbnail, until the van pulls up. HOLLY RIDGE PRESBYTERIAN CHURCH, the logo on the side says. A man gets out, dressed in jeans and a short-sleeved shirt. He speaks to the deputy for a moment, then walks to the door. The ringing of the doorbell makes Bassim sit up straight. Alia calls to him, "I'll get it."

The man at the door has a nice smile and kind eyes, but it's not until he says, "Hi. I'm Ed. I'm Jack's landlord," that Alia can relax even slightly.

She holds out a demure hand. "It's nice to meet you, Ed. Thank you for coming."

The formality seems to amuse Ed, but the smile fades quickly. "Jack thought things might not be safe here. He asked me if I'd give you a ride to his house. While he gets some things straightened out."

"Straightened out." Alia shakes her head. "Did he tell you he was being arrested?"

"Yeah." He looks over his shoulder. The sheriff's car is pulling away. "He seemed to think that maybe that put you in danger."

Alia looks over her shoulder. "Bassim. We're leaving." She turns back to Ed. "Does this put *you* in danger, Ed?"

He smiles at her. "*In'shallah*," he says. *As God wills.*

She looks down and covers her mouth with her hand.

"What?" he says.

She's trying not to laugh. "Your pronunciation is terrible."

The smile doesn't leave his face. "We'll work on it in the car. Let's move."

# SEVENTY-THREE

"So let me get this straight," Fletcher says. "You're protecting the children of a guy who you think stole at least a few million in USAID from Iraq, and there's some kind of renegade CIA operative trying to use those children to get at the guy who stole it?" He shakes his head. "It sounds like something from a novel."

"Except you were contacted by someone trying to get me away from them. Weren't you? When I mentioned the lady who showed up trying to warn me off, you both looked like you knew who I was talking about. Come on, Fletcher. Admit it. This is weird, but it all comes together."

"What about these two guys you talked about?" Cameron asks. "The guys you said looked like military contractors. Where do they fit in?"

"I don't know," Keller says. "I honestly don't know where they fit in. But I don't think they're here for anything good."

There's a brief silence in the interrogation room. Then Fletcher stands up. "We'll be back in a minute."

Outside in the hallway, Fletcher takes a drink from the water fountain, then stands up, rubbing his face. "This shit is nuts. This is tin-foil-hat level conspiracy craziness."

Cameron's voice is gentle. "You know what's different from your usual conspiracy nut?"

Fletcher sighs. "The part where he's right about someone contacting

177

us from the government."

"And if he's right about that…"

"Like the man said. There's some shit coming down." Cameron shakes his head. "We need to kick this upstairs, partner. It's gettin' away from us. We may need to even call in—"

"Homeland Security?" Fletcher interrupts. "I seem to remember that lady saying she was from Homeland Security." He puts his head in his hands. "Fuuuuck."

"We still got a guy in there." Cameron nods to the door of the interrogation room.

When they go back in, Keller gives them a sad smile. "You're in that place where you don't know who to trust. Where up is down and left is right and everything is wrong."

The stock reply sticks in Fletcher's throat. All he can do is nod.

"Gentlemen," Keller says, "welcome to my world. Now let me make my phone call."

# SEVENTY-FOUR

As he approaches Keller's house, MacDonald frowns. There's a truck parked in the driveway that doesn't look like Jack's. He slows the van down. "Hmm. I don't recognize that truck."

Alia looks up from her phone. Her eyes widen. "Drive on," she says in a low, urgent voice.

"What?" MacDonald is confused, but he presses down on the gas and speeds up.

"That truck. With the dent in the side. It was at our house. Watching us."

As they pass the cottage, a man looks out the driver's side window of the truck. As they pass, they're close enough to see his mouth open and hear him calling something to someone they can't see.

"Shit," Bassim speaks up from the back seat.

A man exits the house at a run, headed for the truck.

"Drive," Alia pleads.

MacDonald stomps on the gas. "Get on the phone. Call 9-1-1. Tell them there's a B and E..." As he speaks, the first shot shatters the rear window.

# SEVENTY-FIVE

He's been Adnan Khoury, warehouse manager, for so long, he doesn't respond to his birth name at first when the American woman addresses him. "Fadhil Al-Masri?"

He blinks at her as she stands silhouetted in the open bay door, leaning on her cane and carrying a large leather handbag on her shoulder. "I'm sorry?" He recovers his composure and thinks of the cover he's maintained for so long. "I think you have mistaken me for someone else."

She smiles. "Of course. I should have said Mr. Khoury."

He nods. "How may I help you, Miss…"

"Gray." She leans forward and speaks in a low voice. "Does the name mean something to you?"

He looks around. The workers he manages are busy stacking bags of concrete on wooden pallets. "In my office."

He closes the door behind him as they enter. The office is cramped, with cheaply paneled walls and a bulletin board crowded with thumbtacked work orders and index cards bearing various phone and account numbers. "Where is Mr. Wilson?"

She sighs as she takes a seat. "I'm afraid Mr. Wilson is no longer with us."

He doesn't comprehend for a moment. "You mean…dead?"

She nods. "And I believe the man who killed him was Jack Keller. The man you hired to protect your children."

He sinks into his chair. "That is not possible."

"Really?" She smiles sadly. "How much do you know about Jack Keller, Mr. Khoury?"

His eyes narrow. "I know that he saved my children from a bully." His jaw tightens. "And I have seen the interview he did on that website. The one that caused all the trouble in your," he grimaces, "intelligence community. Whatever he is, I know he is not with you."

She angles her head inquisitively. "Do you not trust us, Mr. Khoury?"

"Should I?"

"We've been trying to keep you safe."

"Who is 'we'? First there is this Wilson. Who works alone. Or so it seems. We believe everything he tells us, but he never provides any answers as to who or what is threatening us. But we blindly move from place to place because he tells us it's not safe. And now he is gone, and you show up." He stands up. "I don't know you. Wilson never mentioned you. So. Get out."

She doesn't move from the chair. "Mr. Al-Masri—sorry, Mr. Khoury, your children are in danger. And Jack Keller is under arrest." She leans forward. "You may not trust me, sir, but right now, I'm the only one you *can* trust." She reaches into her handbag, pulls out a photograph, and slides it across the desk. Khoury sucks in his breath as he recognizes the person in the picture.

"We know you used to be partners. And he landed at Raleigh-Durham airport a few days ago. He's hired a pair of contractors who've done a lot of work in the Middle East. Now do you believe in the danger?"

He looks at her, his eyes hard. "I have always believed in the danger. I am not sure I believe you are the answer to it."

She smiles sadly. "And Jack Keller is?" She shrugs. "Try and call him. Now."

He hesitates, then picks up the phone and dials Keller's cell. He listens, then puts his phone down. "Voice mail."

"His phone's in evidence. They're likely getting a search warrant to do a data dump on it. Meanwhile, he stays in custody. And your children are alone, while Al-Mansour's men hunt them to use as leverage against you." She shakes her head. "We need people we can trust, Mr. Khoury. And that means money."

He gives her a look of pure hatred. "So again, it is the money. All of this has been a ruse to get the money. The money I tell you I do not have."

She shrugs. "It may take a while to convince Al-Mansour of that. In the meantime, your children suffer."

His voice is a low, flat hiss. "You *bitch*."

She smiles again. "Guilty as charged. But I have people lined up. Waiting to help you and your family. All they want to know is how they get paid. And I know you're sitting on far more than it would take to pay them. I'll be taking the rest as…well, call it a finder's fee. So, what will it be, Mr. Al-Masri? What will it take to get you to come off some of that money you've been sitting on? Are you willing to let your children—"

"Shut up. Just shut up." He gets up and goes to the cork bulletin board on the wall. Carefully, he lifts it from the wall and sets it on the floor. Behind it is a safe sunk into the wall. He places his body between the safe and the woman and works the combination. In the silence of the room, the mechanical click of the lock opening sounds like a gunshot. He reaches into the safe and pulls out a large canvas bag. He turns back to the desk and takes a deep breath before tipping its contents onto the desktop. Bricks of cash, bound with paper bands, spill onto the table.

The woman nods in appreciation, then looks over the stack appraisingly. "This isn't all of it. Not anywhere near."

He won't look at her. "This should be enough to hire the men you need."

She reaches out and takes the bag from him. Setting it on the desk, she begins scraping the banded bills into its darkness. "We'll call this a down payment." She sits back down, the bag in her lap, and reaches back into her handbag. She comes out with a short-barreled black semi-automatic pistol. "Now tell me where the rest is."

182

# SEVENTY-SIX

Deputy Seth Childress has always told friends and family that he likes the busy days. They keep him occupied. Not like those long days, or worse, night shifts, on patrol with nothing happening. He wants to be doing something, not just waiting for something to happen. Some of the older deputies rag him about it; they're happy with a slow day, and laughingly accuse him of stirring up trouble where there isn't any. He just smiles and kids them back about being old and lazy. No one takes offense, it's all a way to pass the time and be part of the unit.

All that said, some days make Childress feel like he's scrambling just to keep up. First, he gets sent to the house where some unaccompanied minors are supposed to be, next he's shunted to investigate a supposed B & E. He grew up in this county, so he recognizes the address of the little stone house everyone calls the old Holly Ridge parsonage. He pulls up in the driveway and looks the place over. There doesn't seem to be anyone there, but as he leans forward and looks at the front door, he sees it's slightly open. He frowns and gets on his radio. "Dispatch, this is two-six. I'm at the Holly Ridge parsonage. We got an open door with nobody here. Possible forced entry. I think I'm gonna need some backup."

The crackling of the open channel is the only thing he hears, then: "Wait one." After another pause, dispatch comes back. "Two-six, hold. Working on that backup. Can you confirm why you need it?"

Childress bends and rests his head on the top of his patrol cruiser.

His department is stretched so thin that an officer going into an open doorway situation needs to justify backup. "Never mind," he mutters into the mic.

"Say again?" dispatch comes back.

Childress draws his weapon and advances on the open door. *It's probably nothing,* he thinks, *nothing serious.* He reaches for the partially opened door and prepares to push it open.

# SEVENTY-SEVEN

"What are you doing?" Alia shouts as MacDonald slows the van, then pulls over to the side of the road. There are no houses nearby and nothing but pine woods on either side.

"We can't get away from them," he says, his voice surprisingly calm. "They have guns. We don't. The next thing they do is shoot out the tires."

"So you just give up?" Bassim demands. "Turn us over to these killers?"

MacDonald looks back at him. "Are you sure these men mean to harm you?"

Bassim shakes his head in disbelief. "You're kidding, right?"

MacDonald smiles. "No. I'm not kidding." He looks at Alia. "I'm going to talk to them. But I'm leaving the keys in the ignition and the motor running. You know what that means, right?"

She stares at him. "They'll kill you. And then they'll take us."

He shakes his head. "Only if God wills it."

"For fuck's sake," Bassim mutters. "We're not even all that religious."

Alia's still looking MacDonald in the eye. "You don't even know us."

He nods. "True. But we all have a duty to help the stranger in our land. I think that's something our holy books share."

Tears are running down her face. "That's...that's what they tell me."

He reaches out and squeezes her hand. *"Salaam al-akum."*

She wipes her eyes with the back of her hand. "Your pronunciation is still terrible."

"So, you'll have to teach me better. Later." He opens the door and steps out of the van.

# SEVENTY-EIGHT

Waller and Tench stand on either side of their battered truck, weapons held loosely by their sides, as the man in jeans and a polo shirt stumbles toward them, hands raised.

"Hey, fellows," he says, an ingratiating grin plastered across his face, "what seems to be the trouble?"

They look at each other, an unspoken message going back and forth between them. *Is this guy for real?* Tench is the first one to speak up. "We need to get those children back to their father." He smiles. "We appreciate your looking after them."

The driver smiles back. "Well, that's good to hear. I mean, it's not often in this world that good deeds get appreciated."

Waller interjects. "She's moving! She's in the driver's seat!"

As Tench looks from the man in khakis to the van, the engine of the big vehicle roars, the tires throw up twin rooster tails of dirt, and the vehicle accelerates.

In reverse, smashing into the front of their truck.

# SEVENTY-NINE

Childress is about to push on the door when his radio comes alive again. "Two-six, two-six, we've got shots fired. Repeat, shots fired. Location, Holly Ridge Church Road. All units. Respond."

That's the road he's on, which makes him the closest unit. He steps back from the door and keys his portable microphone. "Two-six, responding. What about that backup?"

"On the way, two-six," dispatch comes back.

"Okay," Childress mutters as he sprints back to his cruiser. "I know I like to stay busy, but this is getting ridiculous." He doesn't know if he's talking to himself, God, or the universe. In any case, no one answers.

###

"*Shit!*" Bassim yells as the church van slams into the truck behind them. "Are you crazy?"

Alia's face is grim as she yanks the gearshift lever to put the van in drive. "We can't let them follow us." She pulls forward for a moment, then stops and looks in the rearview mirror. The men with the guns are nowhere to be seen. She looks around over her shoulder and sees one of them standing up, his gun trained, not on her, but on Mr. MacDonald, who's running around the back of the van, trying to reach the side door. "No," she whispers as the gun barks out a three-round burst. She hears a cry of pain and feels a thump against the back.

"Drive!" Bassim shouts. "Drive!"

"Mr. MacDonald!" she cries. "We have to—"

"They shot him! Go! Go! Go!"

She can barely see the road through the tears in her eyes, but she steps on the gas and swerves onto the asphalt. In a moment, the scene behind them is fading in the rearview.

# EIGHTY

"Damn it to fucking hell." Waller looks at the crumpled front of the truck. Both headlights are shattered and the hood is folded up like an accordion. Water and coolant are puddled underneath the front from the broken radiator. They're not going anywhere in this vehicle. He looks over at Tench. His partner is standing over the man he just shot, cursing him in a low, unintelligible voice, emphasizing his more heart-felt expletives with kicks that wrench groans and whimpers of pain from the man on the ground. Waller sighs. "Tench," he calls. "Stop screwin' around. Finish him."

Tench looks over, his face a mask of frustration and rage. He looks for a moment as if he means to open up on Waller. But then he just nods, turns and puts a final three-round burst into the man on the ground. The whimpering stops. The only things Waller can hear are the sounds of birds in the trees lining the road, and the slow drip of vital automotive fluids into the dirt by the roadside. Finally, Tench speaks. "What the hell do we do now?"

Waller doesn't answer until he hears the sound of a police siren, coming from far away, but clearly getting closer. "The first thing we do," he says, "is get away from a dead body and a broken truck." He grimaces. "After that…we'll have to think of something."

When the patrol car comes screaming up and pulls to a halt beside the ruined pickup, they've vanished into the woods.

# EIGHTY-ONE

Childress sees the body lying beside the road and brakes to a skidding halt that leaves him three-quarters of the way in the oncoming lane. He gets on his radio as he's straightening the vehicle up. "Dispatch, we need EMS, 10-18. One subject injured, lying in road. Repeat, 10-18." It looks like a particularly serious accident, maybe a hit and run, until he gets out and rushes to the body. At that point, the bloodstains on the shirt and the bullet-smashed face of the victim tell him a far different story. He takes a deep breath to still the sudden pounding in his chest. He draws his sidearm and looks around him at the woods before he gets back on the radio. "Correction. We still need EMS. But we've got a subject with major GSW. An apparent 10-31. Repeat, 10-31." *Homicide._*

There's a brief pause, then dispatch comes back. "10-4. Acknowledge. 10-31."

Childress stands over the body, eyes scanning the tree line, looking for any trace of whoever might have done this. He feels his right leg trembling and wills it to keep still. As soon as he relaxes his attention for a moment, the leg begins shaking again. *Maybe I should get off the bulls-eye,* he thinks. That's when it hits him. This is a murder scene. His second this week. He needs to secure it for the detectives. He doesn't want a repeat of the situation where he disgraced himself in front of Fletcher and Cameron. *At least I'm not throwing up this time. That's progress. I guess.* On still-shaking legs, he goes to his cruiser, pops the trunk, and starts pulling out orange and white traffic cones. Placing them around the scene in the precise places he recalls from training helps to settle his nerves. He still pauses from time to time to scan around him. His gut tells him that whoever killed this victim is long gone, but he doesn't want his gut to get him killed, either.

He hears the ambulance coming from up the road, followed by another sheriff's car. His backup finally arriving. He takes another deep breath. This would not be a good time to let anyone know how rattled he is. He's glad to see the deputy getting out of the car is Benny Hires, one of the older guys, and even happier to see Hires stop, regard how he's secured the scene, and give him a quick nod of approval. The EMS people pile out of their vehicle and run to the body in the road, shouting to each other in their own tongue. He walks over to Hires, trying to affect a nonchalant saunter. The sardonic smile on Hires's face tells him he's not pulling it off, but the look in the older deputy's eyes tells him that's okay. "Still like those busy days, young man?" Hires says.

"Sergeant," Childress says with feeling, "I'm beginning to come around to your way of thinking."

Hires laughs, then a distant yet sharp sound makes them both turn their heads and look down the road. It sounds like a crack of thunder, a couple of miles away, but there's not a cloud in the sky, and there's not a following rumble. "What was that?" Childress asks.

# EIGHTY-TWO

Brandon Ochs awakens in the early afternoon, sprawled across his cousin Jake's tattered couch. He sits up and nearly knocks over the beer cans sitting on the floor. His head is throbbing again and his mouth is dry, but the thought of another beer makes his stomach feel as if it's going to climb up his throat. Through the slightly cracked bedroom door, he can hear Jake snoring. Good, he thinks, not wanting to feel the contempt he can feel from his cousin even when the older man isn't speaking. He goes to the sink to try and get some water, but the few glasses he can find have unidentified liquid remnants and cigarette butts, so he drinks straight from the faucet. It's then that he sees the gun, lying on an empty open shelf above the kitchen counter. He picks it up, and the act makes him re-live the flush of shame he felt from his cousin's words: *Instead of shooting at the boyfriend, you shoot at the fucking cop.* He'd been angrier at the bitch for disrespecting him, but he saw now that the real target should have been Keller all along. He looks over at the hook on the wall by the door. His car keys and Jake's are hanging there. At that moment, he decides what he needs to do.

His hands are slick and slippery on the wheel as he drives to the house near the church where his friends told him Keller lives, but he can't tell if it's nervousness, the summer heat, or the hangover making him sweat like a pig. He cranks the A/C as high as he can, but he can still feel the moisture beading on his brow. He grips the wheel harder to try and stop his hands from shaking.

When he gets to Keller's house, there's no vehicle in the driveway and he involuntarily laughs out loud with relief. If there's no one there, he doesn't have to go through with it. Another idea occurs to him; he can break in and fuck some shit up. That'll show Keller and Jake both that Brandon Ochs is no one to mess with.

As he gets out, Brandon can see that the door to the small stone house is slightly ajar. He frowns. Maybe someone's home after all. He goes back into his truck and fetches the gun. Holding it down by his side, he approaches carefully. "Hey, asshole," he calls out. No response. He can't see any light through the opened door. "Hey, asshole!" he calls out a little bit louder. Still no response. Feeling a little bolder, he moves to the door, draws back his leg and kicks it open.

He never hears the blast that kills him.

# EIGHTY-THREE

They've left Keller in the interrogation room rather than take him to the cells, so he figures they've got more to ask him. Either that or they're checking out his story. Either way, he waits. He's gotten better at it over the years.

It's Fletcher who comes back in, and he doesn't look happy. "Your lawyer's here."

Keller nods and stands up. He knows Scott McCaskill will probably chew him out for talking to the cops without him there to advise, but he's ready to explain the situation.

It's not the tall, impeccably dressed figure of his long-time attorney waiting for him in a conference room. The person who rises to greet him is a slender woman, in her late twenties, with curly blonde hair, dressed in a plain gray suit. She looks strangely familiar. "Jack Keller?" she says, smiling and extending a hand.

"I'm Jack Keller," he says, and takes it. "And you are...?"

She smiles. "Addison McCaskill. You can call me Addie. I'm Scott's daughter." She motions to a chair. "I've heard a lot about you."

"Uh-huh." He takes the chair. "And where's Scott?"

"Retired. He's living at Wrightsville Beach and fishing every day." She turns to Fletcher and smiles. "Thanks a lot, Detective. I'll let you know when we're done."

He shakes his head. "Can't leave him unguarded." He moves toward the door. "But I'll wait outside."

She frowns. "I'm not sure that'll work."

He doesn't change expression, but his voice is sharp as he replies. "Ms. McCaskill, we don't know each other, so I'll fill you in. I don't listen through doors. And I sure don't listen in on privileged conversation, 'less I get a warrant." He smiles thinly. "Easier all around that way."

She sighs. "Okay. Didn't mean to offend you, Detective."

"No offense taken. Everyone's just doin' their job." Before she can speak again, he closes the door.

McCaskill shakes her head and sits down. "Touchy fellow."

Keller shrugs. "He's a professional. I trust him to be that, at least. "

"Trusting a policeman." She gives him a wry smile. "Not the Jack Keller I've heard about."

"Things change. And not everything you may have heard is true."

"So, tell me. What's the truth about what's going on?"

"Well, it's true I do have a felony conviction. And I did have a firearm. No getting around either of those things."

"And you had a firearm why exactly?"

He sighs and repeats the story again. When it's over, she shakes her head. "If Dad hadn't told me about you, I'd think you were in the grip of some kind of delusion. But he was right. You lead a pretty interesting life."

That makes Keller laugh. "Yeah. It wasn't something I intended. But that's how it worked out."

"Dad also told me to help you if I got the chance. He thinks a lot of you."

Keller finds his earlier discomfort with her fading away. He realizes now why he found something about her familiar: she has her father's easy confidence and the direct gaze that makes people open up. "Thank him for me. What do we do now?"

"We try to get you an unsecured bond. We're lucky that—" She's interrupted by a knock on the door. McCaskill frowns. "Come in."

Fletcher opens the door.

Keller can tell by the look on his face that something's gone wrong.

"What is it?"

Fletcher hesitates. Keller grows more alarmed at how shaken he is. Fletcher takes a seat uninvited. "Reverend MacDonald...your landlord...was just found shot to death a couple of miles from the church, lying next to a wrecked truck. And Mr. Keller...someone just set a booby trap inside your house."

McCaskill looks as if she's been poleaxed. "Wait, what?"

"You know that interesting life your Dad used to talk about?" Keller says to her. "This is it." He turns to Fletcher. "And you know that shit I told you was about to come down?"

"This is it?"

"Yeah."

# EIGHTY-FOUR

Bassim is in the backseat, clutching the front seat like a drowning man. "Do you even know how to drive this thing?" he shouts at his sister.

"I can drive!" Alia shouts back, just as the right wheels leave the road and the van begins bumping along the shoulder. She yanks the wheel, overcorrects, and veers wildly into the other lane. An oncoming hatchback blares its horn as the vehicles nearly collide, and Alia cries out even as she pulls back into her lane.

"Where are we even going?" Bassim's voice cracks with terror.

"Stop shouting at me!" Alia shouts back. She takes a deep breath as she accelerates. "Get my phone," she says in a steadier voice. "Call Father. Tell him we're in trouble and we need him."

Bassim looks around. "Where is it? I can't find it." He leans over the front, his voice rising again. "I can't find it!"

"Bassim!" she snaps in a tone so familiar he immediately falls silent. She switches to Arabic, marveling at how much she sounds like how she remembers her mother speaking. "Calm down. Look around." She glances over to the front seat and catches a glimpse of a black rectangle. "Look," she points as she looks back to the road, "there it is."

He reaches over and snags it. "This is my phone."

She tries to hold on to the composure she just regained. "Does it matter? Call Father. Now."

"Oh. Yeah." In a moment, he speaks again. "Voice mail."

198

She returns to speaking English, because it's the language she best knows how to curse in. "Shit."

"Language," he admonishes in an exaggeratedly prissy tone. She wants to reach back and smack him, but realizes that if he's trying to make a joke, he's calming down. Not only that, he's trying to make her laugh and feel better. A fierce love for her brother seizes her. She promises herself that she's going to get them out of this. She has to.

"Do you think the same people who shot the reverend have got Dad?"

The thought makes her stomach feel as if someone is twisting her guts into knots. "I don't know. I pray not."

"We haven't prayed in a while."

She sighs. "Maybe we should have. Maybe this wouldn't be happening if we did."

"We prayed a lot back home. I don't remember it helping. Mom still got blown up." He leans over the front seat. "What now? Where do we go?"

The question and the reference to their former life makes her wonder for a moment at how much things have changed for them in America. In Iraq, as oldest male, Bassim would be expected to begin issuing orders as head of the family. But he's asking her advice. She shakes her head. "The only place I can think of is Ben's. Officer Jones can help us."

"Really? I mean, after the whole thing with Ben?"

She fights back the urge to snap at him. "I can't worry about that now. We need help." She takes the next left. "Try to call Father again."

He picks up the phone and starts pressing numbers. "This isn't the way to Ben's."

She nods grimly. "I know. There's someplace I need to go first."

# EIGHTY-FIVE

The man known as Adnan Khoury sits and watches his phone vibrate on the desk. "That is one of my children," he says in a level voice. "Let me answer it."

"I wonder what they want," she says. "Maybe they're in trouble." As Khoury makes a move toward the phone, she raises the gun. "You can answer the phone when you tell me where the rest of the money is."

"You have all of it. I swear. All that's left. This moving around has been expensive."

"I know. I helped pay for most of it."

"That may be what Wilson told you. But—"

She smiles condescendingly. "Trying to turn me against him? Convince me that he double crossed me? Clever. But Wilson wouldn't be capable of that. He had a trait of blind loyalty that would have shamed a dog. It made him useful." She sighed and shook her head. "I'm going to miss him. Truly."

The phone stops buzzing, then gives off the short chirp that signals a voice mail message. Khoury sinks back into his chair, eyes defeated. Finally, he raises them. "Okay. I'll tell you. I'll tell you where the rest of the money is."

"You'll do better," she says. "You'll take me there." She stands, scoops the phone off the desk, and stuffs it in her handbag. "Let's go."

# EIGHTY-SIX

Keller's been through a few court appearances, but this is the first one where he's had the arresting officer standing beside him and advocating as hard as his lawyer for an unsecured bond.

"Mr. Keller is assisting in a sensitive inquiry," Fletcher is saying, "and we believe he has important information on others."

The judge, a short, cadaverous-looking man with gray streaks in his thinning black hair, looks over the paperwork in front of him. "I don't know, Detective. This man's got an interesting record. What I see here is a long history of violence."

Keller doesn't answer, just stares straight ahead, hands cuffed in front of him.

"You'll notice, Your Honor," Addie McCaskill speaks up, "that most of the charges were dismissed. Or ended up with acquittals."

The judge looks sourly at her. "On violent felonies. I see your father's hand in all this."

She gives him an artificially sweet smile. "I'll tell him you said so, Your Honor. I'm sure he remembers you fondly as well."

The judge grunts, looks silently at the paper for a moment, then shrugs. "Ten thousand. Unsecured." He looks up. "Conditional on your cooperation with current investigations."

"Thank you, Your Honor." McCaskill takes Keller's arm and steers him toward the side door. The shackles on his legs reduce his gait to a shuffle.

Fletcher walks on his other side. "We'll process you out downstairs."

"Thanks." Keller raises his cuffed hands. "Think you can get these things off me?"

"Downstairs." Fletcher shrugs at Keller's look. "Sorry. I bent enough rules for one day getting you up here as quick as I did."

Keller nods. "I appreciate it."

"We still need to talk."

"I know. But I need to find the Khourys. They were with MacDonald."

Fletcher presses the button for the elevator. "Let us handle that, Keller. We've got a BOLO out for the church van, and we're working on getting an Amber Alert out for the kids."

"What about the dad?"

Fletcher shakes his head. "Someone came to his job. Some of the workers saw them leave together."

"Was it a woman who came to see him?"

Fletcher nods. "Every time we call him, it goes to voice mail."

Keller grimaces and shakes the handcuffs impatiently. He needs to get out there and on the hunt for those kids, whatever Fletcher says. He knows they're in trouble, and he knows he should have protected them. The elevator arrives, and Keller steps on first, followed by the detective and McCaskill. They make the ride down in silence. At the magistrate's office, a deputy removes the cuffs and leg shackles.

"So about that talk," Fletcher says.

Keller rubs his wrists to get the impressions of the cuffs off. "I need to check out how bad the damage is to my house."

Fletcher's lips tighten in frustration, but Keller can tell that's hard for him to argue with. "Call me when you get done."

"Will do." Addison McCaskill walks out with him. When they reach the parking lot, she says, "You're not going to call him, are you? You're going after them yourself."

He smiles at her. "Your dad really did tell you a lot about me."

She sighs. "As your attorney, it's my job to tell you to stay out of the way of a police investigation."

"I'm not going to be in their way. I'm going to be way out ahead of them."

"But—"

"Addie," he breaks in, then stops. He shakes his head like a man waking up from a long sleep. "I've spent too much time running. Now it's time I got back to what I do best."

"Finding people."

"Yeah." He looks around. "Shit. I need a ride. Back to the Khoury house. My truck's there."

"Okay. But you know I'm going to spend the ride trying to talk you out of this."

Keller shrugs. "Nothing's free."

# EIGHTY-SEVEN

Alia slams on the brakes in the driveway and the van slides to a stop, nearly crashing into the back of Keller's truck and throwing up gravel. She leaps out of the door without turning off the motor and heads toward the house. "Come on."

"What are you doing?" Bassim calls out, but she's already to the door and inside. Bassim follows her at a run.

Inside, he hears Alia yell something from their father's bedroom. He stops in the doorway and regards her. She's kicking the bedside table in frustration. "I came to get Father's pistol. But he's put a lock on the drawer."

He looks. There's a small padlock and hasp crudely screwed into the cheap wood. "We should be going to the police," he says.

"The last time we saw the police, they were taking Mr. Keller away. How do we know they're not on the same side as those men?"

Bassim frowns. "We can go to Officer Jones. We can trust her. Right?"

"I think so. But if those men catch up to us first…" She grabs the knob of the drawer and yanks. The knob comes off but the padlock holds. "Shit!"

"Hang on." He goes through the kitchen and into the laundry room. When he comes back, he's carrying a metal toolbox. Alia's trying to get her fingernails into the space between the front of the drawer and the body of the table. "Here, Let me." He sets the box down with a clank and flips it open. After a moment of rummaging in the disorganized contents, he comes up with a small black pry bar. "Out of the way."

The lock gives way in a moment, and Alia hesitates before reaching inside and pulling out the pistol. Bassim takes a step back. "You sure about this?"

She ignores the question. "Come on. In the backyard."

"Wait, what?" he follows her out the door.

In the yard, she makes a beeline for the disused pile of cinderblocks that they were told was supposed to be a barbecue grill. She puts the gun on the ground and begins hefting blocks from the top. "Help me."

"What the fuck?"

She's almost frantic now. "Help me!"

"Okay, okay, calm down." He begins moving blocks from the top. "Mind telling me what we're doing?"

She grunts with the effort as she picks up another block. "Father hid something out here. I think it's money."

He straightens up, a cinderblock in his hand. "What?"

She's gasping from the effort, sweat breaking out on her brow. "I think the reason people have been after us is because father got a lot of money from somewhere. Or someone. Someone bad, and that's why the government has been protecting us."

He drops the block to one side. "That's crazy."

"I saw Father out here one night. He was doing what we're doing. Or what you would be doing if you were helping me."

Bassim picks up another block. By now, they're almost to the bare ground. "For crying out loud, do we look like we're sitting on a lot of money?" She moves the last block aside. There's nothing there but bare ground. "See?" Bassim says. "Now let's get out of here."

Alia steps forward and stomps on the bare patch of earth. It gives off a hollow thump.

Bassim steps back. "Whoa. What's that?"

She goes to her hands and knees and brushes away the dirt. A half inch beneath the layer of soil, Bassim can see the grain of a piece of wood. This time, he doesn't need to be told. He goes to his knees and helps his sister brush away the rest of the dirt from a large sheet of plywood. Working together, they pull it up like a hatch and let it fall to the ground, leaving them standing in front of a shallow hole. Nestled snugly into the hole are two large, olive drab footlockers.

"Oh, man," Bassim says, "are those full of money?"

"Let's find out." She reaches and tugs at the handle of the footlocker, grunting with the effort. "Heavy."

Bassim joins her, and with difficulty, they manage to hoist the first footlocker out of the hole. Alia stands up and looks at it.

"Well?" Bassim says. "Aren't we going to open it?"

"I'm afraid to," she murmurs. "If I'm right...then Father's been lying to us."

That stops him. Then he leans forward and works the catches on the footlocker. When he raises the lid, he hears Alia gasp.

"Yeah," he says. "That's...a lot of cash." He notices a zippered bag, like a bank deposit bag, lying on top of the banded hundred-dollar bills. Hands shaking, he picks the bag up and unzips it, then dips a hand in. The hand comes out full of glittering white stones. He looks over at Alia. Tears are running down her face.

"All lies," she whispers. "All lies."

He pours the stones back into the bag, then carefully places it back in the footlocker. As he puts an arm around his sister's shoulder, she turns to him, laying her head on his chest and sobbing.

"Come on," he says as he hugs her, "we don't know the whole story here." He pulls her away and takes her by the shoulders, looking into her face. "What I do know is we need to get out of here." He looks at the footlocker. "And we should take this with us. If that's what those guys are after, I don't want them getting it, and I'll bet Father doesn't either. How about you?"

She shakes her head. "How are we going to get these to the van?"

"Truck," he says. "That van, banged up like that, it sticks out. We'll use Jack's truck. I saw one of the cops putting the keys in it when they took Jack away."

She looks shocked. "You mean steal it?"

"Borrow it, more like. I don't think he'd mind. Not if we use it to get away and be safe."

She wipes her eyes with the hem of her scarf. "I suppose."

"I'll bring it around to the back. And we can load these inside." He grimaces as he looks around. "It's not like we haven't already trashed the yard."

"Wait, you're driving?"

He nods. "No offense, Alia, but your driving scares me to death."

She bristles at that. "And you can do better?"

"I sure hope so. We don't have time to argue. Come on, let's go."

# EIGHTY-EIGHT

"Huh," Keller says as they pull up in the driveway of the Khoury house.

Addie McCaskill stops the car and puts on the parking brake. "What?"

"My truck's gone. And that's…" He leans forward. "That's Reverend MacDonald's van."

"Why is the back all smashed up?"

"I don't know." He gets out.

"Keller," she calls to him. "What are you doing?"

He doesn't answer. As he walks toward the house, he sees the ground in the side yard torn up as if someone had been spinning tires in the soft soil. He follows the trail past a tree with a big chunk of bark scraped off. Someone's driven a large vehicle through here, and done it badly. He walks to the backyard, which has even more tracks gouged in the grass. He stops and stares at what he sees.

The untidy pile of cinderblocks that made up the makeshift grill in the backyard is torn down and scattered around a hole in the ground. Keller looks around, eyes and ears straining for any sign that anyone's watching. Nothing. He walks carefully to the hole and looks in. Drag marks in the dirt indicate something heavy has been dragged out of the hole. *Guess he had the money after all,* Keller thinks. *But who has it now?*

He hears McCaskill coming up behind him. "What in the world

happened here?"

Keller turns as she comes to stand beside him. "Remember, Khoury said the people after him were after a pile of USAID money that disappeared out of Iraq a few years ago. He denied having it. I'm thinking he was lying."

"It was buried here?"

"Something sure was. And I think someone took it away in my truck."

"Who?"

Keller looks around the yard. The tire tracks are all over, and Keller can see where the vehicle flattened a low brick wall at the edge of the patio. "I'd say someone who's not used to driving. Or at least not used to driving a big vehicle."

Her eyes widen as she gets his meaning. "Like a pair of teenagers."

"Like a pair of teenagers." He starts toward the house. "I need to check something out inside."

"Wait," she says. "Is it okay for you to go in there?"

"Yeah. I'm the nanny, remember?"

Inside, he walks to Khoury's bedroom. McCaskill catches up with him as he's standing, hands on hips, looking at the jimmied open bedside table. He shakes his head. "Warrior," he murmurs.

"What?"

He nods at the drawer. "That's where Adnan Khoury kept his sidearm. From his police days, or whatever he was." He turns to her. "Here's what I think happened. Whoever's after that money tried to take Alia and Bassim as leverage. That's how MacDonald got killed. Maybe the damage to the van is where they tried to run him off the road. Whatever happened, they got away in the van after he was shot." Keller grimaces. "He was probably out of the van, trying to be all persuasive and nice and convince the gunmen to leave the kids alone."

"Or maybe he was buying them time."

Keller nods. "That fits, too. Anyway, they got away somehow. And came here. For their dad's gun, and his money." He takes a deep breath. "That means they're okay. For now."

She shakes her head in disbelief. "What about the people who tried to take them? Where are they? And who blew up your house? The same people?"

"I think we're dealing with two factions here. The woman who tried to wave me off and the guy who worked for her—that's one. She may be the only one left. From the sound of it, she has Khoury himself. Then there's whoever hired those contractors." He walks past her and out of the bedroom door. "Come on."

"Where are we going?" She falls into step behind him.

"I've got to make a phone call."

"To Fletcher?"

He shakes his head. "Not yet. Not till I know where Alia and Bassim are."

"You said you'd cooperate with the investigation. It's a condition of your release. As your attorney—"

He cuts her off. "I'll share whatever information I get. When the time is right." He picks up his stride as he heads to the car.

She has to trot to keep up. "I don't think you know how this works."

He gets in the car, pulls out his cell phone and scrolls through his received calls. When he finds the number he's looking for, he presses the button. "Come on, girl," he mutters. "Pick up. I know you're out there."

She answers on the third ring. "Jack?"

He lets out the breath he's been holding. "Alia. Are you okay? Is Bassim with you?"

"Yes. We're okay." She pauses. "I'm afraid Bassim may have dented your truck."

In the background, he can hear Bassim yelling at her to shut up.

"It's insured," Keller says. "Don't worry. Where are you?"

"We're on our way to Officer Jones's house. We're hoping to call the police from there."

"Good. Smart move. Wait for me until I get there. I'll call the police and let them know where you are. Just sit tight, okay? It's going to be all right."

"Okay." She doesn't speak, but he can hear her breathing. Then she says, "They shot Mr. MacDonald, Jack. He was trying to help us, and they killed him." She begins to sob.

"I know, kid. Hang in there. We're going to get the guys who did this."

"And I can't find our father. Bassim kept calling and calling, and he didn't answer. I'm afraid." She begins sobbing again.

"It's okay to be afraid," Keller says, "but you guys have to keep it together. I'll try to find your dad, as soon as I know you guys are safe."

She's sniffling now. "Really?"

"Really. I'll be in touch in a little bit. Okay?"

She takes a deep, shuddering breath. "Okay. And, Jack?"

"Yeah?"

"I asked you to stop calling me kid."

He chuckles. "Sorry. I'll try to do better. See you soon." He ends the call, then dials another number.

"I hope you're calling the detective," McCaskill says.

"Yeah."

# EIGHTY-NINE

Fletcher is staring at the fax sheet in his hand, shaking his head in disbelief.

"You know that's bullshit," Cameron says.

"I know it's from a US government number, with a Homeland Security letterhead."

"Uh-huh."

Fletcher lowers the page and looks at his partner. "And that doesn't mean anything to you?"

"I'm just saying. I think we're being played."

"Question is, by who? Keller or our own government? In case you forgot, Lauch, we work for the government."

Cameron snorts. "We work for the county. An' I seem to remember a couple of operations we ran with the Feds where they weren't what you'd call completely up front with us."

"That was that one time." He hesitates. "Well, okay, twice. But that's out of, what? Six, seven times?"

"It's enough that when some stranger claims to be a Federal agent, I ask for references and two forms of ID"

Fletcher laughs in spite of himself. "You've always been a skeptic, Lauch."

"And you should be, too. You're too good a detective not to be." He shakes his head. "C'mon, Fletch. Admit it. You trust Keller more than that lady who claimed to be from Homeland. It's why you helped get him out." He nods at the paper still clutched in Fletcher's hand. "And that paper there's got that shady lady's fingerprints all over it."

The argument is interrupted by the buzzing of Fletcher's cell phone. He looks at the screen. "It's Keller." He puts the fax down on the desk and raises the phone to his ear. "Keller. Where are you?"

The voice on the other end has the strange, echoey quality of a dodgy connection. "I'm at the Khoury house. I found out where they are."

Fletcher scowls. "I thought you were going back to your house. To check out the damage."

"I didn't think it'd do any good. Place is totaled, right?"

"Not as bad as we thought. Someone wired a grenade to the door. Tore up the entryway, but…" He pauses. "We found a body."

There's silence on the other end.

"Keller?" Fletcher says.

The reception is clearer when he comes back. "Who?"

"Still waiting on a positive ID. But he had a wallet in his back pocket. It looks like Brandon Ochs."

"That stupid little—what the fuck was he doing at my house?"

"Why don't you come back to the station," Fletcher says, "and we can talk about it. Bring the Khourys."

"I'm going to—wait a minute. You think I wired my own house? To get to someone I had no idea was coming by?"

"I don't know what to think," Fletcher says, and he means it. "You need to come in. And Bring the Khoury children in, too." The second the words are out of his mouth, he realizes he's said the wrong thing. He looks over to see Cameron grimacing.

"Bring them in?" Keller's voice is tense. "You make it sound like I'm bringing back a couple of bail jumpers. Fletcher, what's going on?"

Fletcher forces a chuckle. "You're just hearing it that way because of all those years bounty hunting."

"You're lying to me, Fletcher. Why are you lying to me?"

"I'm not lying, Keller." He considers his options, then takes the plunge. "We just got a fax from Homeland Security. The Khoury family's been placed on the terrorist watch list."

"All of them?"

"All of them."

Keller laughs. "You cannot be serious."

"I am serious. Look, I know it sounds crazy but—"

Keller stops laughing. "These are *children*, Fletcher."

"Come on in. Bring them. We'll get it sorted out."

"Right. Okay. I'll get back to you."

"Keller? Keller?" Fletcher realizes he's talking to a dead connection. He tosses the phone down on the desk and swears.

"Well, that went well," Cameron observes.

"Shut up."

"Fletch, come on. You had to know what a guy like Keller— suspicious, paranoid—was going to do when you told him that. I'd almost think your heart wasn't in this whole idea of bringing in those kids."

"Spare the Dr. Phil psychobabble, Lauch," Fletcher snaps. "We need to bring these…people in."

"These *kids*," Cameron insists. He walks over and picks up the fax. "Because someone's put the entire Khoury family on the terrorist watch list. Including their teenage children."

"How about we go see them because they're witnesses to Reverend MacDonald's murder?"

Cameron nods. "Now you're thinkin' right, partner. We're goin' out to talk to witnesses. Not apprehend," he holds his arms in front of him and wiggles his fingers as he speaks in the voice of a TV horror movie host, "scaaaaary terrorists."

"If I say yes, will you shut up?"

Cameron smiles. "That usually works."

"Fine. So where are they headed?"

Cameron sits down, folds his hands across his chest and looks at the table, pondering. Then he looks up. "Keller's girlfriend. She's an SRO at their school."

Fletcher nods. "As good a place to start as any."

"And we're just going there to talk to them, right? To interview witnesses in the homicide case of Reverend MacDonald."

"Right. Okay. Can we just go now?"

"Sure."

# NINETY

The man living under the name of Adnan Khoury pulls to a stop behind a van he's never seen before parked in his driveway. The woman he knows as Ms. Gray is sitting in the passenger seat of his compact car, still holding the gun on him.

"What's wrong?" she asks when she sees the look on his face.

"Everything." He opens the door.

"Wait," she says.

He ignores her. He gets out and surveys the scene. The tire tracks in his driveway and yard look as if someone's been holding a demolition derby at his house, then left in a hurry. He sees the open front door and starts to run, ignoring the shout from his passenger seat.

Inside, the house is quiet and empty. There's none of the usual noise and commotion that forms the background any time his children are home together. He leans against the doorjamb in the kitchen, breathing hard. As much as all that chaos used to annoy him, right now, he'd give anything to have it back again. He can see the glow of a light from down the hall. He frowns. *How many times must I tell them to turn the lights off?* Then the reflex fades and the cold knot of apprehension in his stomach returns. He walks down the hall to his bedroom. When he sees the pried-open drawer where his pistol used to be, he lets out a cry of dismay.

It seems to him that the more he tries to insulate his children from the violence he'd committed in his life, the more it falls upon them. Or maybe, this is his punishment for the way he's lived. In his youth, the mullahs had taught him that rewards and punishments only awaited

216

men on the Day of Judgment. It was then, and only then, that every speck of good or evil done in life would be judged by Allah. But while living in the West, he'd heard about the idea of karma, the idea that the things you do in life come back to reward or punish you in that very life. And now, it seems, karma is ascendant. His sins are being visited upon him, and upon his children, in this life.

He jumps as he feels the pressure of a gun barrel in his back. "Don't run from me again," Gray snarls. She leans over to look past him. "What's this?"

"My children," he says, then stops. He doesn't want to tell her any more about his children than he absolutely has to. "Out back," he says, hoping he sounds broken enough to satisfy her. "The money's out back."

But it isn't. He stands in the doorway to the back patio and looks out at the ruin of his yard, and particularly the tumbled wreck of what used to be the backyard grill.

Gray prods him with the gun. "Is that where the money is supposed to be?"

He takes a few steps toward the hiding place he thought was so safe, stumbles, and comes to a halt.

Her voice rises. "What happened here?"

He turns and looks at her. "I don't know. This is where the money was. And now it's gone."

She stares back at him for a long moment. Then she lowers the gun and fires a round into his left ankle.

The pain is like a lightning bolt, all the more agonizing because it's so unexpected. He drops to the ground, howling in pain and clutching with frantic hands at the wounded ankle.

She stands over him, pointing the gun at his other leg and speaking through gritted teeth. "You need to tell me who took that money, Mr. Al-Masri. I am losing patience here."

"I don't know," he sobs. "I swear I don't know."

"Then you need to choose." She points the gun at first one leg, then the other. "Where does the next bullet go?"

"Please," he begs. "Please don't."

"Then tell me. Who might have taken the money? Is it your children? Are they hiding it for you?"

"No," he gasps. "No. They wouldn't…" A sharp report, a sudden brutal pain, and he screams as he realizes she's shot him through the other ankle.

"I think you're lying," she says. "I think you know where they are. And I think they'll turn around and give me that money if you call them and let them hear me making you beg for mercy."

"There were…" He pauses, trying to organize his thoughts through the haze of anguish he's feeling. He knows he may never walk again. He knows that there will be more pain to come, more damage that can't be healed. The despair of that nearly overwhelms him. He's dimly aware of her face a few inches from his.

"The best part of this," she whispers, "is that this is exactly the kind of interrogation you used to deliver. Isn't it, Mr. Al-Masri? Except it wasn't always for information, was it? If I remember the report correctly, you performed this very procedure on a member of the Iraqi national soccer team. To punish him for missing too many shots on goal. Remember?"

"It wasn't me," he sobs. "It wasn't me."

"No," her voice is almost crooning. "It wasn't nice, middle-class immigrant Adnan Khoury, was it? It was Captain Al-Masri of the Mukhabarat."

He looks up at her, eyes streaming with tears. "And how are you any better?"

She smiles, a smile so sweet it makes him want to vomit. "I'm not better, dear. I'm just more honest." She straightens up and points the gun at his thigh. "Now it's time for you to be honest. Where. Is. That. Money?"

He struggles desperately to piece together what he wants to say. In all his years working in the dim basements of the Mukhabarat, he'd never considered that the reason the subject didn't talk was because the pain had short-circuited their ability to put an answer together. Now he knew. What was that if not karma?

Finally, after a few seconds that seem like a decade, he manages a response. "There were two men," he said. "Mercenaries. Keller..." He takes a deep breath as another wave of pain racks his body. "Keller told me. I don't know who they were working for. But I have an idea."

"Al-Mansour," she says, and stands up. "It has to be Al-Mansour."

"Correct," a voice says. "And those men you saw? That would be us."

# NINETY-ONE

Waller and Tench hoof it through the woods, falling into long-practiced techniques of moving quickly and silently in rough terrain. Both know without discussion that the first priority is getting clear of the murder scene. When they think they've gotten far enough away for the time being, they stop.

Waller sits down on the trunk of a fallen tree, the tangle of roots to his left dangling like the tentacles of some nightmare being. He's breathing hard from the run, but not gasping. He lowers his pack, filled with what gear and weapons he could take from the truck in a hurry, to the ground. "Well," he says when his breathing slows, "that didn't go as planned."

"Shut up," Tench snarls.

"Am I dreaming," Waller says, "or did we just get owned by a fifteen-year-old girl?"

"No one got owned here. Except maybe that fucker who tried to distract us."

"You mean the guy who was clearly local, driving a church van, who we just shot?" Waller looks around. "Shit's escalating, bro. We're drawing attention. That's going to raise the operational tempo to the point where we can't keep up."

"Which is why we need to close this operation out. Pronto."

Waller raises his eyebrows in surprise. "You mean walk away?"

"Fuck no." Tench looks around the woods into which they've fled.

"We just need to get that money and go."

"What about Al-Mansour?"

"Fuck Al-Mansour," Tench says without any particular heat. "If that's even his real name. Long and the short of it is, we're making the money. We need to be the ones who keep it."

It's an argument Waller never seems to be able to answer, probably because he doesn't want to. He wants that money as much as anyone. Perhaps more than most. "So where do we go from here?"

Tench frowns and rubs his chin. "First we need a vehicle. That shouldn't be hard."

"So, we take a vehicle. That draws more attention. Which brings us back to our original problem."

Tench shakes his head at Waller. "What's happening to you, bro? You're getting really negative. Tell me the truth. It's this Keller guy. He's got you rattled."

"He's a wild card," Waller says defensively. "I don't like wild cards."

"There are always wild cards. No plan survives first contact with the enemy, right?" He shrugs. "But hey, if you want to bail, go ahead. More money for me."

"Fuck you." Waller stands up. "Let's go find us a vehicle."

It takes them less time than either had expected. After a brief hike, they stumble onto a wooded lot. A dented Nissan Pathfinder sits beside a single-wide trailer at the end of a gravel driveway. The driver's door is unlocked, so as Tench stands guard, Waller hotwires the ignition. When the motor roars to life, Tench raises his weapon and points it at the front door. No one comes out. Either there's nobody home or anyone who is is too scared to come out. Either way, they're soon back on the road.

"Where to now?" Waller says, although he knows the answer.

"Where else? Let's pick up the trail at the Khoury house."

# NINETY-TWO

Gray whirls towards the voice and raises her pistol. When she sees the barrels of the machine guns pointed at her, however, she lowers it so quickly that it bruises her thigh before she releases her grip and the weapon clatters to the ground. "I'm unarmed."

"Smart." One of the gunmen, the shorter one with a narrow, pinched face, nods his head.

The other, a broad-shouldered, broad-chinned bruiser, doesn't speak. He just looks at Khoury, lying on the ground and whimpering with pain, and smiles. Gray resists the temptation to smile herself. The man obviously has sadistic tendencies, and men like that are easy to manipulate.

Gray raises her empty hands. "Gentlemen. I know we may have different agendas here. But I suggest—"

The man with the narrow face breaks in. "What the hell happened here?" He nods at the torn-up yard.

She smiles ruefully. "It looks like the money we're all after has disappeared."

The bruiser frowns. "So where did it go?"

Gray nods at Khoury, lying on the ground. He's only half conscious now, consumed with his own pain. "That's what I've been trying to find out."

The narrow-faced man looks at Khoury, then back at her. "And what have you found out?"

"Before I answer that, let's all figure out who the players are here." She smiles with a poisonous sweetness at them both. "I think you're working for Mr. Al-Mansour. And we're all looking for some stolen USAID money."

The bruiser sneers and starts to speak, but the narrow-faced man speaks first. "We're trying to recover some money. But who we're working for is our business."

"All you've done is confirm what I think. But it's not important. We're all after the same thing. And tell me, gentlemen, considering the amounts involved, and," she smirks, "how much I figure that cheap bastard Al-Mansour is paying you, wouldn't it make more sense for us to work together? And keep the money for ourselves?"

The two men look at each other, the question bouncing between them, and Gray knows she's won. "Let's talk percentages," she smiles. "I think I can better Al-Mansour's deal." She smiles at the bruiser. "Especially if you can get Mr. Khoury here to talk about where the money may have gone."

The bruiser looks down at Khoury. "He hasn't told you already?"

She shakes her head.

The narrow-faced man speaks up. "Well, what does that tell you? Who would he go through that much pain to protect?"

It takes her a second to get it, but when she does, she can't believe how obvious the answer is. "His children."

At that, Khoury's eyes open, still dull and glazed with pain, and he reaches out to clutch as her ankle. "No," he croaks. "Leave...them..."

She avoids his grasp easily by taking a step back. "That looks a lot like confirmation."

The bruiser speaks up. "Either it's the kids or he really doesn't know. Either way, he's no use to us now." He steps forward, raises his weapon, and ends Khoury's pain with a single shot to the head. He turns to Gray, letting the gun fall to his side and extending his free hand. "I'm Tench. My partner's name is Waller. Pleased to meet you."

She takes the hand. "Likewise."

223

# NINETY-THREE

Keller arrives to find his truck already sitting in Marie's driveway.

McCaskill whistles. "Dang. Dented is right. Looks like someone beat the shit out of it."

He gets out to survey the damage. The rear bumper is crumpled slightly, but the major dents are in the front right quarter panel and the left rear fender. "Nothing a little Bondo won't fix," he calls back to her, hoping he's right and that they haven't done something to bend the frame.

McCaskill comes up to stand beside him. "So you're going to go in there and…what?"

He looks into the bed of the truck. A pair of wooden boxes with dirt still clinging to them are resting there. "You don't really want to know."

"I think I already do. And I have to advise you not to do it."

"Noted." He starts for the door.

"Keller," she calls out to him.

He stops and turns around. "The only reason to bring those kids in is to hold them in place. And for what? How much do you want to bet that the next thing that happens is that female spook, or someone worse, shows up with another bullshit paper allowing her to take them away? You comfortable with that?"

"There's a legitimate, legal way to go about—"

"Good. Pursue that. In the meantime, I'm getting those kids out of here." He knocks on the door.

When it opens, Marie's standing there. "Hey."

"Hey. How are they?"

"Shaken. Scared." She stands aside to let him in and looks behind him. "And you are?"

McCaskill extends a hand as she comes up the steps. "Addie McCaskill."

"My new lawyer," Keller explains.

She raises an eyebrow. "What happened to Scott?"

"Retired. She's his daughter."

Marie nods. "Come on in, then."

Alia and Bassim are seated on the couch in the living room. Bassim has his arm around his sister's shoulder. She's hugging herself tightly, looking at the floor. Ben's sitting on the other side of her, looking at her with a worried expression. Meadow's sitting cross-legged on the floor in front of her.

"Hey," Keller said. "How you holding up?"

Alia looks up and smiles wanly. "I've had better days."

"Are the police coming?" Bassim asks.

Keller runs a hand through his own hair. "Yeah. About that."

"What?" Marie says. "What's wrong?"

He turns to her. "We need to go." He gestures toward Alia and Bassim. "Quickly."

Alia stands up, Meadow scrambling to her feet as well. "What? Tell me."

Keller takes a deep breath. "The police are coming here to pick you two up."

"It'll be fine," McCaskill says. "We can get it straightened out."

Alia's looking at him steadily. "Is that true, Jack? Will everything be fine if we go with them?"

"I don't know," Keller answers her. "I'm not taking any chances."

"Wh-why do the cops want to pick us up?" Bassim's voice is shaky.

"Some bogus paper they say comes from Homeland Security. Your family's been placed on the watch list."

Alia's eyes widen. "The...terrorist list?"

"That's crazy!" Meadow pipes up.

"Yeah. I know. Someone's up to something, and I think I know who." He looks at Alia. "Is that the money your dad took in the back of my truck?"

She looks at the floor and mumbles something. Bassim puts his arm back around her shoulder and nods.

Keller shakes his head ruefully. "An old friend told me on the day we met that a big truck, a bag full of money, and a gun was the American Dream. We've got two out of three." He turns to Marie. "I need to borrow your gun."

She stares at him as if he's grown horns. "You really have gone off the deep end."

"Marie, there are people coming after these kids. Not just the cops. Bad people."

She looks over her shoulder at them. "You're frightening them."

"Good. They should be frightened."

"Jack," Marie says, "I'm not giving you my service weapon. You're not supposed to have a firearm at all, or have you forgotten?" She shakes her head. "And do I have this right? The local police have a lawful pickup order and you want me to help you hide these kids from them?"

"Mom!" Ben says.

"Shut up, Ben." She doesn't take her eyes off Keller. Ben mutter something under his breath and stalks out of the room. "There's a legal way to do this," Marie says, "and that's how we're going to deal with it."

"Sorry," Keller says, "I don't have as much faith in the legal way to do things. After all that's happened, I wonder why the hell you do."

"Because I'm a police officer, Jack!" she yells. "What the hell do you expect?"

"I think I'm going to be sick," Alia says. She runs from the room, with Bassim and Meadow close behind.

Francis comes running in. "Mom? What's going on? Why's Ben so upset?" Without waiting for an answer, he starts to cry.

"Now see what you've done?" Marie demands. She walks to him and picks him up. He buries his head in her shoulder as she pats him on the back. "I know the local force, Jack," she says over his shoulder. "They've got some good officers. If there's somebody that needs to be dealt with, they'll deal with it."

"They'll do what they're told, Marie. And not give a lot of thought to who's telling them to do it." He shrugs. "Fine. You won't give me your pistol, I'll figure something out. But…" He stops and inclines his head, listening.

"What?" Marie says, but he's already at the door, yanking it open.

Just in time to watch his truck pulling away, with Ben at the wheel and Alia in the front seat.

"God damn it," he mutters, and runs to the driveway. "Addie," he shouts back, "I think I'm going to need another ride…" He shakes his head as he sees that the front right tire of McCaskill's car has been punctured. A quick look at Marie's car shows the same, the tire still hissing with escaping air.

"My car!" McCaskill cries out as she runs up to stand beside him.

"They want to make sure we didn't follow them," Keller says.

"It gets worse," Marie says as she strides up to them. "Ben's got my gun."

# NINETY-FOUR

"Ben," Meadow says from the front seat, "where are we going?"

He's gripping the wheel, white-knuckled. "I don't know. Away." He glances over at the silver metal box she holds in her lap, the one he grabbed from his mother's bedroom before the four of them exited his bedroom window. "You need to figure out how to get that box open."

"Why?" Alia says from the backseat.

Meadow doesn't take her eyes off Ben. "Because it's got a gun in it. Am I right, Ben?"

He doesn't answer.

"Ben," Alia says. "I can't let you—"

"I can't let them take you!" he blurts out. "There are bad people after you. You heard it. And my mom was going to let them do it."

"And what are you going to do? Shoot them?"

"If I have to." He feels that dizzy, intoxicated feeling again, like the peak before the roller coaster drops. He's starting to become accustomed to it. He almost doesn't hear Alia when she says, "No. I can't let you do that." He doesn't answer, just keeps driving blindly.

She leans forward and puts a gentle hand on his shoulder. "Don't I get a say in what you have to do to rescue me?"

"How about me?" Bassim says. "I get a say, too, right? And I say shoot the motherfuckers."

Alia closes her eyes and rests her head wearily on the back of the driver's seat. "Bassim."

"What? I'm scared shitless, Alia."

She raises her head. "You think I'm not? But I can't ask people to kill for me. Especially Ben, who's been so kind to us." She sighs. "There's been enough killing."

"I have an idea," Meadow says. "And it doesn't involve anyone shooting anyone." She bites her lip. "Probably."

# NINETY-FIVE

"What the hell is that kid thinking?" Keller's fuming as he hoists the spare tire out of Marie's trunk. He grimaces as he sees it's not a real tire, but one of the thin hard donuts of rubber that pass for spares, good only for getting a distressed driver to a store where they can buy an actual fully functioning one.

"I'll tell you what Ben was thinking, Jack," Marie's face is red with anger. "He's thinking, 'what would Jack Keller do?'"

Keller drops the tire to the ground and glares at her. "So this is my fault?"

She stands with hands on her hips and glares back. "Can't you see it? He's grabbed a gun and run off to be someone's rescuer. It's how you've spent most of your life."

"Guys," Addie McCaskill says.

Keller ignores her and snaps at Marie. "I didn't see you complaining when you were the one being rescued."

"He's *fifteen*, Jack." She breaks down and starts to cry. "And he idolizes you."

That makes Keller blink in surprise. "I thought he hates me."

"Guys," McCaskill says again.

"You saved his life. And mine. But the way you did it's given him nightmares ever since."

"I can't help—"

"*Keller! Jones!*" McCaskill's yelling now. They stop and turn to her. She nods toward a car coming up the long driveway. "We've got company."

# NINETY-SIX

Fletcher gets out of the car first, Cameron following with his hand poised near his holster. It's clear to both of them from the posture of the people standing by the vehicles that something's seriously wrong.

Cameron's the first one to see the ruined tires and the inadequate spare. "Fletch," he says.

"I see it," his partner says calmly. He raises his voice to address the people standing in the driveway. "So. I can't wait to hear what happened here."

The three people standing in the drive look at other. It's Jones, the school resource officer who Cameron knows slightly, who speaks up first. "The people you're looking for aren't here."

"Ah," Fletcher says. "And that would be because…?"

"Detective," Addison McCaskill says, "I'm going to have to advise my client—"

"Alia and Bassim Khoury," Marie interrupts, "along with my son Ben and their friend Melissa…" she hesitates, struggling for the last name and failing, "…stole Mr. Keller's truck. I don't know where they've gone." She answers McCaskill's glare with one of her own. "You do what you want, Ms. McCaskill," she snaps. "I'm not lawyering up in front of my fellow law enforcement officers." She turns to them and takes a deep breath. "And my son Ben has my sidearm."

Cameron glances over at Fletcher, who looks like he's aged forty years in the last two minutes. His partner nods. "Any idea where they may have gone?"

"None. But the pistol's secured in a lockbox. They took the box with them."

"The key?" Cameron asks.

She reaches inside her blouse and pulls out a small silver key on a chain around her neck. "I've got a five-year-old in the house, Detective. I'm not completely stupid." She sighs. "Just mostly where my eldest son is concerned."

Fletcher nods. "So, we hopefully have a little time before your son's able to do something even more stupid."

"You're a real comfort, Fletcher," Keller says.

"Not my job to be comforting, Mr. Keller. Especially since I suspect those kids did a runner, with a firearm, let's not forget, because you told them we were coming with a pickup order."

Keller regards them without expression. "Well, you were, weren't you? A pickup order. For children."

"He said we had one," Cameron says. "Not that we were coming to do it."

"That right?" Keller looks from one of them to the other. "What were you coming to do?"

Fletcher speaks up before Cameron does. "I don't need to explain myself to you, Keller."

"Maybe not. But you need to pick a side. And you need to do it right now."

Fletcher's had enough at that point. "Listen here, Keller—"

Cameron breaks in. "Fletch."

Fletcher turns on him, ready to snap at his partner to be quiet. Then he notices the car that's pulled up, and the woman getting out of it. He particularly notices the two hard-faced men getting out with her, the sidearms they wear on their hips, or the automatic weapons they're cradling at port arms.

"Well, hell," Cameron mutters.

# NINETY-SEVEN

Natalya Dudayev pulls the rented van into the driveway of the Khoury house. She frowns at the sight of the open door and the destruction in the yard.

"What happened here?" Liza asks in Chechen.

Natalya puts the car in Park. "I don't know. Follow me." The three of them exit the vehicle, pistols in hand. Natalya always enjoys working in the United States, where weapons are cheap and plentiful and men are stupid about a pretty face. The three of them fan out, approaching the house slowly. Nothing moves. There is no sound except the trilling of a bird somewhere nearby. Natalya stops short of the open door, then advances slowly. With the familiarity of long practice, her sisters take up positions on either side. She enters quickly, pistol held out before her, and scans from side to side, looking for threats. Nothing. As she moves in further, her sisters follow, Liza scanning left and Marina going right. They move quickly through the house, clearing room by room, until they come to the back door. It's Marina who finds the body, lying curled up in a corner of the flagstone patio. She gestures to Natalya, who joins her, followed by Liza.

Natalya is the first one to speak. "*Dermo*," she spits out the curse in Russian, her preferred language for invective.

"The others got here before us." Liza shakes her head. "But which one?"

Natalya feels Marina's hand on her shoulder. She looks up to see her sister pointing at the backyard. The tumbled cinderblocks and piled up dirt tell her the story. "Whoever it is, it looks like they dug up something and took it with them."

"The money."

Natalya nods. "The money." She looks back down at the body of the man they'd come to "persuade" to give up his stolen money. The bullet wounds in the legs tell her more of the story. "Well, at least they saved us the trouble of digging it up."

Liza chuckles. "My dear sister. Always looking for the bright side."

Marina shrugs, spreads her hands, and raises her eyebrows. *What now?* the gesture says.

Natalya ponders the question, then says, "We call the police."

Liza looks at her incredulously. "What?"

"We let the police do the work for us. Then we find out what they know."

"Why would they tell strangers anything?"

Natalya smiles. "Strangers, no. The grieving family, perhaps."

Liza leans back and laughs in disbelief. "We don't look remotely Arab."

"Not to ourselves. But put on a veil, say a few words in Arabic, and these American fools won't be able to tell one Muslim from another. Trust me."

"Of course I trust you, sister." Liza smiles. Marina joins her. "Lead on," Liza says.

# NINETY-EIGHT

Fletcher turns to face the new people on the scene. His hand drops to his own belt where his pistol rides in its well-worn holster. As discreetly as he can manage, he unsnaps the strap. He feels rather than sees Cameron taking position next to him on his right, and he feels slightly reassured. He hears someone else step up on his left, and he's less reassured to glance over in surprise to see Keller standing on his left. "You need to step back, Keller," he whispers.

"I don't think I will," Keller murmurs back.

"You're unarmed."

"They don't know that."

*They're not blind*, Fletcher thinks. *And all I need is a goddamn civilian…*

The woman he knows as Iris Gray interrupts his thought. "Detective Fletcher," she calls out. "I trust you received my fax."

"Yes, ma'am. The office is calling Washington right now to check for confirmation."

She frowns. "This is a matter of national security, Detective. We don't have time for the niceties." She nods to the men on either side of her. "Search the house."

They start forward, but they stop in surprise as Fletcher draws his weapon. Out of the corner of his eye, he can see that Cameron's done the same. He feels the sweat running down his face, feels his heart pounding so loud he's amazed that no one else can hear it. "Sorry, ma'am," he says. "Can't let you do that."

The two gunmen raise their machine guns. Fletcher knows their 9 MM pistols are no match for that kind of firepower. These men look perfectly capable of cutting him and his partner in half, and then doing whatever they please with the civilians. He's been, at best, an intermittent churchgoer, but like a million intermittent churchgoers faced with sudden mortality, he sends up a quick silent prayer. *Lord. Help me do your work here. Help me protect the innocent.*

He notices a strange look on the face of one of the gunmen, the big one with the chin like a boulder. He's looking past Fletcher. "What the hell is she doing?"

He doesn't dare turn, but doesn't need to. He hears Addison McCaskill's voice behind him. "I'm recording this. And don't bother trying to take the phone away. This app I'm using uploads straight to a database maintained by the ACLU."

The gunmen look uncertain.

Gray shakes her head. "She's bluffing. Take her phone."

They hesitate, then move forward.

Fletcher's finger tightens on the trigger. "I'm telling you people to stand down." They don't stop. They're actually grinning. Fletcher raises his gun to firing position and prepares to die.

The tense silence is suddenly broken by the whoop of a siren. Fletcher looks up from the barrels of the guns coming for him to see a sheriff's cruiser bouncing up the rough dirt driveway, blue lights flashing.

"Childress," he hears Cameron breathe. Another cruiser follows the first one up the driveway. This one's silent, without lights. "I think that's...Monteith," Cameron says, his voice shaking as if he's about to laugh hysterically. A third car, this one a battered Ford Taurus station wagon, pulls in behind the other two. "Goddamn if that's not Locklear."

"Locklear's off duty." Fletcher's voice is hoarse with strain.

"Brother," Cameron says, "times like this, ain't no one off duty."

The two gunmen turn to Gray, clearly uncertain what to do. She shakes her head, lips drawn tight as a closed wound with frustration, and they lower their weapons. "You're making a mistake, Detective Fletcher."

He's recovered control of his voice by now. "That may be, ma'am. That very well may be. But I'll wait until I get confirmation from D.C."

She nods at Keller. "This man's been filling your head with some sort of conspiracy nonsense."

He smiles. "All Mr. Keller's been filling my head with is aggravation. But thanks for your concern."

She grimaces and turns around. The three new arrivals have taken up a line behind her car: Childress, tall and blonde and impeccably turned out, pistol held in predictably perfect firing position; Monteith, a thin, bony black woman slowly scanning her 12-guage shotgun back and forth across the targets in front of her; and finally, the hulking figure of Ardis Locklear, nearly seven feet tall, copper-skinned and curly-haired, dressed in bib overalls with nothing underneath, shoeless, and pointing his personal weapon, a .357 revolver that looks as big as an artillery piece, even in one of his huge-knuckled hands. The three look back at her, as impassive as a castle's curtain wall. She sizes up her prospects, clearly finds them wanting, and turns back to Fletcher. "May we go? Pending confirmation of our status?"

Fletcher wants nothing more in the world that to have these three locked up, but he's still worried about what might happen if they are legit. "Yes, ma'am. We'll be in touch."

She studies Fletcher's face, then turns to them. "Sure. Let's go."

Fletcher calls out to his officers. "Move your cars, deputies. Let these folks out."

"You sure, Detective?" Childress calls out.

"Yeah. And stick around a minute."

The three deputies comply, each one taking a turn moving their car to the side of the driveway while the others maintain their overwatch. When the path is clear, Gray and her gunmen leave without further discussion.

"Fletcher," Keller says, "I'm sorry. I underestimated you."

Fletcher gives him a stony look. "I don't care. We just need to figure out what to do next. And by 'we,' I mean everyone here who's a legitimate law enforcement officer." He looks back at Marie Jones, who's joined them. "Thanks, Officer Jones. I assume it was you who called in our backup while that lady and her new friends weren't paying attention."

She nods. "Don't mention it."

"You may want to mention it. It may help with the problem you're gonna have when someone finds out your son stole your service weapon." He sighs, hating what he has to say next. "I have to call that in, Jones."

She nods. "I understand. But please. Let me try to call him before you do."

Fletcher just nods. Marie pulls out her phone and walks off.

"Keller," Fletcher says. "Remember what I said. Finding those kids is our job."

"Yes, sir." Keller's face is bland. "But it seems like you guys have a lot on your plate."

"We can handle it," Fletcher snaps, the adrenaline from his earlier fear fueling his irritation.

"Hey, Fletch," Ardis Locklear calls out. "If we're done here, I'm gonna go on. I got a fence to put up, and I was on my way to the store for more wire."

Fletcher waves to him. "Yeah. We're done. Thanks. Childress, Monteith, meet me back at the station." As the three get in their cars and begin to leave, Fletcher turns back to Keller. "I mean it."

"I know you do," Keller says. Fletcher's about to say something else when Marie walks back to them, her face bleak. "Call went straight to voicemail."

Fletcher sighs "Okay. Well, we'll do what we have to do."

"What if neither of us wants to file a report?" Keller asks. He looks at Marie. "I'm willing to not ask for a warrant on the truck."

"That's fine," Fletcher says, "but there's a firearm involved. Can't let that go."

"I don't want him hurt, Detective."

"Neither do we, Officer. But my people are going to defend themselves." He turns to Cameron. "Come on. Let's go."

# NINETY-NINE

As the detectives pull away, Keller turns back to the task of fixing the tire on Marie's car. He's not sure if she'll let him borrow the vehicle to go after her son. Not in her current state of mind. But he needs wheels of some kind. He doesn't pay any attention to what McCaskill is doing until he hears the clank of metal on metal and a soft feminine grunt of effort. He stands up to see McCaskill kneeling in the dirt driveway next to her vehicle, working the handle on the already positioned jack to raise the car up.

"I can do that," he says, "soon as I get done with this one."

She waves him off without looking back. "I can do it."

"You sure?"

She looks back at him and grins. "Dad taught me." The smile fades as she looks down. "This skirt's going to be a total loss, though."

"Seriously. I can get it."

"Seriously. So can I."

"Okay." He turns back to his task. He's got the car jacked up and is working on the lug nuts to get the ruined tire off when he hears Marie walking up behind him. He stands up and turns around. She's standing there, hands on her hips, glaring at him. "I should have this done…"

She interrupts. "Are you really going to go look for them? Despite what Fletcher said?"

He nods. "Yeah."

She looks from Keller to the jacked-up vehicle and back, and sighs.

240

"Well, you're not doing it in that. Not with that tire. Come on." She turns and strides away, not looking back. Keller glances as McCaskill, who got her own vehicle raised up and is focused on using the jack handle to pry off the hubcap. He shrugs and follows Marie.

Behind the house, the ground falls away down a long grassy slope, ending at a stand of pines being overtaken by kudzu and wisteria. Directly in front of the tree line is an old wooden tobacco barn with a rusting tin roof, the kind that once dotted the Carolina landscape. Keller catches up with her as she slides the wooden barn door open. "Marie," he says, then stops as he sees what's inside. Marie steps into the cobwebbed dimness, onto the close-packed dirt floor, and pulls a thick blue tarp off the vehicle sitting in the center of the barn.

"Well, I'll be damned," Keller says.

She laughs ruefully. "2000 Crown Victoria. Police Interceptor model. Look familiar?"

"Yeah. It does." It's a near perfect copy of the vehicle he used to drive in his days as a bounty hunter, when he worked chasing bail jumpers down. "Your dad's?"

She nods. "Same thing he drove when he was an officer. He loved it. Swore he'd never drive anything else." She wipes her eyes with the back of her hand. "I nearly peed myself when he pulled up in this damn thing." She runs her hand over the quarter panel.

Keller notices there's almost no dust collected on the vehicle. "You still drive it?"

She shakes her head. "I keep it clean. And I come out once a month and turn the engine over, to keep the battery from dying. Sometimes I'll sit in it for a while. Just to remember my dad."

He walks over and puts a hand on her shoulder. "He was a good guy. He loved you a lot."

"Yeah." She looks at him, her eyes brimming with tears. "He was. And he did. And he was crazy about Ben and Francis…Frank."

"Yeah."

"Jack," she says, "I know he said you never brought me anything but trouble and pain."

241

"Well, he wasn't wrong."

She grips him by the shoulders and looks into his eyes. He's struck over again by the savage loveliness of her eyes. "No," she whispers. "He was." She laughs through the tears, now spilling over. "Oh, don't get me wrong. You brought me plenty of trouble and pain. But it wasn't something you planned. It wasn't something you intended. And it sure as hell wasn't the only thing you ever gave me." She kisses him, hard, so hard it nearly takes his breath away. It's been a long time and a number of changes, but it feels like coming home again. The kiss turns into an intense hug, as if they're clutching each other to keep from drowning. She breaks away first, still gripping him by the shoulders and looking into his eyes. "Bring me my son back," she whispers fiercely. "Bring him back to me."

"I'll do it," he whispers in return.

She breaks the hug and steps back, shaking her head like a woman shaking off a vision. "Okay. Just so you know, I'm about to aid and abet a felony here." She laughs bitterly. "But it's not like I have any future in law enforcement. Again. I hear Wal-Mart's hiring." She takes a set of keys out of her pocket and pops the trunk lid. Keller steps around to stand beside her as she removes a long object wrapped in cloth from the trunk. "Remington 870 shotgun," she says. "Police model. Extended magazine, twenty-inch barrel." She hands it to him.

He takes the shotgun and looks it over. It's clearly been as well-maintained as the car. "Thanks."

"You're welcome."

"But what about you? What if those people come back?"

She opens the passenger door and takes a seat, popping open the glove compartment and removing a silver .357 revolver. "Dad's original pistol. Before they went to the 9MM. He always trusted a revolver more. Don't worry about me." She flicks the cylinder open and starts loading rounds into it. "But, Jack, this isn't necessarily a situation you're going to be able to shoot your way out of."

He nods. "I get it. Shells?"

She sighs. "In the trunk. And you're not listening."

242

"Yeah, I am," he replies. "What, you think I'm going to shoot Ben?"

"Would you? If he was pointing a gun at you, would you do it? Would you pull the trigger on my son?"

The question makes him feel as if his head is being put in a vise. "That's not going to happen."

"You know it could. Answer the question."

He pauses for a moment to think it over. "No. No. I'm not going to shoot your son."

"Swear it."

"I swear." Keller laughs. "He probably can't hit anything anyway. And if he does, what the hell, he's probably doing me a favor."

"Don't talk like that," she says, and kisses him, more gently this time. "Now go," she whispers. "Help those kids. And bring my son home."

He takes the box of shells and the keys from the trunk, closes it, and slides behind the wheel. The motor starts up with the first turn of the key, the engine quickly settling into its familiar rumbling purr. Keller nods at Marie. "You've taken good care of it." She just nods back, biting her lip, eyes wide with apprehension. "Come on," he says, "get in."

He carefully guides the car out the barn door and up the grassy slope, then stops and lets Marie off at the back door of the farmhouse. Before she gets out, he asks, "So. This Meadow girl. You got an address?"

"You think they might have gone to her house?"

He shrugs. "Got to start somewhere."

She nods and gives him the address. Then she leans over, gives him one last kiss, and walks inside without looking back.

When he comes around the house and into the driveway, Addie McCaskill is putting her jack and lug wrench back in the trunk. He waves at her as he drives by. All she can do is stare at him, wide-eyed. His tires squeal as he hits the hard road and he can't help but smile at the sound.

# ONE HUNDRED

From down the road, pulled back from the hard surface and half concealed behind a stand of trees, Iris Gray watches the end of Marie's driveway through a pair of compact binoculars, waiting. Waller sits beside her in the passenger seat, with Tench in the back. She's puzzled when she sees a silver sedan pull out and head up the road, going away.

"Was that Keller?" Waller asks.

"I think so. Hard to be sure." She puts the glasses down as a Nissan compact leaves, moving slowly on an emergency spare. As the car passes, she can make out the blond hair of the woman who'd recorded them on her phone.

"Who the hell's she?" Tench asks.

Waller runs a hand through his hair nervously. "More important, you think she really sent video of us to the ACLU?"

"It's possible," Gray murmurs. This whole thing is drawing far more attention than she's comfortable with. This needs to be wrapped up, and soon.

"Do we go back and search the house?" Tench says. There's something in his voice, an eagerness, that makes her uneasy.

She shakes her head. "If the Khourys and the money are there, Keller would still be." Something occurs to her. "And why is he driving another vehicle instead of his truck?" She turns to Waller and Tench. "Did you see a big black truck anywhere around?"

They look puzzled, then shake their heads *no*.

"Of course," she mutters. "Of course."

"What?" Tench asks.

"The marks at the Khoury house showed that someone had driven a large vehicle into the back yard. Someone who was a bad driver."

Waller nods. She's decided he's the more intelligent one. "Like a teenager driving a big truck."

"So…" Tench's face is screwed up in concentration. "The Khourys took the money in Keller's truck?"

"It's a working hypothesis," she says, "and if true, it's a break for us."

Waller looks puzzled. "How?"

"Tench. Reach into the pocket behind the passenger seat and hand me the tablet that's in there." When he hands the device to her, she opens the black leather cover and turns it on. "When I first contacted Mr. Keller, I tried to get him to back off and let me deal with the protection of the Khourys."

Waller nods. "While you waited for Khoury—sorry, Al-Masri to reveal where the money was."

"Correct." She places her finger on the pad of the tablet and it comes to life. "But Keller wasn't what you'd call cooperative. So, I thought it prudent to keep track of his movements."

Tench laughs. "You put a tracker on his truck."

A map appears on the screen. In a moment, a small green dot begins pulsing on a point on the map. "I did. And it seems to be working as advertised." She smiles. "They're not far away, as it turns out. And they're not moving." She starts the car. "Lock and load, gentlemen. It's time we put an end to this."

# ONE HUNDRED-ONE

Alia looks puzzled. "What are the Uwharries?"

"They're mountains," Meadow replies. "Sort of."

Alia's frown deepens. "How is something 'sort of' a mountain?"

"They're not very big," Ben says. "It's because they're really, really old."

"And we're going to hide in these mountains?" Alia shakes her head, clearly dubious.

"Camping out." Bassim sighs. "Great."

"It won't be camping. Not exactly." Meadow takes a deep breath. "I'm going to see if we can stay with my dad."

Ben glances over. "I get the feeling you're not thrilled about this."

"I'm not. He's…kind of different."

"You're not really selling this, Med," Bassim says.

"Tell us," Alia says. "Please. We don't have time for guessing games."

"Okay." Meadow says. "Dad calls himself a 'sovereign citizen.' He doesn't believe the US government is legit."

"You know what?" Bassim says. "I'm starting to agree with him."

"Be quiet, Bassim." Alia turns back to Meadow. "And?"

"And he's got a place up in the Uwharries, way back in the woods.

Bordering the national forest. He doesn't let anyone up there. No cops, no government people, nobody. Except me."

Alia nods. "Your mother lets you visit him?"

"Well, she did." Meadow looks away. "She made me stop a few months ago. That's the other thing you need to know. He's growing weed up there. A lot of it."

"Marijuana?" Alia blinks in surprise.

"That's what weed is, sis."

"Shut up, Bassim." She shakes her head. "No. It's too dangerous."

"More dangerous than wandering around the roads with a government paper out on us saying we're terrorists?" Bassim turns to Meadow. "You think he'll let you bring friends?"

She bites her lip. "I can ask. But we have to go there. He doesn't have a cell phone. He says the government tracks you with them."

"I've read that, too." Bassim looks at Ben behind the wheel. "I say we go."

Alia looks out the window. A car goes by in the opposite direction and she turns to watch, dreading the possibility it might turn around and follow. She feels sick and exhausted with worry and fear. "He has guns, I assume."

"Oh yeah," Meadow says. "Lots."

She closes her eyes. "And how does he feel about, well, people like us?"

"You mean…Arabs?" She looks doubtful. "I don't know. I never asked."

Alia opens her eyes and looks wearily at her. "It's kind of important, don't you think?"

Meadow nods. "Yeah, I know. But I can't think of any safer place to go right now. Dad always said he'd do anything for me."

Alia leans her head against the window. *I'm so tired.* Her answer comes out in a whisper. "Okay."

"Swing by my place first," Meadow says to Ben. "I need to pick up a couple of things." She looks at the box holding Marie's gun. "Like a screwdriver."

# ONE HUNDRED-TWO

As Fletcher and Cameron walk back into the station, the civilian receptionist at the front desk calls out. "Hey, Fletch. You got a message."

He walks over. "Thanks, Lisa." He waits, but she just looks at him. "It's on your computer. The new internal messaging system, remember?"

He grunts in annoyance and turns away. "I hate that goddamn thing," he mutters.

Cameron falls into step beside him on the way to the bullpen, where the few detectives in the tiny department work at desks shoved together in a former meeting room. "You're just irritable because you can't ball up a message you don't want to answer and throw it in the trash."

"That's part of it, yeah." He takes a seat and the desk he shares with the detective on the next shift and stares at the screen.

Cameron leans over his shoulder. "Click on LawTrak, then pull down the menu for—"

"I know how to use it." Fletcher grabs the mouse and performs the necessary commands. He sees the message on the screen. "Huh."

"From Homeland Security. They actually called back. Urgent."

Fletcher turns to him. "You mind?"

"Sorry," Cameron straightens up.

"Here," Fletcher reaches into his desk drawer and pulls out a roll of breath mints as he reaches for the phone with the other hand.

"Nice," Cameron says sourly, but he takes the mint as Fletcher dials. He gets another surprise as the person on the other end picks up immediately.

"Agent Bertone."

"Uh, hi, Agent Bertone, this is Brock Fletcher of the Harnett County Sheriff's Department. In North Carolina. I'm returning your call."

Bertone's voice sharpens. "Right. An inquiry about some people supposed to be on the watch list."

"Right. See we found it a little strange that—"

"Detective, Homeland Security does not confirm or deny whether or not someone is on the watch list."

"I see. So, this Agent Gray—"

"That's actually why I called, Detective. You said the name the person gave you was Iris Gray."

"That's right. She said she was—"

"There is no one matching that name working for Homeland Security."

Fletcher's getting tired of being interrupted, but that information silences him.

Bertone goes on. "Needless to say, we're investigating as well. Is there anything else you can tell us about this person?"

It takes Fletcher a second to find his voice. "You mind if I put this on speaker? My partner's here."

"Yes, I mind. And information about this phone call is not to be repeated. Do you understand?"

"Yeah," Fletcher says. He looks at Cameron and rolls his eyes. Cameron nods. Fletcher goes on. "We know that she's picked up a couple of bodyguards. Carrying automatic weapons."

There's a brief silence on the other line. Then, "We've got a team coming from Charlotte. Until they get there, you should not engage these people. At all. Understood?"

"Understood." Fletcher hangs up without saying goodbye. He notices that Cameron's walked away and is having an intense conversation with Xavier Willis, a black detective who Fletcher had thought was on the night shift.

"Fletch," Cameron motions him over, "we got another homicide."

"God damn it," Fletcher mutters as he walks over. He nods at Willis. "Hey."

Willis nods back. "Hey. Cameron says you might have a connection with this one, the kid who got blown up, and the preacher they found dead in the road."

Fletcher feels a sinking sensation in his stomach. "Who's the victim?"

"Warehouse manager for Dalton Chemical. Foreign guy named Adnan Khoury."

Fletcher closes his eyes. "Yeah," he says. "You could say there's a connection." He opens them. "We'd been led to believe that Adnan Khoury was some kind of US intelligence asset. He was supposedly under the protection of a Homeland Security agent going by the name of Iris Gray. Except I just got a call from the Department of Homeland Security telling us there ain't no such agent."

Willis grimaces. "Great."

"Oh, it gets better. This DHS puke tells me we need to leave Gray alone. They're sending a team from Charlotte."

"We gonna do it?" Cameron says. "Leave her alone, I mean."

"Hell no."

"Guys," Willis says nervously, "maybe we should do that. I mean, if this thing's going Federal…"

"Khoury has two kids," Fletcher says. "Teenagers. They're in the wind along with two other local teenagers. They're afraid this Gray woman is after them. And I'm beginning to think they're right."

"Kids," Willis mutters. "Fuck."

Cameron nods. "That sums it up nicely." He turns to Fletcher. "What about Keller?"

Willis looks puzzled. "Keller? Who's Keller?"

"Used to be a bounty hunter," Fletcher says. "Khoury hired him as a bodyguard for the kids."

"Gray tried to run him off," Cameron adds. "He didn't go for it. Then she tried to get us to arrest him."

"Which we did," Fletcher says.

"Wait," Willis says. "Ain't Keller the guy that got his house blown up?" They nod. "And you think Gray may have done it?"

"Maybe," Fletcher says. "Or the two goons she's got with her."

"Well, we'd like to have a talk with his Keller guy, too," Willis says.

Fletcher raises an eyebrow. "About what?"

"About the pile of cash we found in a duffel bag in the back of the house. And some firearms we found."

"Firearms," Fletcher says.

Willis nods. "You know he's a convicted felon, right?"

Fletcher sighs. "Yeah. We know that."

"You know where he is?"

"We know where he's supposed to be," Fletcher says.

Cameron smiles grimly. "You really think he stayed put like we told him? Out at Jones's place?"

"No." Fletcher pulls out his car keys. "But that's where we're going to start looking for him. Because unless I miss my guess, he's going after those kids. And so is Gray. Find one, maybe we find them all."

"Let's hope we find at least one of them before they all get together," Cameron says. "Because I can't think of a way that ends well."

# ONE HUNDRED-THREE

Keller pulls up outside the address Marie gave him, a double-wide trailer sitting on a clear-cut dirt lot surrounded on three sides by woods. He doesn't see his truck there. What he does see is a pale, red-haired woman seated on the wooden steps of the trailer, smoking a cigarette.

"You just missed 'em," she calls out. She doesn't sound happy. Or sober. Keller can see a couple of empty Budweiser cans on the step next to her.

Keller kills the engine and gets out. The red-haired woman stands, weaving a little in place, as he approaches. She's dressed in a pair of jean shorts and a loose-fitting AC/DC tour t-shirt. "They've come an' gone."

"Who's that?" Keller asks.

She regards him through narrowed, reddened eyes. "Who the hell you think? My daughter. Or whatever she is. An' her boyfriend. Or girlfriend. Or whatever."

As Keller gets closer, he can smell the beer and weed on her. She has a spray of freckles across her face and a pair of green eyes that might be pretty if the whites weren't blood red. "They driving a black pickup truck?"

She blinks. "Yeah. Why?"

252

"It's my truck."

The woman snorts. "So now she's a car thief, too?"

"Not necessarily."

She shakes her head, trying to clear the cobwebs she herself put there. "What the fuck does that mean?"

"There may be some extenuating circumstances."

"Ex-tenuating..." She laughs. "You sound like a lawyer. But you don' look like a lawyer." She steps a little closer to him, close enough that she's looking up at him. She smiles.

"Thanks. You have any idea where Meadow and the others went with my truck?"

"Meadow." The smile disappears. "That ain't the name I gave her."

"It's the name she likes. But let's not go there."

But the name's clearly a sore point. "I thought once she started hanging around with that boy, that Ben..." She stops and cocks her head at him. "Hey, is that your boy?" Before Keller can answer, she's off again. "I thought she'd straighten out. Hell, I wouldn't even mind if they were fuckin'. At least that'd be kinda normal, and he is kinda cute. But nooooo, she's still tryin' to work out her," the woman makes air quotes with her fingers, "sexual identity. Jesus. What kinda bullshit is that?"

"Ma'am," Keller begins.

"I mean, I changed her goddamn diapers for years. I'm pretty damn sure she's a girl."

"Ma'am!" he says louder.

"My name's Debra. Not ma'am." She smiles at him again, seeming to lose track of her outrage. "An' what's yours?"

"Jack. Now about where your daughter went..."

"With Ben. And that Arab girl and her brother."

"Yeah."

Instead of answering, she stumbles back to the steps, sits down heavily, and picks up one of the beer cans. From the way she looks at it, it's empty and she's not happy about it. "Jack," she says. "I need a ride to the store. Can you take me?"

*For god's sake*, Keller thinks. "I'm kind of in a time crunch here. Can you just tell me where you think they might have gone?"

She's lost the thread again, looking off into space. "You know, if the damn sperm donor had just stuck around, she might have grown up likin' men better." She looks at Keller. "Sperm donor. That's what I call her daddy."

Keller's losing patience. "Debra," he says. "I need to know where they—"

She smiles in a way that he guesses is supposed to be flirtatious. "Take me to the store and I'll tell you. But maybe we can party a little before you…"

That's all he can take. He crosses the distance between them in three long strides, bends down, and grabs her by both shoulders. "*Debra!*" he shouts, and pulls her to her feet.

"Ow," she whines. "You're hurtin' me."

"Listen to me," he says between clenched teeth. "Those two kids who were with Meadow and Ben? Those Arab kids? There are people out there, people who are very close, who want to hurt them. Okay? And they're not above hurting your daughter if she gets in the way."

Debra's eyes are wide with fear. Fear of him. He hates that, but he presses on. "I can help them. At least I can try. But to do that, I have to know where they're going. I think you know, or at least you've got some idea. So, you need to pull your head out of your ass and tell me what I need to know."

She swallows, and her eyes brim with tears. "Someone…someone wants to hurt my little girl?"

"They won't think twice about it to get what they want."

The tears are flowing freely down her face now. "But why?"

"Because that's the kind of people they are, Debra."

"No. I mean why would Melissa put herself in danger like that?"

Keller releases her shoulders and stands up. "Because that's the kind of person *she* is. She's a good kid. She cares. She's loyal to her friends."

Debra nods, still weeping. "She is. She's a good girl. She's so sweet.

Always has been. Since she was little." She cries harder. "And I've been so mean to her."

"So, help me find her. And her friends. I can help them."

Debra stands up, still a little unsteady. "Okay. Okay. Come on inside."

Keller sighs. "I don't have time to party, Debra."

She nods. "I know. But you need to come inside. There's a map."

"A map."

"Yeah. To where her daddy is. That's probably where she's gone." She weaves her way up the stairs and opens the door. Keller hesitates a moment, then follows.

Inside, the trailer smells of grilled meat and onions, dirty clothes, and marijuana smoke. Debra gestures vaguely at the piles of clothing on the couch. "Sorry 'bout the mess. Wasn't expecting company."

"It's fine." Keller follows her through the living room and down the hall. She stops at one of the trailer's smaller bedrooms and snaps on a light.

It's a small room, mostly taken up by an unmade twin bed. What strikes Keller most is the artwork on the walls. Instead of the expected pop-star posters, every wall is covered with what looks like original drawings, paintings, and a couple of lithographs, mostly bright, intricate, eye-bending patterns, but with a couple of portraits so realistic they seem to jump off the page. One, a head and shoulders rendering of a dark-haired boy laughing, particularly catches his eye. As he looks more closely, he realizes with a shock that it's Ben. He can't recall ever seeing Ben laugh like that. Apparently, Meadow can. Another, smaller sketch, almost a miniature, shows Francis, sitting on the floor, all his attention on a toy truck.

"Good, ain't she?" Debra says.

"She's amazing."

"Lot of good it'll do her." Debra walks to a metal desk by the window that's covered with tubes of paint, brushes, and paper. Keller realizes that what he'd thought was a dull green abstract drawing pinned to the wall beside the desk is a US Geological Survey topographic map of the Uwharrie National Forest. She reaches up and pulls the map from the wall without taking out the thumbtacks holding it to the cheap paneling, so that the corners tear loose. She holds the map out to Keller. "Here. That's where she's prob'ly gone."

Keller takes the damaged paper. He hasn't had to read a topo map since the Army, but he can see the route Meadow's traced in pen from a state road, through the National Forest, then off that reservation up to a place marked with an X, where the contour lines come together to indicate a steep slope, possibly even a cliff. "This is where her father lives?" Keller asks.

Debra's stumbled backward to a seat on the bed. "Yeah. Drug-dealin' asshole. I'm callin' my lawyer in the morning. He ain't s'posed to see her 'til he turns three clean drug screens." She snorts. "Like that's gonna happen."

Keller folds the map into a square and stuffs it in his back pocket. "Okay. Thanks for the tip."

She squints up at him. "You gonna take me to the store now?"

He shakes his head. "Got to go. How long have they been gone?"

She scowls and stands up. "You said you was gonna take me to the store. I'm outta beer. And cigarettes."

"I didn't say I was going to take you." He exits the bedroom and heads for the front door. "If anyone else comes asking where Meadow's gone," he calls back over his shoulder, "don't tell them. In fact, don't even open the door." He stops to consider. "Except to a cop named Fletcher. You can trust him."

"Wait a damn minute," she fumes. "What the hell am I supposed to do here by myself?"

Keller turns to face her. "Sober up, maybe. Get ready to be at least a little less shitty to your kid when I bring her home."

She puts her hands on her hips and glares at him. "Who the fuck do you think you are, tellin' me how to raise my child?"

Keller doesn't answer, just turns and walks out.

"Asshole!" she yells at him from the front door. She shouts it several times as he pulls away.

# ONE HUNDRED-FOUR

If there's one good thing about all this craziness, Seth Childress thinks, it's the opportunities. The Criminal Investigations Division was undermanned to begin with, and now that there are at least three major murder cases breaking, even road deputies like Childress are getting more responsibilities.

"Deputy Childress?" the female deputy working the front desk calls on the intercom. "There are…some people here to see you. About the Khoury case."

Childress looks up from the report he's typing. "What do they want?"

"They say they're his family."

He frowns. "The family? Wait…Khoury's children are here?"

"They're not children." A pause. "Maybe you'd better come out here."

"Where's Willis?"

"He went back out to the scene. You're the only one here knows anything."

What he finds in the waiting area is something he'd never expected to see in his county: three women, wearing headscarves and veils that show only their dark eyes. He stops short. "Ah, hey. Can I help you ladies?"

One of the women stands up and steps forward. "Yes. We came as soon as we heard about our cousin."

Childress is nonplussed. "Your cousin."

"Yes, Adnan Khoury. My name is Fatima Al-Saddiq."

"Hey. I'm Deputy Childress." He holds out his hand. She doesn't take it.

He looks at her, then and the other two. They regard him in a way he finds unsettling, their gazes flat, without expression or emotion. "Maybe you ladies better come with me."

He leads them to a conference room and motions them to the chairs around the table. They take their seats and the woman who spoke first continues. "We understand that someone killed our cousin. Do you have any suspects?"

He hesitates. "Ma'am, I don't mean to be rude, and I'm, ah, sorry for your loss. But I have to see some proof that you're actually relatives of Mr. Khoury. Preferably next of kin." The three women don't answer, just stare at him. He rushes to fill the silence. "It's just policy. Even more so now that there've been some people contacting us who, ah, well, let's just say they weren't who they said they were."

That gets a reaction. The three women look at one another, and something unspoken seems to pass between them. The spokeswoman says, "What sort of proof would you need?"

"Photo ID, for one. And I'd have to clear it with the lead detective, anyway."

She shakes her head. "We cannot do photo ID. We cannot appear unveiled in public. It is against our faith."

He shrugs. "Well, then I don't know what to tell you, ma'am."

The woman's voice doesn't change in tone. "Perhaps we should contact an attorney. This is religious discrimination."

Now he's annoyed. He stands up. "You do what you need to do, ma'am. In the meantime, I need to get back to work."

The three women don't move until he walks to the door and opens it. Then, they rise at the same time and file out, with the spokeswoman last. "You'll hear from us again, Officer…"

"Childress." He spells it carefully for her to show he's not intimidated. "C-H-I-L-D-R-E-S-S."

She just nods curtly and walks past.

He shows them to the door without further words. "Spooky," he mutters as the door closes behind them. He figures he needs to let Fletcher know about the visit, but the call goes to voicemail. He looks at the clock at the same time he feels his belly rumble. "Hey, Carla," he calls over to the deputy working the front desk. "I'm gonna run to Subway an' get some dinner. You want me to bring anything back?"

She waves him off. "Nah, I'm good. Brought a salad from home."

He rubs at his stomach absent-mindedly. He thinks maybe a salad wouldn't be such a bad idea for himself. He's getting a little thick around the middle.

In the parking lot, he's getting into his cruiser when he hears a soft footstep behind him. As he starts to turn, he sees something pass quickly before his eyes, and suddenly he can't breathe. He reaches up to claw at the cord that's been wrapped around his neck, fighting for a breath he can't catch. Something's pulling him backward like a riptide, and before everything goes dark, he can hear the sound of a large engine.

When Seth Childress comes to, he's looking up at a metal ceiling. He tries to get up and realizes that he can't. He looks around as best he can and realizes that he's lying on the metal floor of what looks like a delivery van, his wrists and ankles bound to the cargo tie-downs. To his further dismay, he realizes that he's dressed only in his boxer shorts. He pulls against the restraints, but he's held fast. The door to the van slides open with a rumble and a figure climbs in, followed by two more. They crouch around him in the crowded space like vultures over a carcass. He realizes with a cold shock of fear in his stomach that they're all women. Women with dark eyes. One of them has a scar down one side of her face, another had some kind of scarring around her mouth. It's the third one who speaks to him, and he recognizes the voice as the woman from the station.

"Now, Mister C-H-I-L-D-R-E-S-S, you will tell us what we want to know." She gestures at the woman with the scarred mouth. "My sister will ensure that what you tell us is the truth." She smiles, and that bright, beautiful smile is enough to make a dribble of piss run down his thigh. She nods at her sister, and Childress is screaming before the knife comes down.

# ONE HUNDRED-FIVE

The drive is only a couple of hours, but it seems to take years. Meadow provides terse directions through the country roads and small towns leading to their destination: Barbecue, Johnsonville, Cameron, Carthage, Robbins, Biscoe. The already rolling and heavily wooded landscape is broken from time to time by corn and tobacco fields, cinderblock convenience stores, tiny country churches with plastic signs, and wood or brick houses with cluttered yards.

In the little town of Troy, she guides them off the main road down a series of ever more winding country lanes. Ben finally speaks up. "Where the *fuck* are we going?"

"It's called Ebenezer," Meadow says. "That's the nearest town at least. It's kind of a town, anyway."

"Wow," Bassim says. "I thought we lived in the sticks before."

Alia chews at her thumbnail and doesn't speak.

Ben looks back at her. "You okay?"

The only answer is a terse nod.

Soon they see brown and white signs telling them they're entering the Uwharrie National Forest. One sign with a dial on it in front of a ranger station lets them know the fire risk is MODERATE today. The houses, farms, and stores are gone now, and the pine woods seem to close in on either side. Meadow leans forward, straining her eyes to look through the gathering gloom for some familiar landmark. A small green sign on a short post by the side of the road says EBENEZER. The only sign of habitation is a wooden building set back a little way off the road, festooned with a collection of faded metal signs advertising RC Cola and Red Man chewing tobacco. The old store looks like it was last open in the 1960s.

"Pull over here," Meadow says.

Ben complies, but there's a dubious look on his face. "Is this the place?"

Meadow shakes her head. "In about a mile, there's a parking lot. We'll need to leave the truck there and walk in."

That startles Alia out of her reverie. "Walk?"

Meadow nods. "The first half mile or so is in the National Forest."

"Half. Mile," Bassim says.

"Yeah. Then we take the path off the main trail. Where the *No Trespassing* signs are."

"Meadow," Alia says. "Are we supposed to make this hike in the woods with two heavy footlockers of money and jewels?"

"No," Meadow says, a little impatiently, "that's why I said stop here. Wait a minute." She opens the door and slips out. In a moment, she's disappeared around the back of the store.

"Where the hell is she going?" Bassim demands.

"I don't know," Ben answers. "Just shut up a minute, okay?"

"Hey, don't tell me to shut up."

"Look, asshole—"

"Both of you shut up!" Alia's voice cracks as she blurts it out.

Bassim puts a hand on her shoulder. "Okay. Sorry. It's going to be okay."

She looks as if she's about to retort, but Meadow appears back at the passenger side door, holding a shiny key in one hand. "Found it.

Come on." Then she's gone again.

The three of them look at each other.

Ben shrugs. "Might as well."

Meadow's standing at the edge of the parking lot. They can see a steep drop-off behind her. "This way."

The ground behind and beneath the ramshackle building falls off precipitously into a deep ravine. The back of the building rests on a foundation of heavy timbers and columns made of native stone that hold up the corners of the structure. Beneath that overhang is a narrow space and a storage area that's walled off by what looks like railroad ties. They pick their way carefully along the edge of the precipice, to a heavy oak door in the center of that formidable wood wall. Meadow's fitting the key she showed them earlier into a padlock securing the door. She struggles for a moment, then the lock gives way with a soft snap and she pulls it off. The door doesn't give way to her first tug, and Ben steps up to help pull it aside. It drags a bit on the ground before they swing it open.

Beyond is only darkness. Meadow steps inside and flips a switch. A dim orange light spills out. Ben looks inside.

The space is empty, with a dirt floor. There are cobwebs in the corners, and a rusty hand truck leaning against the far wall.

"What is this place?" Alia's stepped up beside Ben to peer into the space.

"Dead drop," Meadow says.

Alia looks confused. "What?"

Meadow steps out and looks away from her into the ravine. "I told you. My dad grows weed."

"Marijuana." The judgment is obvious in Alia's voice.

Meadow rolls her eyes. "Yes, marijuana. When he's ready to ship it out, he brings it down here and leaves it. Whoever picks it up leaves him the money."

Bassim peers into the dimly lit space. "What happens if the guy takes the weed and just doesn't leave any money?"

Meadow shrugs. "He doesn't get any more weed. Dad says that's how people were meant to deal with one another. Based on what he calls 'enlightened self-interest.' Not coerced by governments." She looks around at the looks she's getting and shrugs. "Whatever. This is a place to hide the money for the time being. Until we figure out what we're going to do."

"What happens if the buyer shows up?" Ben asks.

Meadow holds up the key. "I'm taking this with me."

Bassim looks doubtful. "Won't this just piss everybody off?"

"Of course it will." Alia's voice is biting. She shakes her head. "Don't we have any other alternative than dealing with criminals?"

Meadow bristles. "If you've got one, Alia, I'd love to hear it. And before you get all high and mighty, you might want to think about where all that money came from. You know, the money and gems buried in your backyard? I don't know how they do things where you come from, but most people I know who make honest money don't need to bury it."

Alia stares at Meadow furiously for a moment, hands on her hips, looking as if she's about to charge. Then her face crumples and she looks down. A sob escapes her.

Meadow looks stunned, then her own face collapses into tears. She holds out her arms and runs to Alia. The two girls embrace, tears running down their faces, murmuring apologies to one another. The young men stand aside, looking awkwardly at one another. Finally, Alia and Meadow break the hug and look at them.

"Come on," Alia says. "Let's get this stuff hidden."

# ONE HUNDRED-SIX

"I'm going to quote your boyfriend, Ms. Jones. You need to pick a side."

Marie glares at Fletcher, who's standing on her porch. "So we've dropped 'Officer' Jones now?"

"Maybe we should."

"If I knew where Jack Keller was, Detective, I'd tell you. But I don't. I know he's going after those kids. That's all."

"And you didn't try to stop him."

"No. I didn't." Francis has appeared beside his mother in the doorway, clutching at her leg and looking fearfully past her at the officers. She puts a reassuring hand on his head as she goes on. "You know why? Because I know he can get the job done. He can find and bring back my son. Alive."

Fletcher grimaces in frustration. "Look at his history. He's unstable and dangerous."

That gets a sharp laugh. "Oh, believe me, Detective. I know his history. Remember who you're talking to. And yes, he's dangerous. But unstable? No. Right now, he is completely focused, completely committed, and probably as calm as he ever gets. Because he's hunting.

That's what he does. And he's only dangerous to people who'd threaten those children."

Cameron speaks up. "Can you just tell us where he might have gone to look for them? Where he might start? Officer Jones, you may not believe it, but we want to protect those kids as much as you and Keller do. We just want to do it the right way."

She sighs. "That's part of the problem. What you call the right way doesn't always do the job, does it?" Fletcher starts to say something, but she silences him with a raised hand. "He asked for the address of Melissa Troutman's mother. Melissa's the one with them who goes by Meadow. He thought that might be a place to start."

Fletcher nods. "Okay. Thanks."

"Now, will that be all?"

"For the moment, yes. If you hear from Keller, let him know he needs to come back in."

She inclines her head curiously. "And why is that?"

"We just have some more questions about the explosion at his house. So ask him to come by the station, will you?"

"You know," she says, "I don't think I will."

As they walk back to their car, Cameron says, "I think I'd look both ways before crossing that one."

"Agreed." Fletcher opens the car door and looks back at the house and its closed front door. "I hear she was a good cop once. I wonder what happened?"

When they arrive at the address Marie gave them, there's a light on inside, but no one comes to the door when Cameron knocks. He frowns and knocks again. "Sheriff's Department." Still no answer. He makes a fist and pounds forcefully on the door. "Open up, ma'am. We know you're in there. It's about your daughter."

There's a rustling behind the closed door, then it opens a crack and half a face looks out at them. The one eye they can see is tinted pale red, as if the woman is stoned or crying or both. "She ain't here," the woman slurs.

"Yes, ma'am. May we come in?"

A pause, and the eye looks from one officer to the other. "She ain't here."

Fletcher speaks in a low, measured voice. "Ma'am, we have reason to believe your daughter's involved in a motor vehicle theft, for starters. She may also be a witness to at least one homicide, and that might put her in danger. Now, if we can come in and ask you some questions, we'll go away and leave you alone. But if I have to come back with a warrant, we're bringing deputies with us who'll search the house. You want that?"

The woman mutters something that Fletcher can't make out, but it doesn't sound friendly. The door opens wide and the woman inside steps back to let them in.

"Thanks," Fletcher says.

"She didn't steal no truck," the woman says. "That was those Arab kids. And the Jones boy."

Fletcher takes out his notebook. "First things first. Are you Debra Troutman?"

The woman just nods without looking at them.

"And Melissa's your daughter?"

Another nod. She wipes her running nose with the back of her hand.

Cameron looks around, locates a roll of paper towels on the living room table and tears one off for her. She nods her thanks and blows her nose.

"So, do you know where she and the others may have gone?"

Another silent nod. Her eyelids droop and she looks as if she may pass out in front of them.

"Hey. Hey." Fletcher snaps his fingers and she jerks awake. "Where'd she go, Ms. Troutman?"

"Her daddy," she mumbles.

"Right. Okay. And where does her daddy live?"

"Woods."

"Wood?"

"Woods. He lives in the woods."

Cameron puts his hand to his head. "Damn." He leans forward. "Ma'am, is her father John-Robert Troutman?"

She nods again, but she's clearly fading.

"Who's John-Robert Troutman?" Fletcher asks.

"Tell you later." Cameron turns back to her. "Ma'am, can you tell us how to find where John-Robert is?"

"Had a map," she mumbles. "Gave it to Keller."

The two detectives look at each other. "Jack Keller? He was here?"

The name gets her attention. Her head snaps up and her eyes are narrowed with anger this time. "That son of a bitch!"

"He was here, all right. You gave him the map to John-Robert's place?"

"Yeah. And then he wouldn't take me to the store." The idea seems to wake her up. "Can you take me? I need beer and cigarettes."

"We're a little tied up right now, ma'am." Fletcher stands up. "You know where this guy is?" he asks Cameron.

Cameron sighs. "I know where he might be. I was kind of hoping I'd never have to deal with that particular pain in the ass again."

"You're not taking me to the store?" she's beginning to fade again. "Assholes," she mumbles.

Outside the trailer, Cameron fills Fletcher in. "John-Robert Troutman's one of those Sovereign Citizens. When I was a road deputy, we locked him up for thirty days one time because he showed up for court and wouldn't acknowledge that his name was John-Robert Troutman. Kept blabbering on about how that name on his birth certificate 'created a corporate shell' or some such bullshit and it wasn't his real identity, till the judge got tired of it and held him in contempt."

Fletcher sighs. "Great. And don't tell me, let me guess. He has lots of guns."

"Last time we checked. But no felonies, and they all seemed like legit purchases."

"So where can we find this whack job?"

Cameron shrugs. "Last I heard, he'd gotten some land in the Uwharries and was living off the grid. And out of our jurisdiction."

Fletcher says nothing, just taps on the roof of the car while looking off into space, thinking.

"We've got a lot on our plate already, Fletch," Cameron says. "Let's put out a statewide BOLO and wait for some other agency to bring them in while we work the local angle on the murders we picked up this week. Keller's firearms problem can wait."

Fletcher runs a hand over his face, trying not to snarl in frustration. He knows his partner is right. They're overloaded and it's time to focus on what they can do. But it gripes his ass that Keller's the one on the hunt and not him. He sighs. "Okay. Let's get back and see what we got."

As they pull out of the clay and gravel drive of the trailer, they turn toward home. But Fletcher can't help but glance over his shoulder to the road going the other way.

# ONE HUNDRED-SEVEN

"This is it," Meadow says. "Turn off here."

Ben has to stand on the brakes to stop the big truck in time. His three passengers are thrown forward by the sudden stop and the tires squeal on the pavement of the hard road. Alia cries out, and Meadow instinctively puts out her hands to keep from crashing into the dashboard before her seatbelt stops her. Ben glares at her. "You could have told me sooner."

She's close to tears. "I'm sorry. I didn't see it. I haven't been here in a while."

"Okay." Ben takes a deep breath. "Sorry I snapped at you."

As he puts the truck in gear and backs up to make the tight turn, she murmurs, "It's okay. We're all on edge."

They've turned onto a gravel road that's so narrow Ben grits his teeth and leans forward to keep from running off the side. Twilight is falling, and he has to grope to find the switch to turn on the headlights. As he does, the road widens out to a tiny gravel parking lot. Ben pulls the truck to a stop. "Is this it?"

Meadow shakes her head. "This is the trailhead. The beginning to one of the hiking trails in the forest. We walk from here."

"Oh boy," Bassim says. "Hiking. *So* looking forward to this."

270

Ben pulls the truck to one side, puts it in park, and kills the engine. The only sounds are the ticking of the cooling motor and the growing rasp of crickets.

"Grab your packs and come on." Meadow does just that as she exits the vehicle. Ben follows, sticking the pistol they'd retrieved from his mother's lockbox during the drive into his waistband.

Alia and Bassim look at each other. Bassim shrugs. "Unless you want to live in this truck, I guess we're hiking."

Alia nods and picks up her own backpack.

Meadow's already started up the trail. They have to jog to catch up. She snaps on a flashlight to guide their way through the gathering darkness. The trees loom overhead, shutting out what little light there is left. The trail is hard-packed clay, but jutting roots and patches of loose gravel cause all of them to stumble from time to time. The terrain dips into shadowed valleys, then climbs abruptly to tall ridges. Before long, they're all panting with the strain. After a while, they start to notice bright yellow signs on either side of the trail, warning POSTED. NO TRESPASSING. PRIVATE PROPERTY.

"I thought this was a national park," Ben gasps, barely able to catch his breath from the exertion.

"It is," Meadow calls back. "At least the trail is." She draws up short at the top of a steep climb, where a group of granite boulders, some of them as tall as a man, just from the clay soil. "We can rest here."

"Thank you," Alia breathes, collapsing onto a chair-sized rock.

Meadow leans against a tree. "The parkland widens out about a quarter mile down the trail. But right here, on either side, is property of people who refused to sell when the government created the park. And the government decided it wasn't worth the effort to go to court to take it." She shrugs. "Or someone paid someone off. Daddy's not sure which."

"Speaking of Daddy," Ben says. "Does he know we're coming?"

Meadow shakes her head. "No. He doesn't have a phone or anything like that. So let me do the talking, okay? And try not to get upset if he says anything, you know..."

"Racist?" Alia's voice bears just a trace of bitterness. "Don't worry, Meadow. Bassim and I have become experts at keeping quiet in the face of bigots."

Meadow sighs. "Daddy's not a bigot. Not exactly. He's not really all that crazy about anyone, to tell you the truth."

"Except you," Ben says. "We hope."

She smiles. "Except me. I hope."

"Except my baby girl," a gravelly voice comes from the darkness. As they leap up to face the voice, a man steps from behind a standing rock a few feet away. He's a little over six feet tall. His hair is gray and thinning on top, but his gray beard is thick and full and reaches to the middle of his chest. He's dressed in tattered jeans and a ragged black T-shirt and holding a black AR-15, the barrel of which tracks from Ben, to Alia, to Bassim, then back to Ben again. "If you're thinkin' of drawin' that piece in your waistband, sonny," he says, "I wouldn't recommend it."

The biggest dog Ben has even seen, a fawn-colored animal with a short muzzle and muscles rippling beneath his fur, steps from behind the man and regards the intruders with baleful pale gold eyes that finally come to rest on Ben. A low growl emanates from the animal's throat.

"You may get one of us," the man says in a growl even more terrifying than the dog's, "but the other one'll kill you."

"Oh, hush, Daddy," Meadow says as Ben raises his hands above his head. "No one's killing anyone." She goes down on one knee and gestures to the dog. "Hey, Zeus. Hey, sweet boy. C'mere. Come see me."

The dog looks from his master to the girl calling to him. Then he breaks and trots over to Meadow, wagging his stubby tail madly and licking her face. She throws her arms around the animal's thick neck and scratches his ears, crooning to him all the while. "That's my sweet boy. That's my good boy."

"God damn it," the man mutters. He looks at Ben and raises the rifle. "Keep your hands up, boy."

"I am, sir." Ben raises his hands even higher as the man steps nearer.

"Meadow!" the man snaps. "Stop playin' with the dog and fetch me that gun."

Meadow gives the dog a final hug and stands up. "It'll be okay, Ben," she whispers as she walks over and takes the gun. As she hands it to her father, butt first, she asks, "Where's Hera?"

The man nods over Ben's shoulder. They all turn to see another dog, with the same massive build as the first, but a streaky dark brindle coat, watching from a dozen feet away. She'd come up behind them without a sound. "She's been a lot more skittish since the pups were born."

"Puppies?" Meadow's voice goes so high it's almost a squeal. "Hera had puppies, and you didn't tell me?"

"Well..." the man begins.

Meadow walks up to him and links her arm in his. This has the effect of impeding, if not completely disabling, his ability to shoot. He clearly realizes and is unhappy about it, but she leans over and kisses his weathered cheek. "Take us to see the puppies."

# ONE HUNDRED-EIGHT

"That didn't take long," Natalya observes.

"It never does," her sister Liza kisses the young deputy tenderly on the forehead and tells him in a gentle voice what a good boy he's been. Then she stands up and wipes the blood off her face with a towel.

They have it down to a science now: Marina wields the knife, inflicting pain with the deft cruelty that comes from long practice; Liza kneels by the subject, cradling their head tenderly in the crook of her elbow, whispering the questions they want answered, commiserating with the subject's suffering, and telling them with a motherly solicitousness that all this foolishness can end if they would just stop being so stubborn and tell the sisters what they want to know. For someone far gone in the wilderness of agony that Marina creates, that soft, soothing maternal voice is a lifeline to a world that may not be better, but at least doesn't hurt as badly. Given that lifeline, most subjects will take it, only some of them knowing that the cessation of pain often comes at the price of permanent darkness.

This time had been no different. It hadn't taken the young policeman long to give up all of the details of the investigation. They're disappointed to find that he's a minor figure, not much more than a report writer, but there's still enough there to proceed.

Natalya looks through the open door of the van and frowns. "And now, what do we do with him?"

A soft whimper from the man tied to the floor of the van indicates an attempt to register an opinion. They ignore it.

"He still has one testicle left," Liza says as Marina tosses the one she's taken into the woods, shaking the blood from her fingers when she's done. "He can still have a life."

Natalya shakes her head. "He can identify us."

"A shame," Liza says with sincere regret. "He was a beautiful young man." She looks to Marina, who nods her agreement. Then she cuts the policeman's throat.

"So," Liza says as she drags the beautiful young man's still-twitching body out of the van and onto the dirt path in the woods where they've pulled it, "where to now, sister?"

"We don't know where the Khoury children are," Natalya says. "But we know this Keller is after them. And we know Keller's center of gravity, do we not?"

Liza nods. "The Jones woman."

"So," Natalya says, "we talk to this girlfriend of Jack Keller. If she doesn't know where he is, I'll wager she knows where to contact him." She smiles thinly. "And hearing the person you love screaming can be a powerful way to motivate someone, right, sisters?"

They all nod. They all have very good, very personal reasons to know.

# ONE HUNDRED-NINE

Keller savors the feel of the tires rumbling on the highway, the big police engine rumbling beneath the hood. It feels good to be back on the hunt. Then he takes a deep breath. This is different, he reminds himself, from chasing down some lowlife who's jumped bail. Before the next dawn, he knows, he might have to kill again. He thinks back on the men he's killed in his life, and suddenly they're all in the car with him, looking at him with accusing eyes. John Lee Oxendine. Willem DeGroot, who'd died on his knees, unarmed, but smiling contemptuously with the knowledge that he'd be back to torment Keller and the people he loved. A nameless team of foot soldiers in an empty place a few miles north of the Mexican border. Jerico Zavalo and the men he'd brought to kill Keller. A pair of gunmen he'd set a trap for and burned to death.

He looks back down the path of his life and sees that it's a path that grows redder and redder with the blood of others. It's true that all of them had been engaged at one point or another in trying to kill him and the people he cared for, but he worries about when exactly it was that killing became so easy for him. He wonders if he hasn't gone completely crazy. You can justify anything, any killing, any atrocity, if you're crazy.

He shakes his head to clear those thoughts. It's time to focus on what's happening now. He made a promise to look after Bassim and Alia. He promised Marie he'd bring her son back. There are people out there who'd hurt them. That means there's work to do. It may be violent and bloody work, but it's work he can do well. He pushes the accelerator to the floorboard and the car leaps forward.

The turn marked on the map comes up so quickly that Keller nearly misses it, and the tires wail in complaint as he takes the corner. He glances in the rearview, hoping that he hasn't pulled the maneuver in front of a lurking highway patrolman. All he sees are the headlights of a U-Haul bound for somewhere else passing the crossroads. He slows a bit, searching for the turnoff identified in smeared ink on Meadow's topo map. He passes by the abandoned country store she's marked STORE, with a large X beside it. Something makes him glance back at the place after he passes. Why would she mark that place? He slows and attempts a three-point turn that the narrow country road makes into a five-point turn. It's gotten dark, and the headlights pick out the worn boards and rusted signs of the old place. Keller stops the car, leaving the motor idling, and looks around. A sudden thought makes him reach into the glove box and fumble around until his fingers close on the long, thin metal cylinder of a flashlight. He smiles. Frank Jones, former veteran cop, wasn't one to go anywhere without being prepared for emergencies.

He gets out, snapping the flashlight on, and walks around the parking lot, not completely sure what he's looking for, but strangely confident that he'll find it. His toe catches in a slight depression and he stumbles slightly, then looks down. A pair of deep tracks scar the clay soil. Keller bends down for a closer look, shining the flashlight beam over the tracks. The dirt to either side is dry and cracked, but the bottom of the track still glistens with the moistness of recently dug clay.

Keller straightens up. So, a large vehicle—say, a pickup—has been here recently. It doesn't have to be his truck, he knows, but this isn't exactly a high traffic area, and this was a place specifically designated on Meadow's map. Tracking, Keller knows, is often a matter of staring at the scattered pieces of a puzzle until patterns begin to emerge. Except sometimes, what he's staring at are pieces of several different puzzles, and the real trick is sorting out which pieces are the ones to his puzzle and which ones are irrelevant. Problem is, Keller doesn't have a lot of time to stare. He plays the flashlight around the parking lot some more until he notices the grassy area to the right of the store, at the edge of the lot. The grass hasn't been cut in ages, but as Keller draws near, he sees it's been trampled down. He moves in for a closer look and almost stumbles down the steep slope behind the store. The bent and broken grass forms a trail down the slope. Keller picks his way along that path until he arrives at the area where mortared stone columns hold up the back half of the building. Someday, he thinks, one of those posts is going to go, and the whole damn thing is going to slide into the ravine. But as he looks closer at the handiwork, he decides that day's probably a long time away. This stonework may be crude, but it was meant to last. He turns and sees the padlocked door set into a dark wooden wall. The light on the hard-packed dirt in front of the door shows the scuffled marks of multiple footprints. Someone's been here. Keller walks over and rattles the padlock. It holds firm in its hasp. The surface of the lock feels rough and gritty in his hands from the rust that covers it, but when Keller examines it closely with the flashlight, he can see the scratches and the bright metal around the keyhole. Keller lets the padlock drop with a rattle that sounds like a gunshot in the closeness of the hidden storage area.

*More puzzle pieces*, Keller thinks. A big truck, a secret locked space where someone—actually several someones, from the look of the beaten path—has recently been walking, and an X mark on a map, like something from a pirate story. X marks the spot, the place where the treasure is buried. Maybe. Maybe these are pieces from some other puzzle. But he has the feeling he knows where the stolen money is hidden. But he won't know for sure until he finds the final pieces. The children. He gets in his car and pulls away, headlights cutting a swath through the night.

The turnoff marked by Meadow isn't far, and it leads to a gravel parking lot with a wooden sign stating that it's the EBENEZER TRAILHEAD. Keller sees his battered and dented truck parked to one side of the lot. He also sees another vehicle.

The rental car he last saw driven by Gray and her two gunmen.

They've arrived before him.

# ONE HUNDRED-TEN

Iris Gray moves through the woods as silently as she can behind Waller and Tench, glad that she brought along a pair of sneakers to replace her flats. Her cane digs into the ground with every step, but she's finding it as much a hindrance as a help. They're only a couple of feet ahead of her, but the woods are so dark she follows them as much by sound as sight, and there's not much sound. The two move slowly, in single file, rifles at the ready, scanning from side to side through their night-vision goggles. "Sorry, ma'am," they'd said as they pulled the contraptions over their heads, "we don't have a pair for you. We weren't expecting company."

They'd arrived at the place where Gray's tracker said Keller's truck would be, only to find the vehicle empty of both people and money. The only way out is the trail that begins beside a large wooden sign standing on a slight rise. The narrow track starts up a steep hill with tall trees and bushes on either side. The thick leaves arching overhead effectively shut out both moon and starlight, making the path ahead of them as dark as a cavern.

Gradually, as her eyes become accustomed to the gloom and the land continues to rise, the overhead vegetation becomes a little less thick and she can see a little better in the ambient light. Still, when

Tench stops dead, she almost walks into his back. They stand still and silent for a second, then a bright red dot appears ahead of them. It's the laser sight on Waller's rifle, and it comes to rest on a figure about fifty feet ahead of them on the trail. Gray catches a glimpse of brown hair in the reflected glow before the light snaps off.

"Deer," Tench whispers. "Quit fuckin' around, Waller."

Waller says something she can't catch, and the three of them move on.

# ONE HUNDRED-ELEVEN

The house in the clearing is the first actual log cabin Alia's ever seen, the rough-hewn structure like something from a history book. "Did you build this yourself, sir?" she asks the bearded man.

He just nods, clearly not happy that any of them are there. He sets the rifle against one of the logs that hold up the roof of the front porch and picks a green Coleman propane lantern off the rough plank floor. The lantern comes alive with a sudden hiss of gas and a quick brightness has them all blinking. He hangs the lantern from a hook, picks up the gun again, and gestures with the barrel. "Y'all sit on the edge of the porch." They look at each other nervously, then comply. There's a large wooden barrel at the end of the porch with a tin cup hanging by its handle on the edge. The man takes the cup and scoops it into the barrel. It comes out dripping and he drinks deeply, noisily, ending with a smacking of his lips. He looks at the children sitting on the porch, sighs, and scoops out another cupful. "It's only rainwater," he says as he hands the cup to Bassim. "Purer than tap. No chemicals in it."

"Thank you," Bassim says, and takes a drink before passing it down.

"We got plenty," the man says gruffly. "Barrel's full. Drink all you want."

In silence, the four of them quench their thirst.

282

"Daddy," Meadow begins when they're done.

"Hush," he barks. "I ain't happy with you, little girl. You know better'n to bring strangers here."

"I know, Daddy," she says, clearly fighting back tears. "But we didn't have anywhere else to go. There are people after us. Government people."

That gets his attention. "Government? What'd you do?"

"She tried to help us, sir," Alia speaks up.

He swings the gun around to point at her. "Did I ask you anything?"

Bassim stands up. "Hey, stop pointing that at my sister." The barrel moves slightly to point at him and he flinches, then straightens up and steps deliberately in front of her.

Zeus, who's been sitting down scratching his ear with a hind leg, springs up and comes to alert, a low growl rumbling in his throat. Meadow's father looks startled at first, then smiles cruelly. "You got balls, little man. But if I pull this trigger, that round'll go through you both."

"Daddy, stop it!" Meadow yells, and now she *is* crying. "They're my friends. And they need help."

Alia's had enough. "No." She stands up and gently but firmly moves Bassim aside with a hand on his shoulder. She looks Meadow's father in the eye. "This is not your problem, sir. My brother and I are sorry to have troubled you. We'll go. Meadow, Ben, you stay here. I'm sure he will keep his daughter safe from the government."

"Alia, no…" Ben says. "Let me…"

"We are the ones they want," Alia says. "They don't care about you."

The bearded man looks suspiciously at her, then at Meadow, then back. "What does the government want with the two of you? What did you do?"

"Nothing," Alia says. "We've done nothing. But they've put out a false report that we are terrorists."

"Terrorists?" the man scoffs. "You ain't no older'n sixteen."

"Fifteen. But that is what the government says we are."

The barrel of the gun lowers slightly. "Fuck the government," he says. "They say the same thing about me."

She smiles sadly. "Maybe we have more in common that we thought. Still. We should leave."

He shakes his head. "I say who stays or leaves here."

Alia sits back down on the porch. "All right. But we don't want to be any trouble."

Meadow's father just grunts. He looks over at the dog, whose attention is still riveted on the line of people standing in front of the cabin. "Zeus. Stand down." The dog relaxes and sits down to resume his scratching.

"You played him good, sis," Bassim whispers.

"Quiet," she whispers back. "We're not safe yet."

"Daddy," Meadow says, "is there anything to eat?"

He looks at her and sighs. "Yeah. Just jerked some venison. And picked some snap beans from the garden."

"Good," she nods. "But first we get to see—"

"Wait," her father snaps. "Quiet." It's then they all notice that Zeus is back up on his feet, peering off into the dark. "What is it, boy?"

Without another sound, the dog springs forward and disappears into the night. Meadow's father snatches up his rifle just as the darker figure of Hera follows her mate straight past them and into the darkness.

"Meadow," her father snaps. "Kill that lantern."

Without a sound, she reaches up and turns the knob. The hissing dies, followed by the light. They sit in the sudden darkness, eyes and ears straining, the only sound the steady rhythmic zinging of crickets calling back and forth across the forest. Then a sudden agonized scream, clearly from a human being.

"Get inside," Meadow's father says. "Now."

# ONE HUNDRED-TWELVE

Zeus moves silently though the nighttime forest, all senses sharp and attuned to the threat he can hear and smell approaching. He knows every noise these woods make, the sound and scent of every creature that lives here, and he knows that what's approaching doesn't belong.

He'd been momentarily confused when his master's offspring, the one who seemed to come in and out of the pack at will, had come up the path; she'd been in the company of those who weren't of the pack. But she'd shown no signs that she regarded them as a threat, so he'd given them provisional acceptance. Then there'd been the confrontation with his master that set him back on alert. But that had been resolved, with a resulting lessening of the tension and fear scent. Humans are confusing sometimes. There's nothing confusing, however, about what's coming toward the pack. The tension, the taste of metal on the air, all scream "threat." And Zeus, in his way, is comforted. No confusion now. He knows what to do with threats to his pack.

To his left, he can sense the dark shape of his mate moving through the woods a few feet away. He growls softly at her to warn her off; the pups will want feeding soon, and this is something he can do. She doesn't respond, but instead melts further into the darkness. Zeus can't worry about her now. The Others, the not-pack, are only a few feet away. There are three of them. Two smell like human males; the third trails behind, smelling of human female, but he gets a slight scent of Alpha from her. It confuses him again for a moment, especially since she seems to be walking on three legs, but he assesses the most obvious threat: the lead male. He's moving carefully, swinging his head from side to side, searching. Zeus crouches down, every muscle taut and quivering. He waits for the moment when the human is looking away, then leaps.

# ONE HUNDRED-THIRTEEN

The dark shape seems to come out of nowhere, a nightmare come to life, as it latches itself to Waller's right bicep and uses that grip to drag him to the ground. His shriek of pain and terror splits the night and silences the forest sounds.

Tench backpedals away from the thrashing pair on the ground, mouth open in a silent scream of terror. The animal lets go of Waller's arm, but only for the second or so it takes to lunge for his throat. He manages to throw his side up so that the beast ends up locking its teeth in the meat of his shoulder.

"Shoot it!" Waller screams. "Shoot the goddamn thing!"

Tench recovers his presence of mind and depresses the trigger enough to activate the laser sight, the red beam illuminating a pair of flailing bodies, one dark and furry, the other dressed in dark cloth. Rolling around the way they are, Tench hesitates, unable to get a clear shot. Suddenly, the animal yelps and thrashes away, growling and snapping at its own belly. Tench's light follows, and he sees the glisten of entrails as the dog writhes in its death agony. He moves the red dot of the laser slightly and ends the attack with a bullet through the dog's head. The animal flops to one side, twitches once, then lies still.

"Thanks for nothing, pal," Waller says hoarsely, wiping his bloody knife on his fatigue pants. "What the hell were you waiting for? That fucking wolf to rip my throat out?"

"I couldn't get a shot," Tench says defensively. "It all happened so fast."

"You're fucking useless." Waller advances on Tench, the knife held down by his side. Tench raises his weapon.

"Stop it, you two," Gray snaps. "We don't know what's still out here. We need to get back on track."

As if to illustrate her words, a tree trunk splinters a few feet away from Waller's head, followed by the flat crack of an automatic rifle. The three of them throw themselves on the ground, hugging the earth in the time-honored manner of people under fire.

A voice comes from the darkness. "This is sovereign territory. You are hereby ordered to get the fuck off my land."

# ONE HUNDRED-FOURTEEN

Jack Keller sits on a fallen tree beside the path, wondering if he's on a fool's errand. These woods are a labyrinth in the dark, a maze without walls waiting to lure an unwary traveler to wander aimlessly or to fall to his death in an unlooked-for ravine. The thing that keeps him going is that the children he's looking for may be as lost as he is. He's been proceeding on the assumption that the path he's been following will eventually lead him to the enclave Meadow's father has established here in the wilderness. That's what her map leads him to believe, at least. He takes the map from his back pocket and turns on his flashlight to examine it. As he traces the dotted line that marks the National Park trail, he sees where the borders narrow, with private property on either side. He knows that the land he's looking for is somewhere beyond those borders. What he doesn't know is how to find it in the dark. But he also doesn't know if he can wait for daybreak. The people who threaten the children he's sworn to protect are also in these woods, and he doesn't know where to find them, either.

Suddenly, from a short distance, he hears the sound of screaming, then a single gunshot. He's on his feet before he realizes he's up, shotgun at his shoulder, pointed at the sound. Well, that's one problem solved, he thinks. As the sound of another gunshot echoes through the forest, he recalls the words of a drill sergeant he'd had in boot camp: "If you get your sorry asses lost," the crusty old bastard had said, "and you will, just quick-march toward the sound of the guns. You can't go wrong."

The advice had been useless the first time he'd gotten lost in battle. But now, after all these years, it's taken on its own urgency.

Keller shoulders his weapon and heads for the sound of the guns.

# ONE HUNDRED-FIFTEEN

With the sound of the gunshot and the voice from the darkness, Waller momentarily forgets the pain in his arm and the bleeding holes that are still seeping blood from the attack dog's teeth. He drops prone, weapon ready and pointed toward the shout. Whoever shot at them must be an amateur, he knows. A professional wouldn't have given them a warning. Sure enough, as he adjusts his NVGs and looks toward the threat, he sees the blurred glow of a figure walking in their direction. The goggles, at this distance, don't give him much definition, but he can see the outline of a rifle held out before the softly luminous figure.

"You got eyes on him?" he hears Tench whisper.

"Affirmative." Waller draws a bead on the advancing rifleman. "On three. One. Two. Three."

He activates the laser sight and acquires the target. The red dots fix the target like a butterfly on a pair of pins. He feels the trigger break beneath his finger, hears the flat report of the rifle as it fires. He hears Tench's weapon do the same, and the figure drops with the boneless heaviness of one who's not getting up again. He manages to get one shot off as he falls, a sharp report that echoes through the night.

"Target down," Tench murmurs.

# ONE HUNDRED-SIXTEEN

On the day when John-Robert Troutman had renounced his 14th-Amendment Citizenship, discarded his Social Security number, and renounced the corporate shell created by the birth certificate designating him—in all capital letters—JOHN ROBERT TROUTMAN, he'd become a free and sovereign citizen—with the "citizen" designation being non-capitalized. But even as he felt that heady rush of freedom, he'd known this day would eventually come, the day when he'd have to assert his rights as a man against the false government. He'd even accepted that he might very well have to do it at gunpoint. He'd always thought it would be in a dispute over the hemp he grew under grow-lights in an equipment shed abandoned by the fake National Park Service, or maybe over the indebtedness to the fake IRS and to the banks, those entities that would mortgage his body to foreign governments. He'd cleverly nullified those false debts by signing the pertinent documents in red ink, but he knew that the rigged courts with their fringed Admiralty flags wouldn't accept that they had no power over a citizen beholden to no law but Anglo/American common law. It surprises him more than a little that the day they finally come for him, the fake government is chasing his daughter and the strange friends of hers he'd never met. But that just makes him feel that his cause is even more righteous. What's more American than defending one's land and one's family against a tyrannical overreaching government?

He snaps himself out of his reverie. From the sounds he's heard, whoever's out there has probably killed Zeus. Or Hera. Maybe both. Whichever it is, his dogs have done their jobs, and done them well. He'll give them a sendoff appropriate for heroes. But right now, he can't depend on the killers just giving up and going away. He's going to have to deal with them himself. For his little girl. For their freedom.

He moves forward, slowly, listening, waiting for the telltale sounds of movement in the woods he knows so well, waiting for the sign that lets him know where they are.

That sign comes unexpectedly, in the form of a red dot that appears on his arm and moves quickly to his chest. Before he can react, another red dot appears, next to the first one. He realizes too late what the dots mean. "Oh, shit…" is all he has time to get out before the bullets tear into his chest. His finger jerks on the trigger as he falls. He never hears the shot.

# ONE HUNDRED-SEVENTEEN

"What was that?" Meadow says as she hears the shots out in the darkness. "What's happening?"

"Wait here," Ben says. "I'll go find out."

"Ben, no," Meadow says. "You don't know who's out there. What's out there. And you're unarmed."

"I'm only unarmed," Ben snarls, "because your crazy father took my gun."

"You don't have to be." Alia kneels by her backpack, rummages for a moment, then pulls out a pistol. She holds it out, butt-first, to Ben. "It's my father's. Pull back the slide to cock it."

"No," Meadow whispers. She hates the eager look on Ben's face as he stares at the weapon. "Please, Ben."

He looks over at her, then does something she'd never imagined he'd do. He walks over to her and gently kisses her on the forehead. "I need to keep my family safe," he whispers. He walks over to Alia and holds out his hand. "Thanks."

She nods as he takes the gun. "Go with God, Ben."

He takes a deep breath and turns away. In a moment, he's lost in the darkness.

# ONE HUNDRED-EIGHTEEN

Marie smiles as she listens to Francis splashing in the bath, making sonar noises as he dives and surfaces the toy replica of The Beatles' Yellow Submarine she'd found in a junk shop. At five, the boy doesn't know The Beatles from the College of Cardinals, but she has hopes he'll learn to love the classics as much as she does.

The knock on the door makes her frown. She's not expecting company, and she hasn't been very happy with the unexpected company she's had lately. "Frank," she calls through the half-open bathroom door, "time to wind it up, buddy. It's bedtime."

"Five more minutes, Mom," he sings out.

She sighs. Whether it's getting up in the morning, playing on the computer, or getting out of the bath, "five more minutes" seems to have become his default response to any maternal request. She knows she needs to put her foot down. She knows she's going to do it soon. Real soon now. But it's been a long day. "Five minutes," she concedes, knowing that the next argument will be over whether it's really been five minutes. But at least it'll give her time to see who's at the door.

She looks through the peephole and frowns at who she sees. A petite, dark-haired woman is standing there, smiling ingratiatingly. "Can I help you?" Marie calls through the door.

"I hope so," the woman says. She has the barest trace of an accent, one Marie can't place. "I'm trying to find Jack Keller. I had heard he might be here."

The woman looks harmless enough, but Marie doesn't like the sound of this at all, given the course of recent events. "Jack's not here. I don't know when he'll be back."

The woman looks distressed. "It's very important that I reach him. It's," she looks down, "a personal matter."

The quick flare of jealousy Marie feels is immediately replaced by deeper suspicion. "And who are you again?"

"A friend," the dark-haired woman says. She smiles, and that smile makes Marie pull back from the peephole and lunge for the table in the entranceway where she's stashed her father's gun. But she's too late. She hears the back door being smashed in, and as she yanks the drawer open, there are two more women in the living room, carrying short-barreled submachine guns. Both of them are dark-haired and dark-eyed like the woman at the door, but one has an ugly scar down one side of her face and the other has a lacing of white scar tissue around her mouth. They have the barrels of the ugly little weapons pointed at Marie's head before she can draw out her father's pistol. The one with the scarred mouth walks to the door with quick, determined strides and pulls it open. The woman outside enters, that terrifying smile still on her face and a pistol held down beside one hip. "Good evening, Marie Jones," she says. "We need to discuss where we might find Jack Keller."

"I told you," she says, keeping her voice steady, "I don't know where he is."

"But I will bet that you have his number," the woman from the door never loses her smile. "You are his...what's the phrase Americans use? Baby mama?"

As if on cue, Francis's voice comes from the bathroom, querulous and uncertain. "Mom?"

The two who came in through the back door turn toward the sound, reminding Marie of hunting dogs on a scent. The woman from the door never takes her eyes off Marie. "Sisters," she says. "Go fetch the boy." She turns to Marie. "And you. Call Jack Keller."

# ONE HUNDRED-NINETEEN

Ben Jones is as frightened as he's ever been. It's man's most primitive fear; alone in the woods, in the dark, with God knows how many things out there who mean him harm. And all he has to defend himself and the people who depend on him is a weapon he barely knows how to use. He doesn't know if he can bring himself to pull the trigger on another human being. If recent experience has taught him anything, it's that he's no Jack Keller. Even when he most needs to be.

He takes a few steps, stops, and listens. All he can hear is the chaotic din of what sounds like a million insects. He walks forward again, into a cloud of gnats, a couple of which he quickly inhales. He flails at the swarming bugs, gagging and coughing. *Shit.* So much for being stealthy. When he recovers, he crouches down and listens some more. He thinks he can hear something moving out there in the dark, but the slight breeze stirring the trees may be playing tricks with his hearing. The movement of the leaves in the sparse moonlight filtering through from the treetops could be doing the same with his vision. Still, it's the only thing he has to go on, so he stands up and starts moving toward what he thinks he heard.

"Hold it right there, kid." The voice comes from behind him. As he turns, he sees a bright red dot appear on his chest. He stops turning and his knees begin to shake as he realizes that it's a laser. "You got another dot like that on your back," the voice says. "Drop the gun, step away, and get your hands up."

For the second time in a night, Ben has a weapon taken away from him. This time, it's by the short woman he saw at his mother's farm. She walks forward, grimacing as if every step pains her, and picks the gun up off the ground. A man appears out of the darkness behind her, a rifle pointed at him. He can see the scarlet glitter of the laser sight, and he begins to shake. The woman examines the weapon. "9 Millimeter Makarov," she says, then looks at Ben. "Where did you get this?"

"I…I bought it."

"You're lying." She walks closer, the gun held in front of her. "This is the model sold by the Russians to the Iraqi army and security forces before the war."

Ben can't meet her eyes. "I didn't know that."

In answer, she points the gun downward at his left foot and pulls the trigger.

# ONE HUNDRED-TWENTY

Keller hears another gunshot, followed immediately by another agonized scream. The forest goes quiet for a few seconds, shocked into fearful silence by the sudden intrusion. As the sounds of the night slowly begin to ramp up again, Keller breaks into a run, headed for the sound, and nearly falls over the body lying across the trail. He crouches down, noting the long beard and the tattoo on the arm, the simple word FREE crudely inked on the bicep. John-Robert Troutman, Keller presumes. He sees the AR-15 lying a few feet away and picks it up, slinging the shotgun on his back as a backup. Another thought makes him turn back and quickly rifle through the pockets of the man's camo pants, coming out with a pair of extra magazines. Weapons ready, blood pounding in his ears, he moves through the night, hunting.

# ONE HUNDRED-TWENTY-ONE

Ben lies crumpled on the ground, sobbing.

The woman stands over him, a look of disgust on her lined, ugly face. "Get up," she says. "You're not even hit. But the next one *will* be in your foot. Or a hand. And then, if you continue this silly resistance, the other foot, or hand. And so on. Now, tell me, young man, where are the Iraqis? Alia and Bassim Khoury?"

Ben sits up, hugging his knees to his chest, his nose running and tears streaming down his face. He tries to say something, but chokes on the words. She sighs and points the gun again, this time directly at Ben's left foot. He looks up at the two gunmen. He can't see their eyes behind the night vision goggles, but he can see them grinning. He closes his own eyes and waits for the pain he knows is coming.

From close by, a female voice calls out. "*Ben!*"

The woman's head snaps around to look for the source of the voice. She turns back to him and smiles. "You can thank your friend for saving you a great deal of pain." She nods to the gunmen. "Gag him. We don't want him warning anyone."

# ONE HUNDRED-TWENTY-TWO

Keller stops at the sound of the new voice. It sounds like Meadow, but he can't be sure. But where she is, the others are likely to be also. He changes his course to move toward the sound. She calls again. "Ben! Are you alright?"

Keller realizes that if he can hear her, the others can, too. He slows, then stops, listening. He hears movement to his left and drops prone to the ground. In a moment, he sees a group of people moving up the path. The one in front has his hands behind his back, possibly bound. His head is down, looking at the path in front. Keller thinks it might be Ben, but he's not sure. Behind the leader are two figures with guns pointed at his back. He can't make out those figures, either, but he has a pretty good idea who they are. That assessment is only confirmed by what he can make out of the last person in line, a short female figure leaning heavily on a cane. He can hear her labored breathing from where he lies. She's struggling in the rough terrain, but Keller knows that doesn't negate her threat. When the group passes, Keller rolls to his back and pulls out his cell phone. He's not surprised to find that there's no signal. These mountains may be old and worn down by the slow grind of years, but anyone roaming in them is on their own. Keller rolls over, stands up, and silently follows the column moving through the woods.

# ONE HUNDRED-TWENTY-THREE

Alia sees Meadow put her hand to her mouth and let out a low moan as Ben enters the clearing, mouth gagged, hands bound behind him, followed by a pair of men with rifles. It's the person who brings up the rear of the column, however, that most concerns her. The woman leaning over her cane, exhausted as she appears to be, is the one in charge. She's the one Alia is going to have to deal with. Neither she nor her family has ever been devout, but she bows her head now. *Allah, the beneficent, the merciful, protect us now from evil.*

The woman catches sight of Alia and her face lights up in a smile that chills her with doubt that her prayer has been heard. "Miss Khoury," the woman says. "At last our charade comes to an end."

Alia stands up, trying to keep her voice steady. "I don't know what you're talking about."

The woman nods sadly. "I know, little one. You're caught up in the madness your father started. But," she shrugs, "here we are."

"Whatever your problems with my father," Alia says, "they don't have anything to do with me or my brother."

The short woman raises an eyebrow. "Nothing? How about the money your father stole?"

Alia sags. "The money. Always with you Americans it is the money."

The woman shrugs. "As they say, it makes the world go 'round.

And, lest we forget, this was money stolen from the United States of America."

"So you say," Alia says. "But I don't care about that, either. All I want is for my brother and I…and our friends to be left alone."

"Yes. Well." The woman smiles with the cold friendliness of a bureaucrat telling a supplicant nothing can be done. "All information has to be corroborated. Especially if it's obtained under duress."

Alia blinks in confusion. "I don't understand."

"It means," the woman says, "that whatever you tell me would need to be confirmed." That cold smile never wavers. "Did you know that the ancient Romans would never accept a confession that wasn't the result of torture? They believed in two things as infallible guarantors of truth. The first was drunkenness, which lead to their joke about *in vino veritas*. The other," she gestures to the man standing behind Ben, "is pain." She smiles with a terrible whimsy. "Since we don't have any wine present, we can only verify what you tell us with pain. Your boyfriend's pain, for one thing. Or perhaps your brother's."

*He's not my boyfriend*, Alia wants to scream, but she knows it won't matter. They just want to hurt someone. Anyone.

One of the men takes off his night vision goggles and re-lights the Coleman lantern, and the sudden brightness has everyone blinking.

The other man whips off his own goggles, then grabs Ben by the back of the head, twisting his hand cruelly in the boy's hair. He uses the grip to propel Ben toward the rain barrel. "Come on, tough guy," he snarls. "You didn't want to talk out there in the woods. Let's see how talkative you get after a quick dip."

"Stop," Alia begs.

The woman shrugs. "Count your blessings. It's just water. Your father died much harder."

"My…my…"

"Oh, didn't I tell you? He, too, was stubborn about where the money was. So, he died screaming." She smiles like a fond aunt. "But you can comfort yourself knowing that he didn't give up you or your brother." She nods at the man holding Ben. "Go ahead."

303

# ONE HUNDRED-TWENTY-FOUR

Keller sees the sudden flare of light ahead and slows down, raising the gun to take aim. He can see the figures in the clearing ahead, but he can't make out who's who until he gets closer. What he sees then makes him grit his teeth in frustration. Alia, Bassim, and Meadow are standing in a line, between him and the men with the rifles. The woman he'd met in the church, apparently the one in charge, is standing to one side, talking, but she's not the main threat. As Keller begins to move sideways, searching for a better shot, he hears a soft growl behind him. He turns slowly, trying not to make a sound.

A huge brindle-colored mastiff is crouched a few feet away, tense and quivering as if about to spring. A shiver runs down Keller's back, the ancient fear of man confronted by a large angry carnivore in the dark. The dog gazes at him, then looks toward the clearing, then back at him, assessing the threats. Keller starts to raise the rifle, then stops, realizing that that might very well move him up on the list. He doesn't want to shoot the animal, especially since that would give away his position prematurely. The two of them, man and dog, stand frozen in place, stalemated.

# ONE HUNDRED-TWENTY-FIVE

"No," Meadow cries out, and tries to run toward where the smaller of the two men is dragging Ben to the rain barrel.

The other man has a sickening grin on his face as he steps between them and drives the butt of his rifle into her stomach. She cries out and falls to the ground, gasping for breath. The man stands over her, laughing. "Business before pleasure, little girl," he sneers down at her. "But when we get done here, you and me are gonna have some…" It's the last thing he says before a monstrous black shape comes streaking out of the forest, into the light, and leaps onto his back. The man screams as Hera's jaws close on the back of his neck and the weight of her body bears him to the ground. He barely has time for one more scream before she whips her great head from side to side and shakes him like a rag doll. She's gotten a better hold on this prey than her mate; The sound of bones breaking fills the clearing, and the man falls silent. Meadow gets to her knees as the dog releases her limp prey and turns to the other gunman. That one's shoved Ben to his knees and picked his own rifle back up. Hera advances toward him, snarling, hackles raised, her fangs glistening red with blood.

"*No!*" Meadow screams again, and lunges toward the dog as he takes aim.

*\*\*\**

Meadow's scream apparently makes up the dog's mind for her. For a huge animal, she moves blindingly fast. She's past Keller and into the clearing before he truly comprehends what's happening. He turns and follows. The line has broken up, but now the dog is blocking his shot as she springs onto the gunman he sees standing over Meadow. He swings his rifle around in time to see the other man taking aim at the dog. Meadow throws herself on the animal's back as Keller and the rifleman fire at the same time.

###

Alia grabs her brother and pulls him with her as the dog attacks the man standing over Meadow. Her first reaction is to turn and flee, but as the second gunman raises his rifle, she sees the woman holding her father's pistol raise it and point it at the dog and Meadow. A flash of rage roars through her. *I have had enough*, she thinks. *I have had ENOUGH*. She crosses the clearing in three quick strides, barely registering the gunshot from the darkness and the sound of bullet meeting bone as the other gunman falls backward, his rifle discharging its second and third shots into the night sky. The woman turns, a shocked look on her face, as Alia slugs her across the jaw, putting all of her fear and anger behind the punch. The woman cries out and falls to the ground, the gun slipping from her slack fingers. Alia reaches down and picks up the weapon, bringing it to bear on the woman on the ground. She sits up, a dazed expression on her face, rubbing at her jaw.

"Stay down, *bitch*," Alia snaps.

The woman scowls up at her. "You don't have it in you, child."

"Don't I?" Alia pulls the trigger and fires a round into the dirt beside the woman, who flinches away and holds up her hands in a gesture of surrender. "Tell me why I shouldn't kill you right now."

"Because you're not a murderer," Jack Keller says as he steps into the light. "She's unarmed. She's helpless. Powerless." The woman glares at Keller as he goes on. "I shot a man in that situation once. I thought I was doing the right thing." He looks over to where Bassim is using a knife taken from the dead man's belt to free Ben from his bonds. "I thought I was doing the right thing," he repeats. "But that's haunted me

306

ever since. It destroyed a big part of me. Of my life. It'll do the same thing to you if you take her life."

Ben looks away.

"I'm sorry," Keller tells him.

"Um, guys?" Bassim says.

Keller looks and sees Meadow's still on the ground, her face white. She's holding her side. The dog is licking nervously at her face, but then she glances off toward the house, trots off and wiggles her way under the porch. They can here the yipping and whining from beneath the house.

"I just wanted to see the puppies," Meadow whispers. Keller kneels next to her, gently pulling her hand away. Her side is red with blood, the stain spreading. She doesn't seem to notice. "I wanted to see the puppies," she says again, clearly in shock.

Keller looks up. "She's hit." He tries to pull the edge of her t-shirt up to look at the wound. She makes an irritated whining sound and shoves it back down. "I need to look at the wound, kid," Keller says.

Her eyes can't seem to focus. "Don't call me kid," she says weakly, but she lets him look. "Meadow," he says. "Does your dad have a first aid kit? Bandages? Anything?"

"F'course," she mumbles. "In th' house. By th' door." She's starting to turn gray and her eyes flutter.

Keller smacks her lightly on the cheek to wake her up. "Come on, Meadow. Stay with me."

Bassim appears at his side with a large green nylon rucksack with a red cross stenciled on it. Keller opens it to find a fully equipped combat first aid kit. Troutman had truly been ready for anything, and Keller's glad of it. He quickly applies a field dressing, wrapping the bandage completely around Meadow's small frame. Some of the shock is wearing off, and she begins to whimper with each movement. "I know it hurts," Keller says. "But it looks like a through-and-through wound. You're going to be fine if we can control the bleeding. Just stay awake, okay?"

She just nods, her teeth gritted.

Keller looks up to see Bassim, Ben, and Alia standing over him, looking down with horrified expressions. He looks beyond them. Iris Gray has disappeared. "Where's Gray?"

"Who?" Bassim says.

"The woman. Iris Gray."

Alia looks around. "Oh no."

Ben picks up the rifle dropped by the dead man. "I'll go after her."

"No," Keller says. "She's alone and unarmed. Any luck at all, she'll get eaten by a bear. Right now, we need to get Meadow to a hospital. Find an ax and cut two saplings, about six feet tall. Someone get a blanket. We'll make a stretcher."

They stand there looking at him for a moment, until Ben speaks up. "Come on. Let's do this."

# ONE HUNDRED-TWENTY-SIX

Iris Gray moves as quickly as she can through the darkened woods, which is not fast at all, especially since she dropped her cane in her haste to get away.

She was up as soon as the stupid Arab girl took her eyes off her, headed back in the direction from which they'd come. At least she thinks so. She tries to get her bearings by looking at the sky, but clouds have begun to roll in and she can see neither moon nor stars. She also doesn't see the ravine yawning in front of her until she trips over a stone at the edge and goes tumbling head over heels, down the nearly vertical slope, crashing through the brush until her head finally smacks against a granite outcrop at the bottom.

When she recovers her senses, she's lying in a shallow stream. Her left leg is screaming with pain. She feels a drop of rain strike her face and tries to sit up. A trickle of blood down her face goes into her eyes and she tries to wipe it away. The rain begins to fall faster, and that helps clear her vision. She looks down at her leg and nearly throws up when she sees the angle at which it's bent. A bolt of lightning strikes nearby, lighting up the night and revealing the gleam of bone poking from beneath the skin. The rain is coming down in torrents now, rivulets cascading down the steep walls of the ravine. She realizes that the stream in which she's lying is beginning to rise.

"Well, shit," she mutters.

# ONE HUNDRED-TWENTY-SEVEN

"Please give me my son back," Marie tries to keep the fear and rage from her voice.

One of the sisters, the one with the scars around her mouth, is holding Francis on her lap. The boy is clearly uncomfortable; he's squirming and fussing, trying to get down, but the woman holds him fast, smiling horribly, and whispering what Marie assumes are endearments in her native tongue.

"You must forgive my sister," the leader says. "She cannot have children of her own anymore." She gives Marie a sad smile that manages to be as terrifying as that of the woman holding Francis. "The one child she did have was the result of a gang rape she suffered at the hands of Russian soldiers. How could he keep such a child? How could she even carry the seed of such monsters to birth?" The leader sighs. "Still, she agonized. And some choices were taken away. Our country was destroyed by the Russians, and if there was a doctor, they were treating wounded. Who cared about a poor raped Muslim girl? Except her family." She walks over and stands beside the woman holding Francis, putting an affectionate hand on her shoulder. The mute woman looks up, puts her hand on her sister's, then pats Francis on the head and lets him down. He runs immediately to Marie, who gathers him up in a protective hug.

310

The leader is still smiling, running a hand through her mutilated sister's thick hair, as she goes on with her story. "On the day the child was born, the three of us took it to the river. It was a boy. We all held it, and kissed it, then we gave it to Marina and watched as she held it beneath the water until it was dead."

Marie clutches her son tighter as the leader lets her sister's hand go and crosses the room to look down at them with cold eyes. "So, do not think that because we are women, we will not do what needs to be done." She nods at Francis, and the threat is unmistakable. "Call Keller again."

# ONE HUNDRED-TWENTY-EIGHT

The storm breaks as they make their way down the twisted uneven path towards the trailhead. Keller takes the lead with his commandeered rifle, while Bassim and Ben carry the stretcher holding Meadow. Alia brings up the rear, carrying her father's pistol, looking back over her shoulder nervously. Keller's stripped the bodies of both gunmen of weapons. The blood-stained tactical vest he took from the one mauled by Hera bulges with extra magazines and flash-bang grenades.

Bassim and Ben keep slipping in the mud bog the trail is turning into, but they manage not to drop the stretcher. Finally, soaked to the skin and near exhaustion, they reach the parking lot. "Put her in the back of my car," Keller tells the boys. "I'll see if I can find the nearest hospital." He pulls out his phone and frowns at what he sees. Five messages, all from Marie. He presses the button to dial back.

She picks up on the first ring. "Jack," she says.

He immediately picks up on the tone on her voice. "What's wrong?"

Another female voice comes on the line. "Jack Keller?"

"Who the hell are you? Where's Marie?"

"I will make you an offer," the woman says, with just a trace of accent. "Sheikh Al-Mansour wants his money. We have your woman and son. We will trade them for what we want."

"What money?"

The answer is a cry of pain in the background, from Marie. "My sister has just broken one of your woman's fingers. If you continue to play stupid, we will break them all. Then we will begin on her with the knife. In front of your son. Do we understand one another?"

Keller bows his head, feeling the tide of black rage bubbling up inside him.

"I said, do you understand?"

"Perfectly," he says.

"Good. If you do not know where the money is, then find the Khoury children. You can make them tell. Or bring them to us and we will find out. But if you try to disobey or trick us—"

"I won't. I'll get you the money."

"—I say, if you try that, then your woman and son will not be dead when you find them. But you will wish they were when you see what we leave behind." The woman on the other end hangs up.

Keller closes his eyes, resisting the urge to scream and throw the cell phone into the night.

"The money."

Keller looks up to see Alia standing before him. Her clothing is soaked and clinging to her, but she doesn't seem to notice the rain. She puts a hand on Keller's shoulder. "I heard your side. What about the money?"

Keller can barely get the words out. "Someone has Marie. And my son. They're going to hurt them if I don't get the money from you and give it to them."

She nods. "Then you must give it to them."

He shakes his head. "I can't. I can't ask you to—"

"Jack," she says gently, "what has that money brought us but pain?" Her voice breaks as she says, "My father is dead because of it." She gestures up the trail. "Three men are dead in those woods because of it. And I don't know how many more." She shakes her head. "That money is a curse. I hope it brings as much sorrow to these people, whoever they are, as it has to us."

"What's going on?" Bassim steps up to stand by his sister.

"Change in plans," Keller says. "The three of you take my car. Get Meadow to a hospital, as fast as you can. I'm going to go get Marie."

"With the money," Alia tells him.

Bassim blinks. "Wait, our money? To Officer Jones? Why?" By now, Ben has joined them.

Keller doesn't have time to dissemble. "Someone else has come for the money. I don't know who they are, but they mentioned the name Al-Mansour." He sees Alia flinch visibly. "You know the name?"

She nods and looks down. "He was...he worked with my father. In Iraq."

"Well, he thinks he's entitled to the money. And he's sent people to take Marie and Francis. To trade for them."

"What?" Ben shouts.

"So, we are giving them the money." Alia's voice is calm, but she's visibly trembling. "If that's all they want."

"Like hell," Bassim shakes his head. "That's our money."

She turns on him savagely. "And it is worth more lives? Officer Jones, who's never been anything kind to us? Francis, that sweet little boy? You'd have them die? For money?"

He looks down. "No." He looks back up at Keller. "Sorry."

Keller nods. "It's hidden somewhere? Like maybe an abandoned store?"

She looks surprised.

"Meadow had the store marked on her map," Keller explains.

She nods. "Meadow has the key. I'll get it for you."

"Okay." Keller turns to Ben. "Take Meadow in my car. Alia will ride with me in my truck. When we get there, I'll load up and take the money to them while the three of you get Meadow to the nearest emergency room."

"I'm going with you," Ben says.

Keller shakes his head. "No way."

"That's my mother and my little brother, Jack."

"Yeah. And you're fifteen. You'll just be in my way."

Ben looks furious as he turns away and stomps off in the direction of the Crown Vic.

Keller looks at Alia and Bassim. "Get moving."

314

# ONE HUNDRED-TWENTY-NINE

"Hang in there, Meds." Ben pulls in behind the truck as it stops in front of the abandoned store. He sees Alia jump from the passenger side, with Keller following. He turns and looks into the backseat, where Bassim is sitting with Meadow's feel on his lap. "How is she?"

"I don't know, man. I'm not a doctor. Still breathing. So that's good."

The passenger door opens and Alia slips in. "Come on," she says. "I looked up where the hospital is on Jack's cell phone."

Ben opens the door. "Can you drive?"

"Why?"

Ben starts to get out.

She grabs his arm. "Ben, no. He said you couldn't come with him."

"I have to, Alia. That's my mom and my little brother those people have."

"Please, Ben." Her eyes are wide and he can see tears glistening in them in the dim glow of the interior. "I need you to help us. And I don't know what I'd do if anything happened to you."

He sees Keller dragging one of the chests they'd hidden earlier to the truck. He pulls away from Alia and goes to help. The earlier downpour had subsided to a few drops here and there and the clouds above are beginning to break up. He grabs the other end of the chest and helps Keller muscle it into the bed of the truck.

"Thanks," Keller says. "But you're still not coming with me."

"Jack…"

"If we stand here arguing and your friend bleeds out as a result, how are you going to feel?"

Ben stands, hands clenching and unclenching with fury, then turns and runs back to the car.

"Five miles," Alia says, "and take a right." Ben just nods and steps hard on the gas, gravel shooting from beneath the spinning wheels.

When they reach the turn, Ben glances in the rearview mirror. He sees the headlights of Keller's truck, then the big vehicle roars by as Ben turns back to the road in front of him. He wants to bang his head on the steering wheel until everything goes dark. He knows Keller's right. He knows his recent performance proves he's not ready for the type of fight that Keller seems to take to as if a war zone was his natural habitat. Still, he can't help but feel like a coward, letting someone else go to help his family. The thoughts go around and around in his head, and he grips the wheel tightly, barely hearing Alia's tersely delivered directions. Finally, they pull into the brightly lit drive of a hospital, beneath a large red glowing sign that says EMERGENCY. The car's barely stopped before Alia is out of the door and running for the glass front doors. Ben gets out and goes around to the side to help Bassim with Meadow.

As they're easing her out of the car, the doors crash open and a pair of men in blue scrubs run out, a large wheeled gurney between them. "Don't move her," one shouts. "We'll take her."

Bassim lowers the limp girl back onto the car seat.

The men shoulder Ben aside, firmly but not roughly, and gently lift Meadow onto the gurney. One of them, a dark-skinned black man, turns to Alia, who's followed them out at a run. "Go back inside, ma'am," he says. "Give the girl up front her information." They begin rolling Meadow into the hospital.

Ben's heart feels like it's in his throat because of how small and frail she looks. "Will she be all right?" he calls.

"If God wills it," the man calls back.

Bassim looks surprised. "He's a Muslim?"

"Maybe," Ben says, "but it's the kind of thing people say a lot around here." He slams the passenger door and walks around the car to the driver's side. "I'll call later," he says. "Go on in and help Meadow." He gets behind the wheel.

"Wait," Alia says, "Where are you going?"

He doesn't answer. He presses the accelerator of his grandfather's old car and the tires squeal on the pavement as he pulls away. Headed for home.

# ONE HUNDRED-THIRTY

Keller pulls into the entrance to the driveway and stops. He can see the lights of the farmhouse, yellow and welcoming in the night, as if everything's normal. He doesn't know how many people are waiting inside. The woman on the phone had mentioned her sisters, but that could mean anything from two other women to an entire crazy death cult. He's got the shotgun and the automatic rifle he'd taken from the gunman at Troutman's. With a start, he realizes he left the other rifle with Ben. Well, it's not like he has more than two hands. He'd like to have had Alia's father's pistol, not to mention Marie's. But he'd been in a hurry, and, he admits to himself, thoroughly taken over by rage. He takes a deep breath. He can't make any more mistakes like that. And, truth be told, one more gun might not make that much difference. He's going to have to go in unarmed, if he doesn't want whoever's in there to murder Marie and his son.

He sees the door of the farmhouse open, with two figures silhouetted in the light, one behind the other. *That's how confident these people are*, Keller thinks. *They know I can't take the shot. Well, maybe I can use that cockiness against them.* He drives the truck slowly down the long drive. As he gets closer, the two figures in the doorway resolve into Marie and a dark-haired woman whose face he can make out over Marie's shoulder, peering intently at the truck. The woman

318

behind Marie is holding a pistol. The pistol is pointed at Marie's head. Keller's hands twist on the wheel as if he's got them wrapped around the dark-haired woman's neck. He pulls the truck to a stop in the dirt just in front of the porch and kills the engine.

"Hands where I can see them," the woman holding the gun calls out.

Keller raises his hands and displays them, palms out.

The dark-haired woman steps to one side, pulling Marie with her, as another woman, shorter, but with the same dark hair and slender build, slides out between them and the doorframe. She's carrying a stubby-barreled submachine gun. In a few quick strides, she's at the door of the truck, pulling at the door handle with one hand while pointing the gun at his head with the other. Keller sizes her up. The scar on her face tells him that she's not a stranger to violence. Still, she's not a big woman, and she's made the common mistake of getting too close. He could knock her down with the door. Jump her. Take the gun away. Come up shooting. But that would just get Marie killed, and he doesn't know where Francis is. There's at least one more player here, maybe more, and he needs to know who that is. The woman with the scar knows that, and that's why she feels comfortable being this close.

Keller's anger is still there, his old familiar companion, but he feels himself floating above it, buoyed up by it over the despair that threatens to drown him, even as he's coldly calculating angles and chances of taking out his targets. It's a place that's become too familiar to him, but he puts the feeling of wrongness that shivers through him aside, all his faculties devoted to getting the people he loves out of this.

He steps down from the truck, hands up. "I've got the money," he says. "It's in the back of the truck."

The woman holding the gun nods. "Come in, then." She steps aside, still holding the gun at Marie's head.

He sidles past them, turning to look at Marie. He looks down at her hand and sees the pinky of her left hand is crudely splinted with what looks like surgical tape and broken Popsicle sticks. "You okay?"

"I've been better," she says grimly.

He just nods and looks around the room. "Where's Francis?"

"In his room," Marie says. "They drugged him. He's out."

A third woman steps into the living room, also carrying a submachine gun. He takes a look at her and sees the network of scars around her mouth. She looks back at him and smiles.

The woman in the doorway speaks. "It seems that Liza has taken quite a shine to your little boy. So don't worry. He will have a good home."

As the implication of what she's saying sinks in, Marie's face goes white. "No," she whispers.

"Marie," Keller says. She doesn't seem to hear him at first. "Marie," he says, still quiet, but more firmly. She looks back at him, her face slack with despair. "Look at me," he orders. It takes her a moment, but after a few long seconds, she manages to focus her eyes on him. "Three of them?" he says.

She looks confused for a second, then nods. "Three."

He nods toward the one standing by the hallway door, the one with the scarred mouth. He doesn't speak. She looks from him to the woman, then back at him. "Do you trust me?" he says.

This time she nods without hesitation. "I do."

The woman with the scarred mouth frowns, then waves her hand at the woman in the doorway, who's looking out into the driveway and doesn't notice. The woman in the doorway calls out something to the woman still outside. Keller doesn't know the language, but it sounds like a question, and he thinks he knows what it is. He's moving before the answer comes in a bright flash and a loud bang, followed by a scream of pain as the flash-bang grenade Keller wired into the lid of the footlocker goes off directly in the face of the woman who's just pried it open.

# ONE HUNDRED-THIRTY-ONE

Keller's moving as soon as he hears the report of the stun grenade, his body aimed straight at the woman in the doorway who's standing, looking slack-jawed at the sight of her sister rolling on the ground, howling like an animal and clawing at her face. The flash-bang is designed to stun, not kill or injure, but Keller figures the magnesium/potassium perchlorate core of the weapon must have gone off directly in the woman's face as she leaned over to examine the treasure chest she'd just pried open. He has to give her sister credit; she recovers from the shock of what's happened within a half second and is turning to bring her weapon to point at the people in the house when Keller tackles her, wrapping her up and bringing them both crashing to the wooden floor of the porch. The barrel of the machine gun rides up, blasting chips of wood from the ceiling. Keller grabs the body of the weapon and pushes it back over the woman's head, another quick burst stuttering into the darkness. She writhes like a serpent beneath him, managing to squirm clear and dump him onto the porch. He manages to maintain enough grip on the gun to tear it from her grasp and toss it away, skittering across the porch. That doesn't stop his assailant; she leaps on top of him, her fists a blur as she pounds at his face. He manages to get his forearms up to block some of the blows, but she's almost superhumanly fast. At least a half dozen punches connect with his face. He feels his nose break under one punch, and the next one coming directly behind it onto the broken bone sends a lightning bolt of agony through his head that leaves him temporarily stunned. The punches stop coming for a moment, and Keller recovers enough of his faculties to see that the woman straddling him has pulled out a long-bladed knife and is holding it in both hands, her eyes filled with triumph as she prepares to plunge the blade into his throat. *Fucking hell*, he thinks, *I'm about to be killed by a girl half my size. How the fuck did that happen?*

The sharp report of a gunshot. The sound of shattering glass. The sudden turn of the woman's gaze away from him. In his dazed state, Keller has trouble putting all those things together. Then the woman's weight is off him. He slowly rises to a sitting position and turns his head.

Ben Jones is standing a few feet away, a pistol clenched in his hands, pointed at the woman who'd been about to plunge the knife into Keller. His hands are shaking so badly that Keller can see it, even through the haze of pain.

"Ben," he croaks.

Ben ignores him. "Put the knife down." The trembling in his voice matches the shaking of his hands.

The woman smiles as if she's been given an unexpected present. "Please, boy," she says. "You missed once. You should not have missed when coming against such as us." She calls back over her shoulder. Keller doesn't know what she's saying, but the lack of answer makes her look uncertain for the first time. She dares a look back over her shoulder. There's no one there.

Keller slowly gets to his feet. "Your sister's not there. Don't know where she's gone, but right now, lady, it looks like you're outnumbered. Maybe we should just end this now."

The uncertain look vanishes, replaced by a wolfish smile. "I don't agree. I don't think the boy will be able to kill me. At least before I kill you. And then I will take the gun he doesn't know how to use and make him watch while I gut his mother and little brother like pigs."

322

She advances on Keller, smiling that ghastly smile, as she shifts the knife from hand to hand. Keller knows the machine gun is lying on the porch behind him. He could turn and dive for it, but the woman, fast as she is, would be on him like a cat. His only hope for survival is for Ben to take and make the shot. To become a killer. Before he's fully considered that, he's charging at the knife.

The woman's smile widens, then disappears in a spray of blood as the round Ben Jones fires takes her lower jaw off. She stops, stunned, and turns toward Ben, her ruined face spraying blood onto the wooden slats of the porch. His next shot misses again, but the third one strikes home, hitting the woman square of the middle of her forehead and knocking her backward against the side of the house. She stands for a moment, then slides to the floor of the porch.

Keller bows his head. He hears the boy walk up onto the porch next to him and raises his gaze.

Ben is looking at the woman he's just killed. His face is calm, and that calm breaks Keller's heart. He takes a deep breath, squares his shoulders, looks around. "Hey," he says, nodding to the truck. "There's a fire over there."

Keller turns to look. The flashbang explosion has ignited a fire inside the footlocker full of money. He sees the glow of the flames, and from time to time, a piece of burning paper flutters out, the flame sputtering and dying on the wind.

"Let it burn," Keller says. "Just let it burn."

Ben nods, then turns to Keller. "Where's my mom?"

# ONE HUNDRED-THIRTY-TWO

The moment the woman Marie's come to call The Silent One runs to the door to see what's happened to her sister, Marie is moving. She rushes into Francis's bedroom, scoops the boy's recumbent form off his bed, and throws him over her shoulder, moving quickly out through the living room. She's into the kitchen and pulling on the back door when she hears the woman with the scarred mouth scream in anger. Marie sobs in terror, yanks the door open, and plunges into the darkness. She runs through the small backyard, then down the hillside, headed for the old barn. Behind her, she hears the inarticulate scream of the woman, then a burst of gunfire that whistles off into nowhere but makes the back muscles between her shoulder blades clench up in anticipation of the bullet. She reaches the barn and stops to look behind her. A dark figure is coming behind her, rushing through the night like a vengeful spirit. Marie sobs and pulls the door open.

Inside, she can barely see her hand in front of her face, but she knows her way around the old shed well enough to find her way in the dark. She makes her way to the far corner, the way made easier now that her father's old car isn't stored here. She lays Francis in the soft earth at the far end of the open space, placing a soft kiss on his forehead before standing up. It's pitch dark inside the barn, but she manages to work her way back across the dirt floor, the rich smell of the packed earth filling her nostrils. When she reaches the other side, her vision has acclimated somewhat to the darkness, but she has to grope along the wall where the tools are hung until she finds the one she needs. Hefting the ax in both hands, she waits for the woman pursuing her.

She doesn't have long to wait. There's a sound of soft footsteps outside of the barn, then a heavy boot kicks the door open. Marie waits, barely breathing, as she feels more than sees a figure enter the darkened doorway. Her hands tense on the handle of the ax.

From across the open space of the barn, Marie hears her son stir. He makes a small, querulous sound, then falls silent. But it's enough that the dark figure turns in that direction. That's when Marie swings.

# ONE HUNDRED-THIRTY-THREE

Keller hears the screams from all the way up the hill, howls of agony mixed with shrieks of rage. "Stay here," he orders Ben.

"That's my mom," Ben says. "No way am I staying here."

Keller can't argue with that. The two of them check the house, find it empty. Without speaking, they move down the hill. The night is waning, and light is rising in the east, enough to see Marie trudging up the hill, her son on her shoulder, an ax dangling from one hand. As they draw closer, Keller can see that the ax is smeared with blood and gray matter. Marie raises her eyes to his, then looks at Ben, who's still holding the pistol down by his side. The look in his eyes makes her knees sag. "Ben," she says. "Did you…?" Her voice trails off into a sob.

"Mom," Ben says. "Let me take Frank. And put the ax down. They're done."

"Done." She says the word as if it has no meaning to her. She looks to Ben. "What did you do, Ben?"

"He saved my life," Keller says, "and most likely yours and Frank's, too."

She turns to him, eyes wild with grief. "I didn't ask you, Keller. Ben," she says, her voice cracking with anguish, "did you kill someone?"

He nods. "Yeah. I did, Mom. I'm sorry. I thought it was what I had to…" He's interrupted by the sight of her falling to her knees, her wail of anguish echoing across the hillside in the rising dawn. Ben steps forward, gently taking Francis from her.

Ben turns to Keller. "You think you can get her to the house? I kind of have my hands full."

Keller nods "Yeah. I'll handle the 9-1-1 call, too. Let me do the talking, okay?" He grimaces. "I've done this more than you."

Ben nods. "That makes sense." He shifts Francis's weight on his shoulder and turns to head back up the hill.

"Ben," Keller calls after him. Ben turns and looks at him steadily. "Thanks," Keller says.

Ben doesn't answer, except to nod and walk up the hill toward the house, his brother sleeping on his shoulder, the nine-millimeter pistol looking more natural than it should in his free hand.

# ONE HUNDRED-THIRTY-FOUR

"So let's review," Addison McCaskill smiles sweetly at the assistant district attorney. "Someone broke into my client's house and planted explosives. Explosives that killed poor Brandon Ochs, bless his dumb little redneck heart." She shakes her head. "Sorry. That was unkind. But are you seriously suggesting Keller booby-trapped his own house? After the evidence that he was attacked and had to kill two so-called 'contractors,' one, who I might add, put himself out there on the Dark Web as a mercenary explosives expert?"

The ADA's lip shows a light sheen of sweat. "I don't see what that has to do with the charge of possession of a firearm by a felon."

She shakes her head, as if dealing with a particularly stupid child. "Brad, Brad, Brad. That search was illegal as hell, and you know it."

Brad's face brightens as if he's suddenly remembered the answer to a test. "Sheriff's department found a cache of weapons on what was left of his premises."

"In the same place where someone who we're pretty sure is not Jack Keller planted a booby trap? You sure you want to take that to a jury, Brad? Especially given the government's very clear desire that all of this crap gets shoved under the rug?"

Brad looks over at Detective Fletcher, who's been silent so far during the conversation. "What's your take on this, Detective?"

Fletcher looks at the blank wall of the conference room. It's a few long seconds before he speaks. "I've got a local citizen, a man everyone loved, dead. I've got an officer…" He pauses, taking a moment to collect himself. "I've got a young officer with a promising career in front of him carved up like a piece of meat and left to bleed out by the river. His funeral's in an hour. And I understand that you," he looks at Keller, "are responsible for taking out the people that did that."

Keller starts to say something. McCaskill puts a hand on his arm and he falls silent. "We can neither confirm nor deny—"

"Oh, for fuck's sake," Fletcher snaps. He stands up and walks to the door. "I've got a funeral to get to," he says. "Do whatever you want, Brad." He looks at Keller. There's clearly more he wants to say. He doesn't. He shakes his head and walks out.

After he leaves, there's a long silence. Finally, Brad sighs. "Okay. I'll offer you a misdemeanor. Carrying a concealed weapon. Supervised probation for eighteen months."

McCaskill puts her hand on Brad's and says with complete earnestness, "Brad, and I say this with all due respect, fuck your misdemeanor. We've got a case I'm absolutely dying to take to a jury." She glances at Keller, who's been sitting silently at the conference table, watching his lawyer work. Keller nods, almost imperceptibly. "But my client wants to get all this shit behind him. Misdemeanor CCW. Unsupervised probation," she says, "six months."

"Twelve." He sighs. "Unsupervised."

"Six."

"Fine," Brad says through gritted teeth.

"And the money in the safe goes back to Keller," she says. "We've got a will and everything that says it's his."

"There's some dispute…" Brad looks like he's going to cry. "Fine. We release the money held in evidence. But we're keeping the firearms."

She nods. "Of course. See you tomorrow in court. Hey, can we get this done first? I've got to be in Moore County by ten thirty."

"Okay."

Keller walks out behind McCaskill. "Your dad would be proud."

She smiles at him. "Oh, he is. He tells me that a lot. Makes a real difference in a kid's life when they know their dad is proud of them."

He smiles. "You trying to give me parenting advice?"

She smiles back. "You think you're going to need it?"

The smile fades and he looks away. "I don't know," he says. "I pretty much fucked up Ben's life. Now I may be doing the same thing for Francis."

"Oh, bullshit," McCaskill snaps. "You didn't fuck up their lives. You saved them. It was traumatic, sure. It's caused Ben some problems. It may do the same for Frank. But if there's anyone who's learned how to navigate through that kind of trauma, it's you, Jack Keller."

He grimaces. "I haven't done the greatest job."

"Then teach those boys not to make your mistakes. Even if it's true that you fucked up their lives—and I'm not saying it is—don't you owe it to them to try to make it better?"

Keller shakes his head. "Damn. You really *are* good."

"Honey, I am the best. You just wait and see. But it always helps a good argument when at least part of it happens to be the truth."

He laughs at that before turning serious. "What's the word on Meadow? Melissa Troutman, I mean."

"I know who you mean. She got airlifted from Montgomery County General to University of North Carolina Hospital. She's doing fine. Lost a few inches of intestine, but she's expected to make a full recovery."

He nods, dreading the answer to the next question. "And the Khourys?"

She hesitates. He stops as they reach her car, studying her face.

"What?"

McCaskill takes the deep breath of someone delivering bad news and turns to face him. "Jack, Alia and Bassim Khoury were here under false papers gimmicked up by a rogue CIA agent. They've got no legal right to stay here. I've referred them to a lawyer that specializes in asylum claims. He's gotten a temporary stay of their deportation. But…"

"But they could end up getting shipped back to Iraq. Where their lives could be in danger from this Al-Mansour."

"That's the basis of the asylum petition." She sees the look on his face. "Keller. What are you thinking of doing?"

He rests a forearm on the roof of her car. "Where are they now?"

"Foster care," she answers. "And that's all I'm going to tell you."

"Fine," he says. "Let's go."

"Jack," she says, her eyes wide with alarm. "Please tell me you're not going to attempt something stupid."

He regards her without expression. "I'm not going to attempt something stupid."

"Do you mean that?"

Keller just smiles.

"Mr. Keller," a voice calls to him from across the parking lot.

The two of them turn to see who's calling. It's a short woman with dark hair drawn back in a long braid. She's dressed in jeans and a khaki uniform shirt without insignia and carrying a pistol in a shoulder holster beneath her left arm.

"What fresh hell is this?" McCaskill says under her breath.

"Relax. I know her. She's FBI."

"Great."

FBI Special Agent Leila Dushane saunters up to them. "Mr. Keller. Good to see you again." She nods to McCaskill.

"Agent Dushane," Keller says. "To what do I owe the honor?"

"You seem to keep popping up on our radar. Usually leaving a lot of dead people in your wake. Can we talk?" She looks at McCaskill. "Off the record."

"Absolutely not," McCaskill snaps. "Not without—"

"Sure," Keller says. McCaskill stops and glares at him. "It's okay," Keller reassures her. "We've met."

"And you trust her."

"Not really. But we can talk." He looks at Dushane. "Where do you want to do this?"

Dushane nods to a black Hummer sitting at the far end of the parking lot, motor idling. "Over there."

"Do I need to tell you that talking to the FBI without a lawyer is a terrible idea?" McCaskill says.

"Something tells me," Keller says, "that I'm not going to be talking to just the FBI."

# ONE HUNDRED-THIRTY-FIVE

Keller climbs into the back seat of the Hummer, Dushane right behind him. He slides over to let her sit down. "Jack Keller," she says, "Let me introduce Special Agent Melissa Saxon."

The woman who turns around from the front passenger seat has an angular, striking face, with arresting gray eyes. She holds out a hand. "First, Mr. Keller, let me thank you."

He takes the hand out of courtesy. "For what?"

"For the Dudayev sisters." She smiles grimly. "I have to say, you've set off quite a turf war, though. The Czech Republic, the French, even the Russians, would like to get their hands on the last survivor of that nasty little trio. And to shake the hand of the people who took the first two down."

"How is she?" Keller says.

Saxon shakes her head. "You are a remarkable man, Mr. Keller. You set a trap that burns half the woman's face off, and then you ask after her health."

"Yeah. Well. I'm an enigma wrapped in whatever. Is she going to make it?"

Saxon nods. "She'll survive. And she could be a real trove of information about terrorist activity, including crimes committed by or on behalf of Mohammed Al-Mansour."

Keller shrugs. "Okay." He reaches for the door handle. "Glad to help."

"Wait." Saxon's command comes as Keller realizes that the door isn't opening from the inside.

He sits back and looks at Dushane. "What the fuck, Dushane?"

It's Saxon who answers. "We'll turn you loose in a moment, Mr. Keller. I promise. But I'd like to ask you some more questions. About Adnan Khoury. Mohammed Al-Mansour. And the stolen money." She leans into the backseat. "You know how interrogation works, Mr. Keller. The more background you have, the more the person being interrogated thinks you know, and the more willing they are to cooperate. The Dudayev sisters are international terrorists. Assassins. Torturers. But they're just tools. Weapons. Help us find the hands that direct those weapons."

Keller leans back in the seat. "Okay. I'll tell you what I know. It may not be much, but there's still a price for the debrief."

Keller's surprised to see Saxon bow her head, even more surprised to see the smile on her face as she raises it and looks for the first time at the person in the driver's seat. "You called it."

"Of course I did." The man in the driver's seat turns around to look at him for the first time. He appears to be in his late fifties or early sixties, but his face is lean and tanned. His bright blue eyes bore into Keller's. "Sergeant," he says, in the voice of one used to command. "I'm Colonel Bishop. And I think I know the deal you want to make."

"Do tell," Keller says.

"Protection for the Khoury children," Bishop says. "Protection from deportation back to Iraq. Protection from Mohammed Al-Mansour."

"You're telling me you can do that?"

Bishop nods. "Mr. Keller. The organization that I'm in charge of can do that and more. Especially when it comes to protecting children who are potential witnesses in a terrorism investigation."

Keller takes a deep breath. He's not used to trusting people who claim to be from the government. But there's something in Bishop's eyes, a dedication that some might describe as fanaticism, that strikes a chord in Keller. "Okay," he says. "What do you want to know?"

# ONE HUNDRED-THIRTY-SIX

Hera stands at the edge of the clearing, unnoticed, watching men she doesn't know moving to and fro around what used to be her home.

Her mate is dead. The man who fed her and her pups is dead. The kind human female who used to ruffle her fur pleasantly and say soothing things to her is gone. None of them are dead or gone for reasons that make sense to her.

Hera didn't have a whole lot of trust in humanity to begin with. Now, she has none. After watching the humans die, then leave, the kind one wounded and possibly dying, she'd decided. There was nothing here for her or her children.

Laboriously, carrying each whining and complaining pup farther into the woods by the scruff of the neck, she'd moved her den to a depression under an over-arching rock where erosion has carved out a perfect little cave.

Now, watching the unfamiliar humans move back and forth across the landscape, calling to one another in their incomprehensible sounds, Hera has had enough. Quietly as a whisper, she fades back into the forest, confirmed in her earlier conviction.

There's nothing in the world of men but death.

## THE END

# About the Author

Born and raised in North Carolina, J.D. Rhoades has worked as a radio news reporter, club DJ, television cameraman, ad salesman, waiter, attorney, and newspaper columnist. His weekly column in North Carolina's *The Pilot* was twice named best column of the year in its division. He is the author of six novels in his acclaimed Jack Keller series: *The Devil's Right Hand*, *Good Day in Hell*, *Safe and Sound*, *Devils and Dust*, *Hellhound on My Trail*, and *Won't Back Down*, as well as the stand alone novels *Ice Chest*, *Fortunate Son*, and more He lives, writes, and practices law in Carthage, NC.